# HEARTBREAK GUITAR

# by Janice Dodge

For information, or to order additional copies,
please contact:

Beacon Publishing Group
P.O. Box 41573 Charleston, S.C. 29423
800.817.8480 | beaconpublishinggroup.com

Publishers catalog available by request.

ISBN-13: 978-1-949472-58-5

ISBN-10: 1-949472-58-5

Published in 2023. New York, NY 10001.

First Edition. Printed in the USA.

For Rick
and
The Dodge Guitar Company
May it Rest in Peace

My writing journey was made easier and my path smoother with the help of technical experts and friends. Foremost is my husband, Rick Dodge, an accomplished luthier, inventor, songwriter, woodworker, and builder of some fine guitars. Editor Adrian Fogelin provided invaluable advice and encouragement. I am thankful for the helpful comments and support from astute readers, Pat Ortega, Geri Dottorelli, Pam Krohn, Sue Wattenberg, and Ellie Hjemmet, and for encouragement of my writing by my sisters, Pat Ortega and Kiki Daniel. Truman Dodge and Dan Adamek patiently recounted notable memories from their trips to Nashville to attend the Summer trade shows of the National Association of Musical Merchants (NAMM), an event that is featured in the story. Dan Del Fiorentino provided useful historic details of the 2002 Summer NAMM show. Details of this particular show are loosely depicted in Heartbreak Guitar as an interweaving of a realistic mileu within a completely fictional account. I thank all of them for their unique and important contributions.

The epigraph is an excerpt of the song lyrics from "Dust Off My Guitar" - written by Janice Dodge (The Dodge Convertibles)
https://www.reverbnation.com/thedodgeconvertibles

and

Truman Dodge (The Repossessed)
https://www.reverbnation.com/TheRepossessed

*Italicized quotes used throughout the novel were taken from the writings of William Shakespeare.*

# HEARTBREAK GUITAR

Get down my guitar
I put away
So long ago
Dust off my guitar
See if she still sings
The bluest notes
Dust my guitar
Of memories
And all the dreams
That never cease
Give her brand new strings
Put her in the spotlight
And let her sing


*Lyrics from "Dust off my Guitar"*

# Chapter 1

June 20, 2002 - 9:30 a.m.

Cole walked up the front steps leading to the entrance of the Edna P. Slate Women's Center and stepped into the shade of the expansive porch. He stepped back as painters exited the building carrying a ladder and bucket past him down the steps and around the side of the building. He opened the door and entered the cool vestibule where it was as hushed as a library. In Jewell's room, he imagined she would be fidgeting with her wedding ring and looking out the window. Perhaps she was sitting on her bed clutching her empty cigarette pack in one hand and pressing the fingertips of the other hand to her hot, swollen eyelids.

Her eyes were her best feature, a clear, pale blue, but today they would be bloodshot from the crying jag that had started last Saturday afternoon and continued almost without a break until he'd brought her here on Monday near dinnertime.

A young woman had met them just inside the entrance and had ushered them into a small conference room where she took Jewell's hand and

1

assured her that she would feel better soon and led her down a quiet hallway. Cole had filled out paperwork and produced his health insurance card without letting on that it had been canceled five months before, along with nearly every other amenity of modern life. For five months, Cole and Jewell had lived in a world without phones or electricity, without TV or stereo or refrigeration or air-conditioning. They washed their clothes in the bathtub, taking turns stomping on blue jeans, underwear, shirts, and sheets in cold water, wringing them by hand, and spreading them across the kitchen countertops or hanging them from doorknobs. They heated their food, including coffee water, on the little charcoal brazier they had been given twelve years ago when Jewell and Cole had married. Until this year, they'd used it only twice.

Their Chevy truck and their minivan had been repossessed and now they drove a shambling, faded blue Mustang that Cole had been meaning to fix up since he'd bought it four years before, when he still had a life before forming The Sweetbird Guitar Company. That was the name that Jewell had suggested, a name he had really liked but had been talked into changing – actually coerced into changing - by Peter and Gary when they had come onboard as investors. Now it was known as The Heartbreak Guitar Company, which Peter had argued would get more attention. Jewell had complained more than once about the renaming and said that she felt pushed out of the business. It had come up again amid her tears last Saturday. Today, Cole would avoid even mentioning Heartbreak…unless she was feeling better. He fervently hoped for that.

Cole walked from the vestibule across a thick oriental carpet in the lobby. Large windows on the far wall looked onto a courtyard, but despite them, the light didn't penetrate well, or perhaps it was repelled by the dark carpet and heavy, dark furniture of the kind he remembered in his grandmother's house in Atlanta. It denoted an era of relative calm, of sensible and orderly lives.

One shouldn't be walking into this stately room contemplating the murder of his company's investors, whether or not they were deserving of it. But Cole didn't have a violent bone in his body. Even when he'd been picked on in middle school, he'd simply put his head down on his desk and refused to acknowledge anyone, including the teachers. He'd spent much of his time banished to the library, and though he hadn't learned algebra or Spanish or history, he'd read nearly every book in the library and even today could quote Shakespeare, with slight modifications, when the appropriate occasion arose. Truthfully, Cole wasn't actually contemplating murder. He was simply mulling over the deliciousness of the idea.

No one was in the lobby, and Cole waited at the check-in counter, a large, boxy cabinet with a poorly made countertop that sat at odds with the careful ornamental woodwork around the windows and doorways, and the imposing furniture. The seams of the countertop were discolored, a circumstance that was completely avoidable, Cole knew, since he had built hundreds of countertops himself. He had built his last one, he hoped, when he quit working for his brother-in-law to devote all of his time and energies to perfecting his guitars.

He heard the brisk clip of shoes on tile, and a diminutive woman wearing a daintily flowered dress walked down a hallway toward him and stood on the other side of the desk, with only her shoulders, neck and head visible above the countertop. "May I help you?" She jutted her chin forward and peered at him through her eyeglasses.

"I'm here to see my wife. They said I could visit after forty-eight hours. Jewell Luce?"

The woman let slip a fleeting smile, reached below the counter, pulled out a ledger, and settled her eyeglasses firmly on the bridge of her nose while she slowly perused a page marked with a paperclip.

"Is she okay?" Cole asked. "No one has told me anything. Our phone isn't working and I tried to call from…"

The woman looked at him through the large lenses of her glasses, then removed them and seemed to study him. Cole realized that he should have cleaned up, taken a cold shower and dressed in clean clothes instead of dashing up the stairs from his shop in the basement and rushing out the door without even combing his hair or shaving his five-day beard. Here he stood in his dusty, wrinkled black T-shirt and his cut-off blue jeans. His tennis shoelaces and the tops of his socks were repositories for fine maple shavings. His wispy, dark blonde hair floated like a dandelion tuft in the faint breeze from the slowly turning ceiling fan. Because of the stares he would receive on a windy day, he rarely went out in public without his baseball cap. But today, in the rush to visit Jewell, he'd forgotten it. He smoothed his hair and tucked it behind his ears. "She was fine, and then…I mean, we've been under a lot of stress. She's probably just exhausted?"

The woman put her glasses back on and closed the ledger. "Room 14. Just down that hallway, take a right." She held up her hand, a delicate but arresting gesture as if she were to bestow on Cole a universal truth. "Your wife needs complete calm."

He walked down the corridor and entered Jewell's room. Jewell was lying on the bed on her side, facing away from him. He stood for a moment just inside the doorway. *"To be or not to be that is the question,"* he declared. *"Whether 'tis nobler in the mind to suffer the slings and arrows of outrageous* investors, *or to take arms against a sea of them and by opposing them, end them!"*

She rolled onto her back and looked at him dully. He continued to stand in the doorway studying her until she sat up and threw her empty cigarette pack at him and lay back down.

"I brought you something." He tossed two packs of cigarettes and a Peppermint Patty on the bed.

Jewell sat up slowly, looking exhausted. Her short, blonde hair was mashed against her head on one side and the dark roots were showing. "Whatever you do, don't say the "G" word," she said.

Cole sat in a preformed plastic chair he pulled next to the bed and propped his feet against the bedframe. "Okay, no 'G' word. How about electric stringed instruments?" No response. "Hey, I understand. We can't keep living like this," he said, picking up on the conversation they'd had on Saturday, before the crying jag had started. "It's just that my electric stringed instruments are almost ready for prime time."

He reached across the bed and took her hand and rubbed his thumb against her palm. She continued to stare at the ceiling, and then rolled onto her side to face Cole. "Peter and Gary have your guitar dream wrapped tight in their sweaty little fists. They stuck to your contract for about – what – six, seven months? They don't give a shit about you or anything you do." They'd discussed many times making one more appeal to Peter and Gary to come and look at the newer guitar models and see how important it was to continue to support the prototyping shop. Gary had come once and walked away with one of Cole's best prototype models to date, which Cole had named "Desire" - a small tele-style electric that ran on batteries. You could use it almost anywhere, but it was not light enough.

Cole had yet to finesse his inflatable guitar design despite its simplicity...basically one long, wood guitar neck and a small – very small – wood body embedded with electronics and inserted into an inflatable cushion. It had a tiny clip-to-your-belt amp and speaker, and was run off batteries, so no outside power source was needed. If you lived in a cardboard box, you could still use the Inflatable, as long as you could panhandle some batteries and had enough breath to blow up the inflatable body.

"I don't want to talk about them anymore," she said, "except to say that you're better off without them. I wish you'd never met them." Before Peter and Gary, Jewell had been enthusiastic about the inflatable guitars. She had watched Cole build both acoustic and electric guitars over the years. This new design, an inflatable body guitar, struck her as fun, different, and interesting.

Cole's friend, Constantine, had a completely different response. It had become Cole's mission to satisfy Constantine, a most difficult connoisseur of electric musical sound. If Constantine approved, anyone would. Cole was haunted by the humiliation of his first inflatable guitar unveiling, when Constantine had exploded into laughter, slumped to the floor and rolled around, clutching his stomach. The fact that Constantine still was not convinced that the world needed an inflatable electric guitar only meant that the product needed more refinement. After all, Constantine only knew what he liked. He was not aware of the whimsical nature of the guitar world, a subculture unlike any other in its simultaneous drive for novelty and retrogression. Cole felt that he had satisfied this dual nature of the guitar playing public by outfitting the inflatable electrics with classic Telecaster electronics, and offering it with an optional tremolo, while pushing, of course, the novelty of the new "feel" of the guitar – light, sleek, melodious as a songbird - and portable when deflated.

Jewell continued, "Seriously, I know you can make guitars, and maybe you can even sell them, but not with Peter and Gary. I'd be just fine never hearing from them or anything about them,"

Cole tapped his foot against the bed frame and watched maple shavings drift to the floor. "Not to worry. We have no phone, remember? So, no communication with the boys?" In fact, he'd attempted periodically to call Gary from Constantine's apartment and leave invitations on voice mail to meet over coffee, though he couldn't tell Jewell that. Gary played in a garage band on weekends with his Prudential rep and the owner of Fast Copy, and Cole felt that if it were up to Gary alone, an actual guitar player, things would be very different. His dream would be on the verge of fruition. But Jewell did not see it that way. In her view, Gary was a manipulator and simply told Cole what he wanted to hear. In her view, Peter, whose money was predominantly funding the venture, had shown from the beginning that he was unwaveringly cheap, without vision and thoroughly difficult. Thus, he was the straight arrow.

Cole lightly stroked Jewell's hand and then sat back in his chair. She was not crying, Cole observed. Not even close, though she was clearly depressed. Hadn't she every reason to be depressed, considering the circumstances?

"How's Frankie?" she asked, still staring at the ceiling.

"Frankie's great," he said. "Though he misses you. I come home and he's all over me to get petted. Then he parks himself on the back of the loveseat looking out the window, waiting for you to come home. It always amazes me that he can even get up in the window. He may be small, but his heart is not." Cole chuckled. "Neither are his ears."

"Give him a hug for me," Jewell said softly. Cole looked for tears - this would be the time - but there were none.

There was a rustling at the window. Cole and Jewell watched as painters stood outside and papered over her one large window, blocking the view of the large oak trees, and beyond them, a line of cars stopped behind a city bus.

"Richard will take you back," she said. "Just for a while." Cole had built kitchen countertops for over ten years - first for his own business and then after he had sold it to his brother-in-law. Richard was a businessman and Cole was not…that was clear to just about everyone. Cole was already building guitars at night, so when Richard offered to buy the business, Cole was ecstatic.

Richard had expanded the countertop business to employ nearly a dozen shop workers. He needed Cole to stay on and run the shop, and so Cole had worked for Richard, training new employees, supervising the fabricators, and building the more difficult tops from complicated templates...until two years ago, when Cole had quit to devote all of his energy to Sweetbird Guitars...now of course, Heartbreak Guitars.

"You could work with Richard during the day, maybe part-time," Jewell said. "And still build guitars at night, like you did before."

Cole *could* go back to solid surface work - part-time like Jewell said – until he got some guitar sales. It was hard to imagine how to make it work when he did everything by hand, without money, and now without power tools, electricity or help. He often worked fourteen hours a day as it was. Still, he might be able to squeeze in a few small kitchen or bathroom countertops, if he pushed it. But he'd had nightmares already, in which every countertop he built took days to install while the customer complained about the inconvenience and the dust.

Cole had gotten up yesterday and written half a song about it before his first cup of coffee. "I'm writing a new song," he said. Jewell didn't move. "A blues song."

She sighed. "Don't tell me - I think, therefore I jam." She stared at the ceiling, as if reading words only visible to her that were written on the high, smooth surface. "No, no, that requires too much effort...I blink, therefore I jam." She sighed and looked at him, but he refused to be offended. She wasn't feeling well, after all.

He started tapping his foot. "It's called "Solid Surface Man", he said.

"I don't sit around and worry or think,
cause thinking will bring a man to drink,
With me you know just where you stand
cause I'm a solid surface man."

She turned onto her side and looked at him. There was a hint of a smile. "Wait a minute, there's more." He hummed a few bars until the words came to him.

"My neighbor's asking for a helping hand
cause her old man is just a vegetarian,
And Lady, I'll fix it as fast as I can
cause I'm a solid surface man."

Jewell's smile drew tiny wrinkles at the corners of her eyes. She closed her eyes, still smiling. With horror, he realized she might think he was singing an anthem to solid surface work. That he was going to fix things by going back to working for

Richard building countertops. He could think of nothing to say.

# Chapter 2

Cole exited the cool and quiet Women's Center and stepped into relentless sunshine. There was a steady rumble of traffic a block away. A raucous quarrel among blackbirds erupted in a Japanese Maple next to a small pond, where they were vying, Cole thought, for the coolest branch, the one with dense leaves and the heaviest shade. Even with the windows down, the Mustang was an oven, and the air-conditioner produced an anemic flow of cool air. Cole drove home the long way to avoid sitting at the traffic lights on Monroe Street and overheating the engine.

At home, Cole scooped up Frankie, who wiggled and squealed in his arms. "Frankie, boy. How's it going?" Frankie continued to squeal, bark, wiggle, and lap at Cole's arm while Cole walked to the ice cooler and tipped back the lid with the toe of his shoe and looked inside: a package of bologna, a head of lettuce and a jar of mustard sunk into four inches of icy slurry. He pulled out the dripping package of bologna and set it on the counter. Frankie squirmed and nearly leapt from his arms onto the counter as Cole held him with one arm and broke

pieces of bologna with the other. "Gentle...gentle."
Frankie quivered with anticipation but politely took
the pieces, swallowed them whole, and looked
eagerly at the package for more. Cole put Frankie on
the floor, dropped a few more pieces of meat into his
bowl, walked down the hallway to the large bedroom
on the end, started to make the bed, but got no further
than removing the bedspread when he slipped off his
shoes and lay on the crumpled dark green sheets in
his clothes. The blinds were still closed, and the room
was dim, with strips of sunlight falling across the
sheets and the pillowcases and onto the maple
headboard. It was stiflingly still and hot. He heard the
hum of his neighbor's air conditioning, a car door
slam, and the roar of an upshifting Mack truck on
U.S. 27. He reached for the phone, wanting to call
Constantine, but then remembered there would be no
dial tone.

Sweat tickled his armpits and the backs of his
knees. He would have to contact Richard and see if
there was a little work. There was no way around it.
He rolled onto his back, reached over to Jewell's side
of the bed, and grabbed the ruby-colored electric
guitar, Desire, which he'd flung there in disgust last
night, when he couldn't remember the lead to
"Moses Smoked that Mother".

Cole lay on his back and picked a few notes.
The batteries were weak, but he managed a wavering,

tinny rendition of the "The Star Spangled Banner" a la Jimmy Hendrix before the batteries failed altogether and he let the guitar slide off his stomach onto the bed and pushed it to the far side. He lay still, rivulets of sweat soaking into the sheets. Frankie trotted into the room and whimpered by the bed. Cole scooped him up with one hand and lowered him onto the middle of the bed, where Frankie rolled against Cole's thigh and licked his knee.

"Frankie, Frankie, we're in big trouble here." Cole scratched Frankie's head and ears gently. "But you already knew that."

Cole groaned, rolled out of bed, and put on his shoes. He couldn't lie around while Jewell was waiting for him to get their finances out of the gutter. He trudged downstairs, into the basement, which was relatively cool, though he knew that it was probably in the 80's. He glanced at the humidity gauge and groaned again. Eighty-three percent. The maple blocks he had stacked in the corner, ready for shaping into custom-order guitar bodies for guitars he would someday make, would be moisture saturated.

Cole had learned about humidity and wood the hard way, when he was building electrics in his pre-Inflatables days, and had placed several guitars locally in Music Masters and Ray Wiley's, the two best music stores in town. The ebony finger boards had shrunk in the dry, air-conditioned store, leaving the frets to stick out to either side or the neck. Cole had bought an oversized air conditioner and two humidifiers for the basement, which had pulled the humidity down below sixty. Now without electricity they sat unused, providing more flat surfaces for collections of picks and screws and coins coated in wood dust.

Cole picked up the bridge he had been prototyping and set it on a shelf. He had set up a worktable on sawhorses at the back of the basement, where there was a sliding glass door that opened onto a small deck in the back yard. Fortunately, this door and several windows on the back wall provided some light. He could work with enough light into the early evening. Then he would go over to Constantine's, where he would spread a towel out on the coffee table, lay one of the guitar bodies on it, and do some light sanding while they watched TV and drank beer. Constantine had also permitted Cole to use his garage for spraying the finishes. Cole had entirely taken it over, with his spray guns and non-explosive fan, the racks for hanging guitars, the pickle and mayonnaise jars cleaned and filled with polyester resins and aniline dyes.

But recent events – with Jewell in treatment – required that Cole rethink his game plan. He would talk to Richard about work, but if he had any chance whatsoever of getting his guitars out the door, he had to finish those in progress and market them to get some sales, BIG orders the proceeds of which he would find a way to wave under Peter and Gary's noses just to show them what they were giving up. Cole's best shot at success was to get his product into the NAMM show - the biggest trade show in the U.S. for musical instruments - with deluxe models of Desire and the new, even lighter inflatables, which he had for the moment named Despair.

Cole studied the finished guitars he had hung on a rack in the corner of the basement, carefully spaced apart, like clothes in a closet hung on hangars, each separated by six or eight inches. There was thick dust on everything. With his finger, he swiped dust off one of the inflatables, on the wood part surrounding and containing the pickups and potentiometers, removed it from the specialty hook he had made for it, carried it outside and examined the finish in bright sunlight. It had to be as smooth as glass at purchase time, even though the customer was likely to leave it in a hot trunk for two or three weeks at a time or balance a lit cigarette on the edge or poked between the strings while waiting for the big solo or lay it on the floor in the middle of a raging party. In the store, it had to gleam like a rare gem. Cole had battled problems with fine scratches in the finish, scratches which could not easily be polished out. His finishing problems would be minimal with the right equipment, but Peter and Gary would not spring for it.

Cole wiped off more dust with the hem of his shirt. It drifted down and stuck to his sweaty legs. He held up the guitar to the light and examined the glossy surface for scratches. "Shit," he said softly. "Shit, shit, shit."

From the basement, Cole heard footsteps in the main part of the house accompanied by the rat-a-tat of Frankie's nails crossing the living room, passing through the dining room and into the kitchen. Without the hum of electric lights and appliances, he could have heard a mouse scamper across the floor upstairs, but these were wildly clomping footsteps on the hardwood floor of the living room, moving through the dining room and kitchen, heading toward the stairs to the basement. The erratic pace of the footsteps of kids, followed by the sedate, almost shy, scrape of a woman's sandals. It had to be Maureen, Cole's sister, with her younger kids, Christine, age four, and CJ, age seven.

"*Hark!*" Cole yelled. "*What* foot on *yonder* stairway stomps?" He heard them clatter down the stairs to the landing, then thunder down a few more steps and suddenly stop while still just out of view. He saw a small, pale hand grip a black, plastic weapon with a long barrel. It turned and took aim at his heart. "You'll never take me alive," Cole yelled, and threw toward them a roll of toilet paper he had been using for shop rags. It bounced off the wall and left a ribbon of paper behind as it rolled away from the stairs. A moment later, CJ leaped down the last two stairs, his gun emitting the rat-a-tat of machine guns, explosions and sirens all at once. "Hey man," Cole said. "Let me see that thing." CJ handed over the gun. There were two battery compartments, Cole noticed. "Pretty cool," he said, though he was disappointed to see that it held only "C" batteries. CJ would surely have loaned him the batteries if he had asked, but he needed eight AA for Desire.

"Why is it so hot in here?" Maureen asked from the bottom of the stairs. She had the roll of toilet paper and was carefully re-wrapping the unrolled sheets. "And dark. It's depressing. No wonder Jewell's depressed."

"The electric's out," Cole said. He didn't know how much Maureen knew about Jewell or about their current struggles. Although he and Jewell hadn't hidden the fact of their financial troubles, exactly, they hadn't gone out of their way to share the grim details. It would have resulted in visits from Maureen and Richard with bags of groceries and offers of loans. But there would be strings attached. Richard was a successful businessman. He would have wanted to know all about Heartbreak Guitar per-unit-costs and projected sales and market penetration. "You can't run a business without the numbers," he had said more than once. But he had inherited the money for his own business from his father and had lucked into acquiring a business that Cole had already made successful - building and installing countertops. Nothing had to be invented. No one had to take a lump of wood and few more lumps of metal and some wires and turn it into a work of art that produced a set of characteristic sounds with the exact tonal qualities of the Fenders of the world, yet somehow better, and priced for the budget of the average American thirteen-year-old. Richard didn't have a clue. Even Jewell hadn't once suggested they confide in Maureen and Richard. That said just about everything.

Cole handed the gun back to CJ and waved at Christine, with whom one had to be reserved, or face the helplessness and guilt of watching her lower lip tremble and tears pool in her round, gray eyes. Chrissy came over, walking haltingly, and hugged his leg and he stroked her hair. When she stepped back, he noticed a knee-shaped smudge on her yellow, cotton top and grime on one side of her face and under her ear.

"You mean the whole neighborhood's out?" Maureen asked, handing him the roll of toilet paper, then taking it back and tearing off a few sections to wipe Chrissy's face and neck.

"No," Cole said. "We didn't pay the bill. When a worldwide computer shut-down hits, and the electric grid goes, we'll be ready," he said, chuckling, as if it was a good plan. Maureen frowned as she dusted the front of Christine's shirt. "It'll be all right," Cole said quickly. Maureen would have Cole employed in Richard's shop by dinnertime if he wasn't careful. In fact, he needed to work something out with Richard, but if not handled correctly, Richard and Maureen would take over his life, ditch guitars, drag his wife out of treatment into the bosom of their family and their busy lives in their two-story house - when he was so close to success, he could taste it. He shouldn't have waited so long for Peter and Gary to get the sales and fund a real shop. They were worthless. He would have to do it himself, like he did everything else. But it would take money to make money. If Maureen and Richard were so anxious to help, they could provide the seed money and Cole would do the rest.

Cole ran his hand through his hair. "Is Richard going to be home tonight, or tomorrow?" It would be best to bypass Maureen. Of the two, Maureen was more financially conservative - the one who clipped coupons from the Wednesday paper, did her own oil changes and recycled everything from string to paint. Richard was the more likely candidate for a loan. "I need to ask him something."

"Yes, he'll be home around five-ish," she said. "Or just give him a call at the office." Before Cole had a chance to confess that the phone was out, too, she added, "Why don't you come over for dinner tomorrow? We haven't seen either of you in forever."

Was this what Maureen had come to convey, a dinner invitation? He watched her watching him, studying him silently like she often did her oldest, Jason, when he was expected to come clean on why he had misplaced his history textbook or left his report card in his school locker. As she stood patiently, her brown eyes both sympathetic and penetrating, Cole felt the panic and rebelliousness that certainly Jason must feel - she was so certain that nothing important could take place without her guidance. It would be best to get everything off his chest now, while she was in a motherly calm, but something inside him insisted he wait and talk to Richard. "Yeah, okay," Cole said. There was no way Jewell would be home so soon. "Sure, we'd love to." He didn't have a clue how he would pull it off. "What time?"

# Chapter 3

Early that evening, Cole locked the back door of the basement, closed the windows, shook the wood shavings off an orange towel, and used it to wipe the sweat and wood dust off his neck, arms, and legs. He whistled for Frankie and went upstairs and out the front door. He sat on the edge of the flowerless brick flower box in front of the house and repeatedly threw a rolled-up sock for Frankie to retrieve from the tangle of tall grass and dandelions in the front yard.

He smelled grilled hamburgers and heard the laughter of the new neighbors on their back patio two houses away, and the shouted taunts of three boys who rode past on skateboards. Despite the nearby activity, he was struck by a deep sense of loneliness and loss. Jewell was depressed. He had hoped that she was just exhausted, but her misery went deeper than that. It was clear to him now that he would need to make some money fast to set their lives back on track. Once he got his guitars in the NAMM show, and was racking up purchase orders and contracts, he was certain that their troubles would subside, but that didn't help Jewell today.

Frankie raced back with the sock, and Cole dispiritedly cast it toward the nearby camelia bush that Jewell had planted several winters ago. After fifteen minutes, he locked Frankie in the house and drove over to Constantine's with three black-stained guitars of the newest design, the last ones he'd cut out and sprayed and hung on the rack. All of them needed fine sanding and polishing, along with several of those he had thought were already completed until today's close inspection. He was toying with keeping the working name for this model - "Despair" - that would appeal to at least half the guitar players the world over. It featured a pickup under the saddle and would have, once he got the money to buy one, a 4-track recorder/player connected to a built-in speaker, which would attach to a player's belt or guitar strap. The guitarist could put down a bass run first, then lay down blues progressions to his heart's content, with no requirement for any other human within a hundred miles. There was a certain beauty to the concept of utter and complete aloneness, when one could wallow in self-pity, saturated with the music of a heavy heart - a wispy, string-bending whine accompanying a penetrating bass line that was rolling around in one's brain.

Cole hesitated before opening Constantine's front door and listened for a moment to an opera emanating from within. Cole wasn't a fan of opera and couldn't possibly have identified which opera this was. As in all operas, a soprano was exercising her voice in a range not to be approached by most mortals.

"Hey," Cole nodded as he entered the small living room. It was wonderfully, deliciously, extravagantly cool. He sighed and slumped down on the overstuffed chair next to the door and closed his eyes. He kicked off his tennis shoes and stretched his toes against the cool, deep pile of the carpet.

Constantine was lying on the sofa with a cushion behind his head against the armrest closest to Cole, his feet propped on the opposite armrest. He brushed his thick, black hair out of his eyes. "Hey man, what happened to you?"

"Life," Cole mumbled and with effort opened his eyes, but let them flutter closed again. "It isn't working out."

Constantine reached past his head and over the arm of the sofa and turned down the CD player. In the corner, next to Cole's chair, was a tiny refrigerator. Constantine nodded toward it. "Grab yourself a brew."

Cole was a leaden lump in the chair. Nothing could budge him at that moment, not even a cold beer. With his eyes still closed, he listened to Constantine shuffle through some CD's and put one in the CD player. The raspy voice of Bob Dylan singing a love ballad filled the room. Cole was a great fan of Dylan, though he liked to make fun of his on-stage playing – at times loud and out of tune. Guitar players could relate to that. Cole was reminded of a song he and Jewell had written, when she was still smiling and hopeful and filled with creative energy…many, many months before. The last verse went something along the lines of:

I want to do a Dylan thing,
and sure enough, that's how I sing,
or so they say.
The neighbors call for 911
and think that they have really done
a good turn today.
Officer, I'm simply trying to sing.
I wouldn't call it bellowing.
What I meant was
these handcuffs really sting.

Cole felt a heavy wet cylinder - a cold beer - nudge his fingertips. He opened his fingers and allowed Constantine to place the beer against his palm, resting it on his stomach.

"How's Jewell?" Constantine asked.

"As well as can be expected," Cole said. Jewell had been Cole's biggest fan in the beginning of Heartbreak Guitars, and actually, she'd been an avid supporter of all his schemes and inventions, even before they were married, but now she had reached the end of her rope. She was completely worn down. They had both been enthusiastic about the Cole's guitar-building aspirations, but their energies had unwound steadily, month by month. The last straw for Jewell had been the UPS delivery the week before. Inside the box was a custom order guitar - not an Inflatable, but nevertheless a lovingly crafted Cole original, with a highly figured wood grain stained an emerald green, and with abalone fret markers and gold-plated hardware - that had been returned by John Ford Sagen, a Nashville studio player and songwriter who had wanted to endorse Cole's line. He had commissioned the emerald model, which was to be named after him. With the returned guitar, he sent a letter of apology with a vague explanation. Reading between the lines, Cole and Jewell determined that the PR company behind John Ford's label had frowned on his activities on behalf of Heartbreak. It seemed he wasn't free to select his own instrument.

Cole had related this story to Constantine last week, before the impact of it had fully sunk in, and now he resumed. "You know…it isn't just John Ford, but every music store, every music writer, every music magazine, every up-and-coming musician –

they have to go with the big guys to survive. Fender, Gibson, Ibanez, PRS have the market locked up tight. Even Gary and Peter can't overcome that fact." Cole momentarily felt a sense of fond sadness for Gary and Peter and their brave folly for investing in a guitar start-up company. They had had no idea what it was all about. No clue. Unless they could throw themselves into promotion of Heartbreak products with tons of advertising, promotional giveaways, wining and dining of the music store executives, and profit-sinking prices, they would never break through the brand loyalty barrier and get any real sales. Heartbreak would always be an oddball enterprise, with novelty guitars essentially custom-made in a basement.

"Lots of people want our guitars when they first see them," Cole said, his eyes still closed. He fingered the pop-top on his beer but didn't open it. "They just want them yesterday – without a blemish, custom-made and free. Other than that, they aren't picky."

"Jesus, you've got it bad," Constantine said. "It'll happen, man," he continued. "These things take time."

Cole opened one eye. He wanted to ask Constantine what he possibly knew about launching a business. Constantine was a high-school chemistry teacher, who in his spare time cooked, played chess and volleyball, studied Buddhism, wrote poetry and, of course, played guitar. But in fact, Constantine was usually on target about Heartbreak matters. It had been Constantine who was the sole naysayer to the partnership between Cole and Gary and Peter. If only Cole had listened.

"Yeah, I know." Cole said. "But it's taking too long. We can't go the distance. Jewell can't go the distance."

"You can't look at the distance," Constantine said, reaching over his head to turn off the CD. He withdrew his feet from the sofa, sat up, and sipped from his beer. "No one can see that far. It's too overwhelming." Constantine's voice was deep and gravelly, with the kind of authoritativeness that could get his 11th graders to stop talking when he was ready to begin class. "You and Jewell just have to get through today and tomorrow. Let yourself worry about next week on Monday."

Cole popped his beer open and slugged back four large gulps. Tonight, he had to sand the three guitars. Again. He groaned and stood up, putting his beer on top of the small refrigerator. "I'm just going to the car," he said. "Have to get the Despair sisters. You can tell them what you just told me."

They watched the news, the weather, and part of a biography on Louis Armstrong. Cole didn't care, really. He sanded mechanically, and occasionally would lightly brush the fine dust onto the towel he had laid across the coffee table while he let fatigue settle upon him. He became pleasantly drowsy, and Constantine invited him to sleep on the sofa. It was tempting, very tempting, rather than return to his own baking bedroom, but he couldn't leave Frankie to fend for himself. After all, the house was empty enough without Jewell.

Before their recent struggles, before the electricity was turned off, when she was still feeling hopeful and at peace, Jewell would come in the door after work with an ebullient smile and a bag of groceries and a plan to surprise them with a new recipe. On weekends, she specialized in finding new trails in the Apalachicola forest, or planning picnics at Shell Point or to local music festivals. And on some evenings, before the heat and mosquitoes were onerous, she just wanted to sit on the back deck with a glass of wine and make up nonsensical lyrics to Cole's newest melodies. Now – except for sounds from the neighborhood - the house was eerily quiet.

Cole and Frankie just had to stick together until she was well and was home again. "Thanks, man," he said. "Another time." He gathered up his sanding paper and guitar bodies and trudged out the door that Constantine held open for him. Constantine stood in the doorway while Cole loaded up his car and backed out of the driveway, and as Cole drove slowly away, he glanced over his shoulder and saw that Constantine was still standing there despite the mosquitoes and moths attracted to the lights inside, a gesture of support.

# Chapter 4

Cole returned home to his dark house and carried his guitars inside while he let Frankie spend a few minutes outside. He took a cold shower and headed for bed, but despite his fatigue, he could not sleep. He lay in bed and stared through the open window at a night sky with a scattering of stars. It was unusually quiet. Even his neighbor, a woman in her fifties who had immigrated from Russia decades before, had not yet initiated her middle-of the night call to the homeland, which she seemed to think could only be conducted on her front porch, her fierce assertions rolling down her sloped yard and into Cole's bedroom windows. Had she always done this ritual midnight shouting, or did she start – as it seemed - when the oppressive May heat forced Cole and Jewell to open their windows to let in the humid but slightly cooler night air? When she had awakened Jewell last week, who already was tossing and turning on their sweat-soaked sheets, Cole had been so enraged that he had run through the house, out the front door, and stood in the street sending curses up the hill. It was effective, a lesson in neighbor-problem management, because for a few nights afterward, all was quiet. But now, with no Jewell to protect and his sleep too elusive to defend, he lay on his back, bathed in sweat, listening to Martina's first throaty exclamations and Frankie's faint snoring.

He thought again of Jewell's hopeful smile. That sealed it. He would call Richard tomorrow. He would discuss countertop building, perhaps set up a date for working some small jobs, and then explain the need for a loan. But what could he really say that would not trigger the lecture about business savvy and lack thereof? Richard had a regular seminar going with an audience of one - maybe Richard should take it on the road now that his delivery was well honed, start an inspirational speaking tour for the self-help business start-up crowd, the multitudes of creative minds and eager hearts who had not yet been touched by the Peters and Gary's of the world…the gullible enthusiasts who still held their eight-to-five, paycheck-every-Friday ability to bankroll the first patent.

Undoubtedly, Richard was right to say, "do not let go of that steady paycheck until your business is on sound footing." He could be very right, but he had inherited his business, at least the money for his business, and had not suffered the suffocating day-to-day tedium of a job that sapped all the energy – mind, heart, and spirit – from someone who yearned for something different, something that welled up from the base of his spine and took over his body and brain as if he was possessed.

Cole listened to Martina's vociferations, greetings to an elderly parent or hard-of-hearing uncle half-way round the world. This was followed by a fit of coughing and then more shouting, apparently without concern that the whole world was privy to her communication, provided they could speak Russian. Cole wondered how any of his neighbors could sleep given the onslaught of exclamations that erupted from across the street. But of course, the neighbors were all comfortably tucked under blankets in their crisply air-conditioned, windows-closed bedrooms, sleeping as peacefully as Rip Van Winkle.

He should talk to Richard...not Maureen. Despite everything Richard professed, Cole had detected a sympathetic leaning, and maybe even admiration, for the fervor with which Cole and Jewell had met their challenges. Richard was left speechless – a true rarity – when he learned that Cole and Jewell had written and submitted their own patent application for the Inflatable. Obtaining a patent without an attorney was impossible it turned out. Indeed, the patent application had been rejected, but then without one single change, it had been resubmitted by their newly hired patent attorney, who had greased the wheels in some way mysterious to Cole and Jewell, and it had then been approved.

So, although the mechanics of steering the application through the patent office was not within their skill set, the writing of it was essentially perfect, a feat that Jewell was especially proud of.

Frankie yipped in his sleep and his paws twitched against Cole's thigh. Cole gently slid Frankie across the sheets, about a foot away, opening enough space to let some sultry air circulate between them. If Jewell had been here, tossing and turning in the heat, Cole was certain that Frankie would have hopped off the bed by now and found a more restful spot.

Lights, air-conditioning. If only Cole had spent less time in the basement, he would have seen the despondency that had slowly enveloped Jewell. But now he knew, and he would do something about it. Richard would definitely be the best person to tap for assistance, just a little help, some work and a loan…just enough to get them to the NAMM show.

Cole reached across Frankie until his hand rested on the ruby tinted Desire, which lay on the far side of the bed. He had supplied her with some used batteries from a very old Walkman, though he doubted they were any good. He pulled Desire carefully around the sleeping Frankie, whose tail whacked the bed sheet although he appeared to be sound asleep. Wagging his tail with such little effort – since it wagged now, even during sleep – Frankie probably kept in better shape than most marathoners.

Cole settled Desire on his belly and strummed the strings. "I got a new song Baby," Cole said softly to the missing Jewell.

> You say that you love me
> I believe that you do
> You just don't want to tell me
> What's troubling you

> You'll work it out someday
> I'll see your mood lift
> But the guards 'round your heart
> Work an overtime shift

Through the window came the guttural exclamations of Russian greetings winging their way on muscular photons toward the homeland. To carry halfway round the world, apparently each word must be forceful and loud. But there was a hint of happy mischievousness followed by bellowing laughter that indicated that Martina had been into the vodka. Russians had invented vodka, apparently, to overcome the somber and authoritarian vocalizations that comprised the natural utterances from their native tongue. But spontaneous, explosive laughter – they definitely knew how to do that, too. He hoped that the breeze from some of Martina's most exuberant laughing…coughing…"Nyet, nyet"…more laughing - would roll down the hill toward him. If anyone could send a breeze his way just from happily expelling the entire volume of her lungs, Martina could. If so…God bless her. Talk away.

> You say that you love me
> I believe that you do
> I would do anything
> In my power to do
>
> I will come like a whirlwind
> And I'll circle around
> And pick up the dreams
> That fell to the ground

Desire wavered on the final "C" chord and lost battery power altogether, but he continued to strum the strings that now mostly sounded like a matchbook clothes-pinned to slowly turning bicycle spokes…very deeply tuned bicycle spokes, ones made from a nickel core wound with bronze to achieve a richer resonation. Wait a minute. Could it actually be possible to tune a bicycle and then learn how to play it? He should try it. That was absolutely something Maureen and her kids would be interested in.

Another fit of laughter erupted and boomed down the hill, rippling Palmetto fronds and Mexican Sage and a sweet-smelling summer blooming grass Cole could not name - so abundant in his yard since he had abandoned mowing. Martina was happy, he could tell, - maybe his earlier assessment of her as "somber and authoritarian" was a little harsh. One could apparently also be happy in Russian. Of that, he was glad.

# Chapter 5

Early the next morning, Cole drove over to Constantine's, although he knew that Constantine would have left for school already. Cole just needed to use his phone to call Richard, a fact he was not eager to share with Richard, although really, what difference did it make, considering the confessions of their dire circumstances that would be required to justify the favor he planned to ask: a loan for the past-due electric bill so they could restore their air conditioning, stove, refrigeration and hot water heater…a little for pickups and tuners, maybe a small amount for sales literature, and just a little more for gas, food and lodging at the NAMM show next month where he would make it or break it for all the music industry to see. He had already, reluctantly, taken the NAMM show registration money that Constantine had pressed on him. He would go to the NAMM show and get some sales. He would pay back Constantine and Richard. It would work out because it had to.

He retrieved Constantine's spare key from under a toad statue near the corner of the garage and let himself in. He sat on the arm of the blue chair in

Constantine's living room and thought about what he would say. It was quiet with the windows closed. He could hear the faint hum of the ceiling fan, and a soft ticking of the house as the sun warmed the roof. Cole sat, staring at the phone, deciding how much he would be required to explain, and bracing himself for Richard's generous thoughts on guitar sales. Constantine would be better at this conversation. He would simply explain the facts in a logical and cohesive story so that by the end, the correct course of action would be obvious.

Cole stood up, picked up the phone and dialed. "Richard, it's Cole."

"Cole, what the hell time is it?" Cole knew that Richard's shop opened at six-thirty, but apparently Richard, in his management role, was not expected to be present so early, or even awake.

"Sorry, I thought you'd be up," Cole said. "I wanted to catch up with you today to talk."

He so hoped that Richard would not require that they talk over the dinner Maureen seemed to have in mind, for which Cole had already decided he would beg for a rain check, so he was enormously relieved when Richard said, "Sure, how about lunch? My treat." Really? What was Richard up to, barely awake yet so cheerful and even generous? What did he already know? Cole was immediately on guard, imagining that Jewell must have called Maureen, and

41

now the shit would hit the fan. Was he just walking into a well-designed trap? If he could somehow spring Jewell out of treatment for the evening, his wife, sister, brother-in-law, and their kids would sit around the dinner table, and all eyes would be on Cole when he was asked at dinner if he was ready to build and install countertops. "Anyone can install countertops," he wanted to say…no, to shout. "But not anyone can invent Desire, or imagine Desire, or even have Desire!" It was a pointed insult – he knew that. Everyone had Desire, but not everyone struck out in the world to express it. They were afraid. Not every single person in this world, but many – perhaps most - were too afraid to express true Desire in the face – more likely the high probability – of spectacular failure. That fear was what he had worked so hard to overcome, and why Richard was so fascinated with the whole Inflatables adventure that he was nearly on board, despite his stuffy businessman's platitudes. Everyone had Desire, but few of them acknowledged it, nurtured it, or sacrificed for it, for God's sake.

They met at "The Hungry Dog" for lunch, where they ordered foot-long hot dogs topped with medium-hot chili and a mound of slender-cut cheese fries. Neither Maureen nor Jewell would even in an extreme famine consume such food - if it could still be called food. It was delicious. Cole wiped half of his hot dog clean of chili and wrapped it in a napkin, along with some cheese fries, to take back for Frankie's dinner.

"Ok, Cole. So, what'cha need?" Richard was surprisingly affable when he was sated by chili hot dogs and fries, a fact Cole felt he should tuck away for future use.

"I wanted to let you know that Jewell isn't feeling well, so we won't be over for dinner tonight. She's ok, essentially, but maybe next week would be better. Can you let Maureen know?" He was planning to check in on Jewell during afternoon visiting hours and hoped that she would be ready to come home tonight or tomorrow if the electric was back on. Surely that would be true once Richard came to their aid. With the electric back on, their doors and windows could be closed to contain the crisp coolness of the A/C and dampen the sounds of traffic and kids shouting, a neighbor's incessantly crowing rooster – and of course Martina's deep bellowing – and Cole and Jewell's ship could be righted. He just needed a little help from Richard. He swallowed hard. "So, you probably know we've been struggling financially. Now the electricity is off, and I was hoping you could help me with a small loan to get it back on, and perhaps some other funding. And of course, I could give you a hand at the shop."

Richard had not stopped a mechanical hand-to-fries-to-mouth repetitive movement, slowly but steadily reducing the mound of fries on his plate while Cole watched in fascination. How was it that Richard stayed so trim? A tall and large-shouldered man, but trim, clean shaven, calm, and poised, wearing pressed tan slacks and a garnet button-down shirt with the sleeves rolled up to keep them free of contamination from the greasy fries and chili sauce that somehow had dripped onto the front of Cole's grey t-shirt. Cole rubbed at the spots with a napkin wetted in iced tea. But Richard was thinking while he was eating, Cole could tell, in that businessman's way of investment thinking, a special kind of calculus that went on for a long, intense, moment during which most of the neurons of the prefrontal cortex were fired nearly to exhaustion. And then it was done. "How much are we talking?"

"Just for now, about seven hundred and fifty-nine dollars, plus a sixty-dollar reconnect fee." Cole didn't tell him that the overdue amount was for five months and the electric had been off nearly that long. "That's the most important thing, but I also wanted to talk about Heartbreak, maybe a little investment opportunity?" What Cole really wanted was a loan, not an investor. Not after Peter and Gary. But this was Richard sitting across from him now, still friendly and charitable, and if anyone knew how to carve out a new investment opportunity, it would be Richard. Otherwise, what was all that business savvy worth?

"Okaaaaay," one simple word Richard dragged out, cautious but not commanding, waiting for more. It was a perfectly reasonable stance.

"Okay, so I think we need to take the Inflatables to the NAMM show. I told you about it, I'm pretty sure...the National Association of Musical Merchants. It's where everyone goes who has any musical product to market. Products are displayed, and reps from the chain stores, online distributors, investors, manufacturers, players, you-name-it, are there to see what's new, what's in. They're there to network, to buy. I think we need to be there." Cole let this sink in. "Of course, the Winter NAMM is bigger, but I'm aiming for the Summer show next month. And I think you should come," he added to sweeten the deal. It would be exciting to go, and Richard would be in his element...wheeling and dealing and racking up the orders, while Cole would be free to talk to the players who wandered into their booth with confused expressions and walked away with grins on their faces and business cards in their pockets.

"Okay," Richard said. "Yes, to the electric bill." He pulled out a checkbook and started writing. "And we'll talk about your NAMM show idea." That was it. Simple. Sweet. Cole had a check that he would soon turn into cash he would hustle to City Hall to pay the electric, hoping against hope that it could be turned back on that very day, and they could be restored to modern life, or at least one that is cooler, cleaner, and with renewed hope for the future. Jewell would be elated. She would come home, and they could resume their normal lives and pursue their plans and dreams.

"Hey, do you have time to help me at the shop next week?" Richard asked? He was still being reasonable…do you have time…knowing full well that Cole had only himself to answer to. What could Cole say, but yes?

When visiting hours commenced in late afternoon, Cole was the first one down the corridor; energized by his news…all paid up, the electric would be turned on tomorrow. Jewell could come home. Please, please, let her want to come home.

"Hey, Babe," he said, when he was barely through the door.

She was lying on the bed reading a book, her short, blonde hair neatly combed back. She was dressed in the clean pair of jeans and a pink t-shirt and yellow socks with small, black diamonds that had been damp when he brought them yesterday, having just washed them in the sink. He'd draped them to dry across the back of the only chair for visitors, one that was a hard, slippery plastic, without any welcoming cushions. Clearly, the treatment center wanted the visit to be minimal. They wanted the residents to rest and contemplate without the emotional uproar that might be triggered by a long visit with close family members or friends, during which they were certain to venture into rough seas - bad memories, petty accusations, and emotional turmoil.

Jewell looked up and offered a smile - if it could be called that...sad, rueful, cautious? He couldn't tell, just a slight upturn to the corners of her mouth. "What are you reading?" he asked.

"'One Flew Over the Cuckoo's Nest'...and I have 'The Bell Jar' on the shelf there." Cole didn't quite know what to say. Didn't this place have any idea of when to censor the reading material? Jewell laughed, the first he had heard in weeks, perhaps. She was getting better...that was clear. "I love it...the expression on your face. Actually, I'm reading "'Be Here Now'. Maureen brought it."

"Maureen was here?" Cole waited. He would love for Jewell to pack up her book - Be Here...something "- and her other belongings and come home with him, but God, please don't say they were having dinner at Maureen's. And anyway, how did Maureen find out Jewell was here, and why hadn't Richard said anything? No, if they were going to dinner, Jewell would have already been packing.

"Listen to this," Jewell read from the open book in her lap…"'as long as desire pulls you or pushes you, you are like a flame which flickers in the wind'."

This clearly meant something to her, but what it meant outside of these drab walls and dim light was not obvious to Cole. Nevertheless, if she was happier, more at peace, with or without desire, that was probably a good thing. He, Cole, was not through with Desire and it was not through with him. It burned inside him like a lighthouse beacon, thousands of candle flames - perhaps millions - that merged into one, without a flicker of hesitation or regret.

# Chapter 6

Visiting hours were over. Cole reluctantly allowed himself to be ushered from Jewell's room by the institute's Director, who had ten minutes previously stopped in to remind him that they kept to a strict schedule, and to let him know that she needed an updated insurance card. "For some reason," she'd spoken while peering at Cole over her heavy glasses, "we have an outdated one." Cole had looked at Jewell, and she had glanced at him, then looked down at the book still in her lap and sighed. "I'll take care of that," Cole had said to the Director. Before he left the room, he gave Jewell a reassuring smile, and she had gingerly smiled back, a good sign, a hopeful sign.

It was dinner time rush hour, and Cole sat at the Tharpe and Monroe streets intersection for two light sequences, prompting him to cut behind the old mall now used as offices for the Driver's License bureau and Florida Department of Health. From there it was just one street past the Spay-and-Neuter clinic to Constantine's where he could drink a beer in sumptuously cool air and visit with Constantine and wait for the traffic to clear out.

Constantine ushered Cole into the living room. The house was effused with the aroma of cooked onions, carrots, celery and chicken. "You're just in time," Constantine said, and led Cole through the dining room, into the kitchen, where he removed the lid from a pot of home-made chicken-vegetable soup. "Can I interest you in soup?" Who could turn that down?

Constantine served it with slices of asiago cheese, sliced pears, and white wine while he regaled Cole with the details of a political struggle at the high school. The school administration wanted the teachers to eat their lunches in the lunchroom with their home-room students rather than place those students in the care of Teacher's Aids, under whose oversight the school cafeteria volume gradually and steadily increased during the lunch hour to cocktail party volume, a cocktail party for one hundred and fifty, all of them under the influence of wildly fluctuating hormones. "Some serious frowns and "zip-your-lips", Constantine mimed the lip-zipping, "pretty much works. The TA's are just too timid."

Cole nodded his head. "Frustrating." There was really nothing more he could add. "Jewell would love this soup, by the way."

"Any idea when she's coming home?"

"Maybe tomorrow," Cole said dolefully. He put his spoon down and looked up at Constantine's puzzled expression at his lack of excitement. Now would be the time to confess the lack of insurance and Cole's nagging concern about Jewell's readiness. This was Constantine, after all, who had no agenda but being a friend. Cole picked up a small slice of pear. "We'll see," he said softly.

"So, what's up in the land of Heartbreak?"

Cole slowly shook his head. "There are eight guitars I want to take to the show, but six, at least six, need work." He placed the pear back on the plate and ran his finger over the stem of the wine glass. "That's not all. If they're going to be more than a novelty item, I need some kick-ass electronics. Maybe some hand-wound humbuckers... some active electronics." He stared at the light reflecting from the glass, reluctant to look at Constantine. "I almost drove over to Gary's house today. He still owes me...both a real explanation of where we stand officially, *and* he literally owes me."

Constantine rested his spoon in his soup bowl and sat back in his chair. "You know what I think."

"I know. I know." Cole lay a sliver of asiago cheese on the pear slice. "The thing is...I can't make these guitars myself and make any money. I know that and they know that. Mine was always a prototype shop. So I don't understand why *they* don't

51

understand that the NAMM show is where you make connections, partner with a bigger company, send the prototypes to a shop that has capacity to build hundreds a day."

"You can still do it," Constantine said. "They've already bailed, but you can figure it out. You don't need them."

It was shortly after dark when Cole arrived home. When he first pulled into the driveway, he was struck briefly with the notion that he had turned at the wrong house. The whole house was joyfully ablaze with golden light. Every curtain and every shade were open, and the rooms were on view as if it was a cutaway dollhouse wherein their furniture, paintings, television, all that they owned was on display. If he had only known the electric would be back on, Cole would have brought home some soup to put in the fridge for Jewell, who was almost certain to come home tomorrow or the next day, because she was well and she wanted to - not, he hoped, because they had no insurance. Surely, they wouldn't release her if she wasn't ready. But she would be ready. Of that Cole was certain…hopefully, wistfully certain.

Frankie leapt, danced, and whirled, and who could blame him? The temperature was already down, maybe into the eighties even with the windows open. With Frankie dancing around him,

Cole stood directly under an air-conditioning vent. It was an incredible, indescribable, sensory delight. Everyone who ever needed and used air conditioning should experience an outage, a serious outage, so that when the cool air was restored, they could fully appreciate what they had every day, all day, simply by pushing a button or turning a dial. Cole went from room to room shutting windows, pulling closed the curtains and blinds, and luxuriating in the drying, cooling air and the bright light that fell on the dust-covered bookshelves, the wood shavings that peppered the dark green bed sheets, and the polyester fluffs from a once-stuffed dog toy that Frankie had torn apart in his frustration and loneliness.

"Frankie, come here boy," Cole spoke softly, almost whispering as he scooped Frankie up and stroked him from his head to his tail. Frankie wiggled with delight and licked Cole's neck and chin. "You're a good sport, buddy," Cole crooned. His voice cracked and he whispered, "and a good friend." He carried Frankie to the kitchen where he broke the hotdog and fries into small pieces and put them in Frankie's bowl. "That's the last cheese fry you'll see for a while, maybe in your lifetime," he said. Jewell would be home soon, and the chaos of their lives would be calmed. They would sleep better, eat better, *feel* so much better!

He went out to the car and brought in the Despair sisters and laid them on the kitchen table. It was so tempting to sand them there in the kitchen, luxuriating with them in the cool, dry, and quiet house, but he toted them downstairs into the basement, placed them on his workbench, and turned on the dehumidifiers and the window air conditioner. They were lovely to look at with an arresting three-dimensional rippling effect in the curly-maple mini-bodies, and he envisioned using a red or green stain mixed with lacquer to achieve a translucent glossy finish. But they needed more work before he could spray them and polish the finish. All of his guitars needed more work. Richard hadn't yet agreed to fund their NAMM show venture or purchase needed guitar electronics and hardware, but Cole knew that he was on board. The NAMM show was scheduled to begin July 19 and end on the 21st. Vendors with display booths must arrive to set up their products the day before the show, display their wares and schmooze for the next three days, and then they would have a few hours at show's end to pack up everything to ship or carry home. Today was June 21st. He had just under a month to get ready to head north – twenty-eight days to be exact. Somehow, he had to perfect the guitars and do a little work for Richard on the side. The schedule was tight, but he could do it.

The next morning, Cole awakened late. Frankie was pacing from the bedroom door down the hallway, seeming to deliberately rat-a-tat his nails against the oak floor, a sign that he needed to go out. Was it that late? Cole usually awoke before Frankie, before it was light, before the birds started up their morning salutations and the rooster three doors down had yet to warm up his egocentric cry – "I'm *wai*ting!"

Cole was almost groggy, though he had had only two glasses of Chardonnay with dinner at Constantine's, followed by the tiniest glass of too-sweet dessert wine that Cole had quietly accepted but wondered why anyone would bother. They usually consumed beer, but Constantine had recently announced that certain food should not be paired with beer. Lately, Constantine was determined, Cole discovered, to utilize the crystal and china that had been given to him by his mother, Eve, before she divested of her possessions and her Miami Springs home and moved to a writer's retreat in the woods of Virginia.

Cole had knocked over his wine glass in the middle of his rant about the mystery and downright unprofessionalism of Gary and Peter's silence. Miraculously, the glass had fallen between his soup bowl and fruit plate onto the turquoise tablecloth and had remained intact. "No worries," Constantine had said. "Mother made us promise to use all of it – china, crystal, silver – use and enjoy." Eve had used it, treasured it, and passed it to Constantine, his sister Annette, and their younger brother, Fabian, hoping that it would help them celebrate their special but transient place on this earth. These items would mean little to the next generations, she had said. That was a relief, because there was only one child in the next generation so far, Annette's two-year old Tyson, who so far had displayed his father's stocky build and overbearing loudness and no affinity for delicacy.

Now, without the heavy sleep induced by three or four beers, nevertheless, a deep and peaceful sleep was made possible by the cool air and the quiet stillness of Cole's bedroom…that was the only explanation for eight or nine hours of unruffled, intoxicating sleep. That and a lack of Russian expletives sent through open windows to jar him awake in the middle of the night and set him wondering about the state of national security, given that in the middle of the night - of many nights - Russian could be shouted at full volume to the star-filled Tallahassee skies, wing its way to the Moscow Oblast, perhaps with Russian operatives listening in, and cause not a ripple in the U.S. except in his own life and to his own disturbed peace.

Cole opened the blinds and looked out at a bright and blistering summer day. Ok, that was an exaggeration. Out there it was probably very warm and humid, with clouds of torpid mosquitoes hovering in the shade of the two massive oak trees in his front yard and beneath the azaleas that were bursting with fuchsia flowers...but it was not blistering...more like slowly simmering, cooking down the creative juices of anyone unlucky enough to be without air conditioning on this moist, summer morning air.

He went downstairs and noted right away how much drier the basement was than yesterday. Last night, he had turned on both dehumidifiers and the 12,000 BTU window air conditioner that blasted the basement with cold air. In the past, running the basement air-conditioner on high would make the basement so frigid that Jewell had let him know that he would have to do all the laundry, since the washer and dryer were in the basement, and she wasn't putting on a jacket to go down there.

He examined the Despair sisters and tried to gauge how moisture-saturated the wood might be. He had started working on them in March and had recognized almost immediately from the look and feel of the curly maple that these guitars would be special. In the hands of any true-blue guitar player, they would spring to life with their rich tones, and bend to the artist's musical whimsy. The players would be seduced by the Sister's outstanding complexions, then by their willingness to deliver tonal ecstasy with the lightest touch, but also fully withstand the hard down-strokes of more intense musical geniuses, even those about whose mental health one might worry. He did not wish to subject any of the Sisters to the petulance and rudeness of the most extreme among the can't-possibly-be-pleased guitar playing phenoms, one of whom Cole had met when he was performing delicate guitar repairs for some of the players in Tallahassee. Most guitar players were great…they were accomplished, interesting, and typically humble. But that one encounter – actually it was many encounters trying to please one player without success - had convinced Cole that guitar repair wasn't worth squandering one's serenity.

He had tenderly brushed off some wood dust from one of the Sisters and silently promised he would watch over them, and eventually put them in the hands of someone sane, or at least tranquil. This wordless conversation had taken place weeks before the humidity had reached intolerability. With the air conditioning back on, he was hopeful they would recover quickly.

He had let Gary and Peter know last January that his electricity was about to be turned off and warned them what it would mean for his prototyping endeavor. They had stopped supporting the shop activities a few months before that. It was baffling, because at that time, Cole still had infrequent but friendly phone conversations with Gary, who had continued to express enthusiasm about their overall chances of success, although he had repeatedly warned Cole that the shop budget was a problem. Then, after the previous more-or-less congenial first year, during which they seemed fully behind Cole's prototyping efforts, they had re-interpreted the routine shop operations-support-clause in the Heartbreak contract. In their view, routine support no longer would include costs for electric or phone service. Neither did it include a new sander when his worn motor shaft developed a wobble, or router bits, or a planer, or a non-explosive fan for his small, homemade spray booth. And last Thanksgiving, they had announced that until they realized some profit, it would no longer include a stipend for Cole, even after Cole had tried to renegotiate the amount to practically minimum wage.

The costs of *real and meaningful* shop support would have been small, Cole believed, but Gary and Peter had a successful business model, they told him, that required blood, sweat and tears from "their" inventors. Is that what they really wanted? Sweat was easy…just let the electric bill go unpaid, guys. Taken care of. Good job. Tears were almost certain to follow. But blood? If only it could be theirs! They had not suffered like Cole, Jewell, and Frankie. They had not suffered like Desire or the Sisters.

Cole had come upstairs, broom in hand, to check on Frankie when he heard a knock on the door. He watched as the door pushed open a foot or so, and Maureen stuck her head in, then pushed the door fully open and walked through, carrying a sleeping Chrissy, who was draped onto Maureen as gracefully as a sack of potatoes. Cole had yet to wipe the dust from the shelves, the television, and pretty much everything. He knew Maureen would notice, but for some mysterious reason, she decided to hold fire, and instead eased onto the loveseat, peeling Chrissy off her shoulder to gently place her onto the seat cushions. "I'm so glad you're home," Maureen said. "I thought you might have already gone to see Jewell."

Clearly, Maureen knew about Jewell, and she wasn't in lecturing mode. Cole was curious as to why. He quickly wiped the dust from the coffee table with his hand, and then sat on the sofa just a few feet from Maureen, wiping his hand on the hem of his t-shirt. "Sorry, I have to get this taken care of before she comes home," he said. "I'm hoping she can come home today." It was simple, talking to Maureen, when you didn't have to make up wild stories about – really – anything. "I'm glad you came by," Cole left it a little light, not sure why Maureen would bring the dead-to-the-world Chrissy, and not her other kids, to visit. Maureen was usually far too busy for that. The other kids normally would be in school at this hour, he guessed, but no…this was the summer break. Still, even when they were in school, Maureen savored her freer daytime hours, saying she couldn't get anything done aside from being a maid, cook, laundress, accountant…Cole couldn't remember the entire list, but he was convinced that Maureen wouldn't easily give up even thirty minutes of her day for small talk.

"Hey, I know you're struggling," Maureen said. "Richard told me that you wanted to go to the NAMM show and needed a small loan. I think you should go."

Could she be serious? This was Maureen, the campaign manager for practicality in the race against wishful thinking and empty dreams. "You're not saying anything," Maureen observed. She sat further back and looked around the room…neat, sort of, but dusty. Still, she held fire.

"Yeah," Cole said. "I think I really need to go, but to do it, I need a little help. Did Richard say anything?" And why was Maureen here instead of Richard? That was what Cole was really wondering.

"Actually, we want to help," Maureen said. "With the money."

"Hey, that's great," Cole said, but he still wasn't sure that he and Maureen were on the same page. "I'll have a small booth at NAMM, the smallest they provide. And there's a bridge manufacturer who offered to make a contribution if I used his bridges," Cole said, wishing to allay potential concerns that he might not be careful enough with Maureen's money. Her puzzled look prompted him to explain: "Guitar bridges. This guy – he sells guitar parts, bridges. You know…it's where the strings are attached to the guitar body." Cole was pretty sure that she wouldn't understand the further importance of the bridge in relationship to sound. She nodded as if the description he had provided - the bridge as an anchor for the strings – was good enough. So be it. "And there's the booth," Cole continued, not mentioning that he had already registered for it and would be paying back Constantine, "and I need a little more for a room and some meals. And transportation?"

"Ok, we're on board," Maureen said. She sighed and stroked Chrissy's leg, and it was then that Cole knew that Maureen had more in mind. "It's just that Jason is almost fifteen." Cole knew that. He remembered Jason's September 6th birthday, an aberration from Cole's usual lack of interest in remembering birthdays – Jewell typically took care of that task – but he remembered Jason's because at the time of Jason's first unabashed and slightly early arrival in the world, Richard was on a business trip in Atlanta. Jason had not been expected for another four weeks when Maureen called Cole and made a pretty strong case for him to leap into his car and take her to the hospital. Cole knew it was too early in the pregnancy and was worried beyond belief as he ran around the house looking for his keys. He'd driven at breakneck speed to Maureen's and rushed her to the ER, where he had been swept with her into the examination room so he could answer questions; then they were rushed to the obstetrics/delivery ward where he was told to hold Maureen's hand while she struggled with waves of pain. "It's like surfing," he remembered saying to her. It was stupid - just something to say…waves of pain…waves. But to his surprise, she was on board with surfing, which they had both attempted as teenagers whenever a tropical storm sufficiently disturbed the placid Gulf waters off St. George Island.

"Keep talking," she said as she gripped his hand.

"So, you're measuring the wave," Cole said. "You're standing up on the board, and the sun is rising at your back, and the seagulls are sweeping in and calling your name." She squeezed his hand harder. "And a soft wind is on your face. You're riding the wave…all the way to the top…all the way…it's beautiful there… and then you glide down the other side." Her grip had loosened. "Take a little time to rest." Cole carried on in this way for more than three hours. In the vision he tried to impart, Maureen easily rose from her knees to stand on her steady surfboard, rode on top of the waves, and looked to the distant shore at the morning light falling on hermit crabs, seaweed, and delicate sea grass anchoring white sand dunes. He was hoping that – amid her moans and her tight grip on his hand – she would see the perfect small child on the shore…who would become the golden-haired toddler with the funny swaggering gait that was still so recognizable in Jason – and that focusing on that tiny, already-loved human being - even when she cried out that she couldn't go on – she could get to the other side. It happened at 8:49 p.m. on September 6, 1987.

"What I was hoping was…" Maureen patted Chrissy's leg. "What I was hoping," she repeated to make sure that Cole was paying attention, "was that you could take Jason on – you know, as an apprentice of sorts - for a few hours each week. He could help around the guitar shop?" She looked away. "He needs a new interest," she said. Frankie ran up to her and jumped up to have his ears stroked. "He needs something," she said to Frankie as she pushed his earflaps one direction and then another and cocked her head as if evaluating a new hairdo. "He's at a crossroads, and he just needs the right spark."

She didn't have to spell it out further. Cole already knew that Jason struggled like Cole had done at Jason's age. Like Cole, Jason spent many idle hours pretending to pay attention in class and do his schoolwork. But they continually floundered – Cole and Jason - from lack of interest in the subjects taught and from some difficulty in mastering concepts dripped onto their brains by teachers who seemed to speak in monotone, at least that is the way Cole and Jason's ears heard it. Like Cole, Jason learned more from hands-on exploration. At the park, Jason packed rocks into his pockets to be examined at home under a bright light with magnifying glass, first having cleaved them with a chisel and hammer. When he was eight, Jason had taken apart the popcorn popper and Richard's watch, just to see how they worked. He welcomed the arrival of new appliances. A product's instruction sheet, with descriptions of interesting dangerous outcomes, was for Cole and Jason just an invitation to see what physical laws might be perturbed or provoked if one violated the prohibitions described in the manual.

Why wouldn't anyone, for example – intrigued by what could happen - put a metal object...let's say...an incandescent light bulb in his new microwave oven?

"Yeah," Cole mumbled, hoping Maureen had more to say. In theory Cole was on board with having Jason as an apprentice, someday, though right now it was next to impossible. He didn't have time to teach anyone anything, even how to sweep the floor. Later would be good...would be fine. In fact, he was somewhat jazzed about the idea, since it indicated that Maureen had some trust in him as a mentor and thought he had some worthwhile experience, or at least some hard-won wisdom, to impart. But now it was impossible.

"Thank you," Maureen said, pausing her arrangement of Frankie's ears. "Just do your best to encourage him. And really...thank you!" She patted Frankie as she stood, took a few steps toward Cole, and to his dismay hugged his head close to her bosom. The deal was sealed. Jason would be coming over after lunch on Monday. And could Cole be at Richard's shop by eight a.m., maybe eight-thirty? Richard really needed him. "Thanks so much Cole," Maureen said as she sat again on the loveseat and skillfully worked to position Chrissy's appendages such that Chrissy could be pulled into a compact blob of humanity onto Maureen's lap, and then stretched across Maureen's torso to rest against Maureen's shoulder. Cole wished that he could have filmed this graceful dance of limp limbs and bending torso to be played afterward in slow motion. He would have to remember it - to mention to Jewell that he had not before realized the synchrony of motion and the engineering savvy of materials leverage, and the biological instinct for low and soothing - but meaningless - vocalizations that were required of parents of young children.

Cole helped to position Chrissy onto Maureen's shoulder. "Here, let me get her... leg." He helped with Chrissy and then picked up Maureen's oversized purse, opened the door for her, and scooted in front of her to open the front patio gate and Maureen's car doors, so she could slide Chrissy into her car seat.

As Maureen drove away, Cole walked to the end of the driveway and waved. He would have the funding to go to NAMM, and Jewell would be coming home to some good news. There would be a price, but he was willing to pay it. It would just take hard work and an incredibly high degree of good luck.

# Chapter 7

25 days until the NAMM show

On Monday morning, Cole had gotten up early and hoped to be able to drop in for a few minutes at Richard's shop but ended up spending the entire morning talking to the shop guys (and one woman) and watching them work. Richard was right. They needed help, serious help. The shop was dim…a third of the lights were out. The fabricators had too little space, and what they had, they didn't use well. One guy worked with his cell phone glued to his ear, moving slowly as he constantly adjusted the phone clamped between his cheek and his shoulder so that he could shout into it while running the router. It was a miracle he still had fingers.

Cole would need to work overtime for months – not just a few hours a week - to get things right. With Richard's help, he picked a tall, lanky dark-skinned Jamaican, whom everyone called Mr. Bean, but whose real name was Carson, to be the shop supervisor. Mr. Bean would get a raise, Richard assured him, "which is already well deserved."

Richard smiled his smooth salesman smile and clapped Mr. Bean on the shoulder.

Mr. Bean's expression did not change with this news, but he nodded his assent and headed back toward his work area where multiple clamps held a long Corian countertop - glued up and ready for routing.

Cole followed him. "We gotta talk about the shop," he said. "Apparently, a third of the tops already need repairs before they leave the shop. Worse, somebody here's going to get hurt." He stared out the raised warehouse door as one of the new workers rode by on a forklift with a teenager balanced on the forks, one foot on each, nimbly absorbing the jostling as the forklift rode across the gravel loading area, the kid maintaining his balance with his arms out like a surfer. "Let's start with some safety training. Jesus!"

Just before lunchtime, Cole managed to get away and drive over to Richard and Maureen's house to pick up Jason and embark on their new partnership – mentor and apprentice. Within minutes, Jason was bored, and wandered around the basement, drawing faces in the dusty surfaces with his index finger. Upon their arrival just after lunch, Cole had put a broom in Jason's hands and showed him where the shop rags were. There was wood dust everywhere. "We don't need to eat off this workbench," Cole said, "but maybe you could help with the dust. I mean, look at this!" He wiped a finger across some of his tools. However, for Cole, the shop dust was the least of what he needed help with. He wanted to send Jason upstairs where there was far more important dust to deal with before Jewell's return. Not that the shop had not also sunk into housekeeping hell with mounds of wood shavings, dust everywhere, tools on every surface, and general disarray. He easily spent two or three hours a week putting things in order and taking stock. He could have spent an hour each day, but he didn't have even a spare minute to show Jason how to do it. "And if you could take care of the floor... start with that." Cole pointed to the broom.

Jason swept with enthusiasm for about five minutes, and then gradually his broom slowed until he was scarcely moving it. "Ok, Jason. How 'bout you just straighten the tools. Don't rearrange anything! Just line them up. Keep similar tools together and even them up," Cole said as he straightened screwdrivers that were inserted into slots on the back of the workbench. "Then you can just watch what I do. I think it's the best way to see how these beauties," – he touched the neck of one of the Despair sisters – "learn to strut their stuff."

After fifteen minutes of work, Jason was through with his assigned tasks. He wandered the basement with a shop rag, snapping it at rasps, planers, the clothes dryer, and the band saw. After a few minutes, Cole noticed that Jason was following him around the basement, mimicking his dispirited posture, and then standing next to him with a grimace when Cole held one of the Sisters directly under the light to check for scratches. When Cole took a step back, Jason stepped back. When Cole placed the guitar back onto the work bench with a sigh, Jason shifted from one foot to the other and sighed. Jason pointedly stared at Cole when he stood in the middle of the basement wondering if he had time to spray another coat of finish on the Sisters before he had to return Jason to the bosom of his family. "Very funny," Cole said. Jason continued to stare at him, a slight smile betraying his pretend earnestness.

"You said to pay attention to everything you do," Jason said.

"Smartass. If you keep this up, I can find more fun things like sweeping to entertain you," Cole said. "Maybe you need to go outside in the heat and humidity and mosquitoes…tote this wood trash to the curb."

"I'm good," Jason replied. He walked over to Desire, which was hanging on the back wall, a Siren whose haunting sound would frequent anyone's dreams. Desire – which Cole had developed after working for two years on the earlier prototypes named Destiny, Daedalus, and Delight - now would lead the way to musical nirvana.

"Oh, I see," Jewell had said when the guitar name game had begun. "They all have to start with a 'D'." She pulled a dictionary off the shelf. "How about 'diaphoresis'. It means perspiration. Here we go…how about 'diarrhea'. I think you know what that means. Whoa! How about 'diathesis'…ha! A constitutional predisposition toward abnormality or disease. 'Disbelief'…you can't get any better than that, and I'm only halfway into the D's." Jewell pointed the dictionary at Cole. Cole should have understood then that Jewell would not be able to go the distance.

Cole had soldiered on, naming each subtly different prototype, but Jewell was right. There were so many more disparaging words that started with D. Distemper, distort, doddering, doldrums, drab, dry rot – my God! Maybe those were terms that exactly suited – even appealed to - the guitar playing consumer. At that moment, those were the terms that appealed to Cole. Still, he had searched the dictionary, as any good guitar builder, gimmick peddler, wild dreamer would do. In the middle of all the D's was the embarrassingly stereotypical "dreamy." Cole had more self-respect than to use that! Now Destiny, Daedalus, and Delight rested in boxes under one of Cole's work areas. The crafting of each had offered something new to his guitar-building insight. Destiny taught Cole that he needed to install truss rods to allow him to adjust the necks. Both Destiny and Daedalus had neck-through-body designs. But a bolt-on neck would make scaled up manufacturing easier, so Cole purchased some custom necks from Musikraft and installed the first one on Delight.

It was when building Desire, that Cole realized that he could create a guitar you could play on a mountaintop, far away from electric power, if you included a small amp that you clipped on your belt or guitar strap. Desire had everything the inflatable needed. Most importantly, it had a great sound.

Jason carefully pulled Desire off the wall pegs, sat on a stool, and without plugging it into the amp sitting just five feet away, quietly picked at the strings. Cole noted with surprise that Jason had fingered a C chord, G chord, B-seventh, back to C, and had a decent pick/strum going. "Hey man, sounding good," Cole said. "Where'd you learn that?"

"School," Jason said. "I took two semesters of guitar last year."

"Play something," Cole said and resumed sanding lightly, not really needing to do much more, but certain that Jason would play only if ignored. It was one thing to learn shop skills, maybe even the artistry of instrument building - but playing…that would transport you to another dimension, spark new neural pathways and spiritual growth. It would let every cell in your body swell with a feverish purpose. It would turn your body electric. That was music.

Jason played through the dozen or so chords he knew, strummed with an easy rhythm, and did a pretty good job of running up notes on some of his chord transitions. He played for about twenty minutes and then stopped and looked at Cole. "Not bad," Cole said. "What kind of music are you listening to…"? Cole was curious if Jason was playing what he heard and liked – a tried and true method of music education – or if he was being directed by his guitar teacher, or by Maureen and Richard. Jason shrugged and returned Desire to her wall pegs, and with his hand brushed the dust off the headstock, the curvaceous body, and blew on the electronics, releasing a puff of dust.

Cole stopped sanding and called Jason over. "Look at this," Cole said. "See how this bridge needs to fit into this slot in the wood?" Jason nodded, definitely interested. "See? All the electronic parts have to fit into slots routed into the guitar body. In this case, they all have to fit into this." Cole indicated the wood piece into which he would embed electronics and attach the bridge and around which he would attach the inflatable body. "I have to rout out these slots for the pickups." That was all Jason needed to know for now. But he was interested, Cole could tell. Jason leaned forward to examine the slot that Cole had cut into the wood, and Cole caught a glimpse of Jason's profile, so like Maureen as a kid when she avidly studied insects that she would bring inside and place in jars. Once they were captured, she was compelled to figure out what vegetation they liked, what temperature and humidity, what insect friends they might wish for – and how to identify those - and how long they could be expected to live. That was before she had gotten snooty in high school and would barely speak to Cole. It was before she had gone to college and then dropped out after two years to marry Richard. It was before the arrival of Jason, CJ, and Chrissy.

There is always that moment in a young person's life – like the one in Maureen's when she gazed at dragonfly wings under a microscope she had received for Christmas. In that moment, questions had flooded her young mind…long before the more dire and all-consuming grown-up issues of finding an affordable home near a good school or determining when a child's fever required a visit to the clinic had overtaken these questions. There is that one moment full of questions, full of possibilities, all paths leading to further inquiry. Then in an instant, it seems, without even noticing, one's life could be turned to other things, maybe satisfying things, maybe predictable things, maybe boring adult settled-for things.

Cole pulled Desire from her high station – thought about it – replaced Desire on her pegs. He pulled a guitar case from a box under the workbench, checked to make sure that in it rested the lovely, black-tinted neck-through-body Destiny, and handed the case to Jason. Then he tucked a mini-amp and some headphones under his arm and said, "good enough for today. I'll give you a ride home." They trudged upstairs.

By the time Cole had dropped Jason back home that afternoon, visiting hours at the Edna P. Slate Women's Center were nearly over and traffic was barely moving…everyone was leaving the downtown state offices at the same time. Cole raced down as many side streets as he could, weaving around slower cars when he could, in the general direction of the Women's Center, but it was useless. He could crawl there faster than this. Now is when he wished he had a cell phone…stuck in traffic and just running a little late. Jewell had had a cell phone before...when they had a lot of things, but Cole had always sought out and savored the time he could be away from everyone. When he had his own shop, before Richard acquired it and moved operations to a large warehouse, there was a landline for the small office, but no actual shop phone. How much contact does a human really need? Just now he needed more. Just now, he needed a break.

He arrived at Edna P.'s ten minutes past visiting hours. The director at first refused to let him speak to Jewell, but he pleaded his case until she relented – since dinner had not yet been served – and allowed a five-minute visit.

"Hey, Babe," Cole said as he entered the room where Jewell was sitting, reading, with her back against the pillows, and her knees drawn up. She appeared placid enough. Maybe she hadn't noticed that visiting hours were over. "I would have called to let you know I was running late, but...you know." Jewell looked at him and raised one eyebrow, waiting for more. "No phone," he said. Surely, she didn't need reminding. "I wondered," Cole continued, "if you were ready to come home. Maybe tomorrow? They don't tell me anything here."

Jewell sighed, put a matchbook in her book to mark her place, and placed it on the bed next to her. "I don't know. It all depends." She sighed again. "It can't be like before."

He wasn't exactly sure what things had to change that he hadn't already been working on. "Oh, yeah, I get that." He waited, but she didn't say anything. "First of all, the electric is back on…thanks to Richard and Maureen. It's pretty awesome." Jewell swung her legs off the bed and sat on the edge. Cole continued, "in return, I'm helping Richard in the shop for a few hours each morning, and Jason is working with me at home in the afternoon." Jewell waited, still silent. "And in return for *that* – for working with Jason – Richard and Maureen are providing some funds for the NAMM show. Richard might even come with me."

Jewell groaned and slumped back onto her pillow in mock exhaustion, or maybe true exhaustion - how could you read that? "It was Maureen's idea," Cole said, hoping that this would make the idea more sound, more acceptable. "But I'd rather you came."

She rolled over to face him. "You go with Richard," she said. "I want you to." All indications were that Jewell had lost energy for the endeavors of Heartbreak. Twenty-five days before the NAMM show.

# Chapter 8

After leaving the Center, Cole drove over to Constantine's. "Maureen came over again today," he told Constantine, who was holding the front door open with one hand. A quilted hot-pad mitten on the other hand was raised in greeting. "Jesus, something smells good," Cole said.

"I just took lasagna out of the oven." Constantine closed the door behind Cole. "I'd ask you to stay but Jasmine will be here…" He glanced at the wall clock he had inherited from his grandfather, a notable wood worker and luthier – in Cole's eyes, practically a god, someone who understood the incredible diversity of tonal qualities derived from wood, and specifically from certain wood species. Constantine's grandfather had pointed out the wood that he predicted would yield exquisite musical articulation. He believed one could trace their savant characteristics to a specific grove of trees, or even to an individual tree, maybe one that was more fully exposed to the sun, yet shielded from the wind? Or maybe it needed the wind and was strengthened by it. Perhaps even the surrounding landscape of arboreal sound when the wind brushed through the highest branches of neighboring trees imprinted tonal genius on a youthful spruce, mahogany or walnut. Cole had many times discussed with Constantine's grandfather what might have made a sound board great – pliant, resonant, melodic…and of course, beautiful. So many woods were beautiful and so many others were resonant, but when the two were combined…Constantine's grandfather kissed his fingertips and flung them into the air.

The clock struck six chimes. "Any minute," Constantine said. "We're having a glass of vino before dinner. Do you want to stay for one? Cole had met Jasmine only a few times. He didn't like her, and he wasn't convinced she was good for Constantine. He couldn't put his finger on it at first, but later realized that her habit, or need, or whatever it was, to change the facts of a story to suit what she wanted the outcome to be, one in which she could be outraged at her mistreatment or be admired for her grit, was a trait he recoiled from. He first had detected the bullshit in her story because he had actually been at a school event she was recounting. He had attended because he knew that Constantine would be getting some kind of recognition, and so he knew that Jasmine hadn't arrived late and been reprimanded by the PTA president in front of everyone as she later recounted, because she hadn't been there at all!

Jasmine was relatively new in Constantine's orbit. She was pulling some substitute teaching gigs at the high school while she was writing her dissertation for a doctorate in Biology. "I can't really say what it's about," Constantine had told him. "Something to do with fruit flies. Fruit flies and sleep disruption. Who knew?"

"Actually, why don't you stay?" Constantine asked. "There is way more lasagna than we can possibly eat." Lasagna sounded good, actually, it sounded wonderful. But Cole knew that he had arrived at an inopportune moment and that Constantine's heart was somewhere else, and anyway, he still felt uneasy about Jasmine. Although he tried to convince himself he didn't know her well, truthfully, he just didn't want to.

"It's okay," Cole said, feeling in small part rejected…the third wheel, despite the warmth in the invitation. "I'll call you tomorrow if my phone's back on." He headed for his truck.

"Hey, come by tomorrow for leftovers," Constantine shouted. "Bring the Sisters…kinda miss them." He smiled that great smile. Jasmine would be crazy not to fall for that.

Cole needed to get home to Frankie, anyway. It was nearly dark, and Frankie's dinner was overdue, so Cole waved, and then got in his Mustang to return to his own electricity powered, air-conditioned, almost-too-quiet house. As he backed out of the driveway, he saw a small, rust-riddled, green truck pull into the driveway. A woman with long, dark hair stepped out and waved at Constantine. She either had not seen Cole or was deliberately ignoring him. Whatever.

Cole drove home, disappointed that he had not been able to complain about Maureen. Now she would pay for Cole's landline to be turned back on, with an added extension phone in the basement. After all, Jason can't be working in a shop with no phone. How would they get help if something happened? "Nothing's going to happen," Cole had told her. He knew this only because he was not going to let Jason get anywhere near a power tool. Maybe that would come later. Maybe Jason would become the apprentice that all artisans, craftsmen, and tradespersons dreamed of – but for now, Jason would play music. He could watch Cole build a guitar, and he could assemble his own guitar when the time came, but Jason had to catch the guitar-building fever first. His temperature was rising, Cole could tell. It was just a matter of time.

Nevertheless, now there would be a phone soon in case of "emergency." It wasn't a bad thing so much as it would extract one more pound of flesh from Cole. That's all.

On the drive home Cole reflected: the phone wasn't really a problem. It was just that Maureen had not really come over to talk about a phone. Paying the phone bill was her apology for asking Cole if he would stand in for Richard, who had volunteered at CJ's school summer carnival to sit on the "dunk" board. On the dunk board, Cole would sit and smile and wait for some kid with a good arm to hit the magic bulls-eye target that would release Cole into a tank of unheated water…not ice-cold by any means, but not bath water. Maureen told him that she understood perfectly if he did not agree to this. Perhaps he could just take over supervising the shop while Richard risked the wild throws from elementary school would-be pitchers who could drop him in the drink.

The next morning, Cole was sitting atop a board over the dunk tank, where he brushed his toes back and forth across the water surface. The tank had just been filled that morning and was plenty cold, even in June. He remembered all the pitching instructions he had freely provided to CJ. CJ already had a remarkable arm for a seven-year-old, and early in the spring had been moved up from the peewee league because of it. "Hey, CJ," Cole shouted at the small kid standing about twenty feet away with determination written all over him. "Go easy, man." But Cole could see that CJ was out to impress. There were not many seven-year-olds who could hit that bullseye, but CJ could. Five bigger kids had failed, however, although a few slow arcs had fouled off the edge of the target and might have tempted a real swing from a real batter. Maybe the dunk target mechanism was stuck. He watched as CJ's perfect strike sped toward the target.

Cole came out of the water sputtering. "Jesus, that's cold!" CJ's look of triumph and his carefully casual walk to the back of the line, with high-five's along the way, made it all worthwhile. An hour later, Cole was released from dunk duty, and walked back to his car parked in a grassy field next to the school. Sweat was running down his face and neck, and although he had changed out of his wet clothing, his new, dry t-shirt stuck to his back by the time he arrived at the car, but it didn't matter. That was just summer in Florida.

Cole remembered the trips he and Constantine would take in the summer to the freezing swimming holes south of Tallahassee: Cherokee sink, Blue sink, sometimes Wakulla Springs, and Dave's sink where everyone who wanted to swim for free had to bring beer, and no one was allowed in the water with clothes on. Beer kegs, bonfires, music. Free beer if you played music. Cole was all about free.

That afternoon, Jason was going to the beach with a friend, so Cole was looking forward to uninterrupted time in the basement. To begin with, he desperately needed to survey the guitars he would take to the NAMM show. But first he visited with Jewell, who wasn't yet ready to come home and didn't want to talk about it. They carefully made small talk, mostly about Frankie and CJ, and then Cole headed over to Constantine's, whose school day ended at 3, for leftover lasagna. To overcome Cole's worry about the time he needed to spend in the basement shop, Constantine promised to have the lasagna hot and steaming on the plate when Cole arrived.

An hour later, Cole thanked Constantine for the lasagna, and headed home. The traffic light gods were smiling, and he made it home in twelve minutes, having been stopped by only one red light, nearly a miracle in the annals of Tallahassee driving, where typically one gazed at the green light a block ahead where there was nary a car in sight, while he waited impatiently with a dozen other drivers at a red light where there was no cross traffic. Maybe PhD students in FSU's Psychology Department had designed the traffic light conundrum for research. It's a study called 'The Boundary between Patience and Practicality in the Typical Law-Abiding Citizen."

Frankie greeted Cole as enthusiastically as ever, but it was clear that he detected a new and intriguing odor, the lasagna. Cole snapped his fingers for Frankie to follow him to the overgrown front yard where Frankie investigated nearly every grass blade to find the perfect one on which to relieve himself.

There were azalea bushes blocking the view of Martina's house and front porch, but Cole could hear her holding forth in Russian. It was late enough in the day for vodka on the rocks with lime. She sat on her porch nearly every afternoon and many evenings, even in the roasting summer heat. She had stamina, and maybe that required vodka on ice with lime.

Now Frankie was sniffing the small purple flowers that were blossoming from some of the many weeds in his lawn. If not for the weeds, Cole noted, there might not be a lawn - and Frankie nibbled several of them, then looked at Cole for reassurance. Maybe there was a nutritious meal right here in the front yard. He could be onto something. "Oh Frankieeeeeee," Cole called in his best impression of Julia Child, a high falsetto that had always made Jewell laugh. "Oh, Frankie dear, a suspicious stomach, uneasy with worry, cannot digest properly. Have at it, dear."

A phone was ringing some distance away, and Cole realized that it was in the house, his own house. Now there were lights, air conditioning, *and* a phone. He should be happy. Jewell should be happy. If he could but convince her to come home, all would be well. He whistled for Frankie and headed into the house but arrived too late. He studied the now silent phone. There was no message, and it didn't make sense to just start dialing…unless it was Jewell ready to come home. A quick call to Edna P's and he learned that it had not been Jewell. He hung up the phone, scooped Frankie onto his lap and slowly stroked Frankie's ears.

After dinner, Cole sat on the sofa and quietly picked out a new tune, and whispered the lyrics:

There are lines suddenly drawn
On a summer afternoon
And tears are shed later
Under a lopsided moon
There are hearts too tender
And so easily bruised
There are truths revealed that
Won't be forgiven or excused

It was probably too late to call Gary, just to see if he was still the guitar enthusiast he once claimed to be. Perhaps by now he had wrested his guitar manufacturing dream from the downbeat, get-it-out-the-door-yesterday businessman that was Peter, and was up for another run. Maybe Gary would be experiencing greater remorse over having abandoned Heartbreak than it had seemed six weeks ago, when Cole had finally gotten through to Gary by phone and convinced him to meet him for breakfast at The Pancake House.

That morning, Gary had shifted in his seat and mostly looked past Cole out the window where the cars and trucks on Monroe Street rumbled as traffic moved at a crawl. "We just couldn't get it off the ground fast enough," Gary had said. He'd drummed lightly on the Formica table and fidgeted in his seat, as if eager to be out the door and on to the next meeting with some other hapless inventor. But maybe he'd just had too much coffee, and the nervous energy that practically poured out of him would evaporate out there in the May heat and rising humidity.

Maybe if they had met instead for lunch, Gary could look Cole in the eye. They could think about a renewal of their partnership, one without Peter. Guitar player to guitar player. They could discuss whether to go with Seymour Duncan or EMG pickups, Lace Sensors or Harmonic Design. They could decide whether to send Desire or one of the Sisters to *Guitar Player Magazine*, or maybe to *Guitar World* for a review – free advertising. And they could mull over whether to continue to get ebony fretboards or switch to rosewood for a warmer tone. Together they could just savor the satisfaction of having invented and built a new product, one that would win the hearts and minds of many guitar enthusiasts as it had won over theirs. But in fact, it had never been like that with Gary.

Cole glanced at the clock. He could call, but some people went to bed at nine. Unlike Jewell, who could not fall asleep before 2 a.m. If Cole got up in the middle of the night for water, she would be sitting in the rocking chair in the living room, reading a true crime story or a novel by an unheard-of-writer that her book club had nominated for that month's reading. Somehow, the book club had learned of that new writing talent. Cole needed to find out how an unknown writer without connections, with no advertising budget, and no one to champion his or her cause managed to connect with avid true crime consumers in small towns and cities far away. That information could be very useful right now.

Frankie, who had been pressed against Cole on the sofa, softly snoring, suddenly sat up facing the door. His ears were hitched up like small tents and he quietly growled. The front gate banged shut and Frankie leapt off the sofa, his feet sliding out from under him on the hardwood floor and his chest hitting the floor with a thud.

Cole rose from the sofa and opened the door. "Take it easy, boy." Jason stomped past them wearing a backpack and carrying his guitar case. He propped the case against a bookcase in the corner, flung his backpack onto the sofa, and sat heavily next to it and glared at the floor. Frankie leapt up and down in front of Jason, wagging his tail, then dancing in a circle, fully expecting Jason to scoop him up and rub his head.

"See?" Cole said to Frankie. "He comes in peace." He refrained from saying "And that's his regular look." Not exactly true, though it was not unfamiliar either. Jason did not crack a smile. Cole paused in the doorway, looking into the dusk at the empty driveway, wondering how Jason had magically appeared in his living room, four miles away from Jason's own house. Then he shut the door. "What's up, Bud?" he asked. He moved the guitar case to a safer perch on the dining room table and then sat in the chair opposite Jason.

"I'm never going back," Jason said. Sweat rolled down his flushed cheeks and dripped onto the front of his t-shirt.

"Are we talking school or…?"

"Richard and Maureen's," Jason declared.

"Whoa, must be pretty serious if they aren't even 'Dad and Mom' now. Speaking of which, do they know you're here?"

"They don't care," Jason declared. His arms were crossed on his chest, and he sank further into the sofa cushion, still not acknowledging Frankie, who now slowly wagged his tail and politely waited with his front paws up on the sofa cushion. Neither was Jason looking at Cole but staring across the room at the bookcase on which Jewell had placed CJ and Chrissie's plaster handprints and the small, fired-clay dog that Jason had made in Kindergarten. The set of his jaw loosened a little. "Only CJ and Chrissie care."

Now Frankie had brought a small red ball and dropped it at Jason's feet, but Jason didn't budge.

"So, I guess they don't know you're here," Cole said. Jason glared at him. "It's cool," Cole said. "We can remedy that."

"Can I stay here?" Jason croaked.

"Sure." What else could he say? "But we have to tell your parents."

"I don't want to talk to them!"

"No sweat," Cole said. Jason would eventually tell him what happened, but the timing had to be right. "Why don't you go get a shower while I talk to them."

When Cole hung up the phone, he was only slightly more enlightened than before speaking with Richard. They were enrolling Jason in a private school for the fall – smaller class sizes and no timed tests, work-at-your-own-pace philosophy – a school that Jason had liked when they all had checked it out two months ago, before school had let out, but now Jason didn't want to go to any school where he couldn't take guitar classes or be in the band. The thing was, Richard noted, he rarely even played the guitar, and he wasn't in the band and had never played a band instrument, so Richard and Maureen thought he was joking. Richard confessed that he and Maureen had burst out laughing. Jason had stormed out of the kitchen, but Richard and Maureen couldn't stick around to talk it out. They had practically wolfed down their food, left the dishes in the sink, and rushed CJ to meet his best friend for the 7:30 p.m. showing of *Spider Man.* Obviously, Chrissie had to go with them, but Jason had gone in his room and slammed the door.

It was settled. Jason would spend the night with Cole, and they could all talk about it tomorrow. Cole hoped that Jason wouldn't want to stay the weekend. The guest room where Jason would sleep was Jewell's meditation room, where she wrote in her journal, performed yoga, and sometimes did a little drawing. She had always needed a place she could go to be alone. Especially in the last year, when Cole spent much of his day in the basement talking only to Frankie and would come upstairs for dinner and some human conversation, Jewell may have already eaten yoghurt and grapes for dinner. She would be in her room, burning incense, maybe listening to music, sometimes with the lights out, sometimes using a candle or maybe quietly reading using the light from a small, ornately bejeweled lamp with a red shade and low output. Could she really read under that light?

There were three bedrooms: the master bedroom, the bedroom made into Jewell's meditation room, and an even smaller third bedroom that had been given over entirely to storage. Cole opened the door of the storage room, flipped on the light, and stared at the stacks of exotic wood he had scored from Red Bay Lumber. You couldn't pass up bubinga or padauk and the future guitar beauties they would become. There were instruments as well. These were the acoustics and electrics he had built steadily since high school – nearly two dozen custom guitars, most now lacking the electronics and hardware that he had cannibalized for the Inflatables.

Over the last several years, he had sold a handful of electrics, and had sold three acoustics, but had let them go at bargain prices, only because he needed to fund the next instrument. He had not sold the antiques that he had been given by Constantine, a mandolin and a bass ukulele that Constantine's grandfather had made in his own early days as a luthier. Cole would go out of business before he did that.

There was not much that could be moved to the basement, but maybe with a little restacking, he could clear room enough for a sleeping bag and a small shelf unit for Jason's stuff. Although Cole had a feeling that Jason would only be staying one night, he didn't truly know what Jason was thinking yet. He didn't know how Jewell would feel about it. He didn't even know how he felt about it. Leave it for tomorrow.

# Chapter 9

June 28th, 2002 (Friday)
21 days before the NAMM show

It was just before lunch, just after Cole had driven from Richard's shop to rouse the still-sleeping Jason and take him home, when the phone rang. Cole still wasn't used to having a phone, and its emphatic ring startled him. Surely it would have been true that Alexander Graham Bell believed in quiet and polite discourse, and he would be appalled at the derelict state of conversation today and the harsh and piercing ringing that his phones now emitted, as bone-penetrating as a dentist's drill. They were loud. They were relentless. As if invented by the Russians! Cole sighed as he walked across the living room to answer the summons, mumbling "Calm down, I'm coming."

It was Jewell, and she was ready to leave Edna P.'s and needed him to pick her up. Cole had wondered how long they would let her stay without insurance. The Center Director had reminded Cole about payment every time she saw him. But his mother believed Edna P.'s would not boot Jewell out

95

before they thought she was ready. He had hoped she was right. "Sure, definitely…I'll be right there…thirty minutes or so," Cole said.

He hung up the phone and looked at Jason, who lay on his back on the couch with his head resting on a small throw-cushion. His legs stretched along the length of the sofa and his feet were hanging over one armrest. Jason's Walkman rested on his chest, and he was wearing small earphones and playing air drums. Should Cole leave him here? That was tempting. Despite Jason's seeming dedication to maintaining a supine position with his eyes closed, Cole felt uneasy about leaving a now awake Jason alone with power tools in the basement. There was the band saw. Jason had commented that it looked like it could do some serious rock cutting. "No, it can't," Cole had declared with alarm. "And it won't."

Cole could either bring Jason along to Edna P.'s or take him back home. This was as good a time as any to find out how angry Jason might still be over this private school thing. "Jason," Cole said. "Jason," a little louder. "Remove those things glued to your ears. Hey, you! I have to take you back home and pick up Jewell. It's a day off, Bud."

Jason groaned and sat up. "Why did you wake me up, then?" he mumbled. Could it be that easy? Last night, Jason was "never going back," but this morning…his more placid, if not cheerful, alter ego had returned.

"*I must be cruel, only to be kind*," Cole said. "Bill Shakespeare wrote that."

Cole helped Jewell pack her collection of clothes and books into a paper grocery bag that he had begged from the Edna P. staff. He hadn't thought to bring a travel bag from home since Jewell hadn't carried anything with her when he had brought her here, but over the eight days of her "incarceration", as she had put it, she had accumulated clothing, books, cards, photos of Maureen's kids, drawings made by Chrissy and CJ, the Aztec-print vase filled with azaleas Cole had picked from the yard, and a travel kit containing a toothbrush and toothpaste and deodorant that he had brought her, but that was now bulging with shampoo and conditioner, a small hairbrush and other essentials Edna P. might have provided or perhaps Maureen had brought.

Who could have guessed that it would take over two hours to complete Jewell's discharge papers? They waited in her room while someone somewhere was doing the paperwork. By the time they walked out the front door, it was just after 3:00 p.m. and the traffic from the shift change at Tallahassee Memorial Hospital had jammed up Centerville Road going northeast, Seventh Avenue going west, and Meridian going northwest. Cole got in the long line of cars crawling north on Meridian.

Cole matched Jewell's quiet reserve at first, but then tried to engage her with tidbits of news she might appreciate: Constantine's increasing chumminess with Jasmine; Jason's blow-up and potential reconciliation; CJ's baseball future; NAMM show preparations. After he had recounted what he had to do to still get ready for the NAMM show - a lot...a whole lot – he fell silent for a moment. "I just have to get in the show. The Inflatables will do the rest." Cole got the green left turn arrow onto John Knox Road and sped through the intersection and merged with the traffic heading west. Traffic was thinning out a little and he could resume a reasonable speed. "I know you already said that you didn't want to come to the show with me, but you know you can change your mind at any time. Heartbreak is yours as much as mine." That was true, but only in principle. It was Cole's dream, and Jewell was along for the ride. They both knew it.

Jewell sat slumped in her seat, looking out the window as they passed a bus stop where a young woman was sitting on the bench with a toddler in her lap and a bag of groceries beside her on the bench. "You have to go to NAMM. I know that," she said. Cole noted that she hadn't said that she *wanted* him to go. That would have been a welcome thought.

"Gary and Peter gave you a little boost. That's about all they did…extended a break from building countertops," she said. "Just enough to keep your hopes up. For them, it's just business. For you, it's your whole heart breaking every day that you can't get Desire, or whomever you're in love with now, out there in the world."

"Whoa! Whoa, whoa, whoa!" Cole exclaimed. "I am not *in love* with any guitar. I just love building them. It's just what I do. Maybe you hadn't noticed, but the craftsmen and women of the world are dying off. Where are the artisans? What do factory machines know about seeing the true beauty and quality sound in a maple with grain distortion or a hardwood with an exquisite natural complexion? Are we supposed to grind all those up for paper?"

"Seriously, Cole, you don't think I've heard this rant before?" Jewell said. Cole started to protest, but she held up her hand. "It's ok. Go to NAMM. You have to. I just can't do it anymore. I can't even talk about it." Her voice was increasingly dispirited. "Go to NAMM. See if you get your big break. Then we'll talk."

Cole remembered that Jewell had just been released from treatment and had yet to experience being home with electricity – air conditioning, hot water, refrigerator, lights at the flip of a switch. That alone might restore her easy smile and her enthusiasm for Heartbreak Guitars. Heartbreak was his idea, and maybe it was his dream, but they were in this thing together, and success at the NAMM show would make all their sacrifices worth it – in just three more weeks.

But even when they arrived home, even with Frankie's leaping and yelping, Jewell's smile remained mostly hidden. Cole looked at Jewell and decided to give her a few minutes to relax, maybe have something to eat, or a glass or two of wine.

"I got you some white wine," he said, "And some crackers and cheese." He pulled a bottle out of the cooler that held the wine, opened the rosemary flecked crackers, brie, and a small Tupperware container half filled with tuna fish salad, all of which Maureen had pressed on him when he'd dropped Jason at home.

Frankie made a whining sound in the back of his throat that sounded pretty much like singing. "Do you think he's happy you're home?" Cole smiled at Jewell. "Hey, but no more than I am."

"I don't see you racing around the house while wiggling your butt," Jewell said, and sipped her wine. Before Cole had learned that Jewell was to be discharged, before he'd locked Frankie in the house to go get her, he had quickly picked azaleas and plumbago that were so abundant in the front yard, and some yellow daisy-like flowers – probably weeds, but how can you really tell - that were growing around the mailbox and in the drainage ditch by the street, and put them in a large vase on the dining room table.

"Frankie didn't pick flowers, now did he?"

"No, he didn't," Jewell said, "and I'm guessing he didn't buy the wine." Prosecco was one of her favorite wines, Cole remembered, but he would have taken anything Maureen had given him. Jewell placed her wine glass on the end table and leaned forward to pick up Frankie, who wiggled in her lap and tried to lick her face. "Oh, no you don't," Jewell said, but she was laughing. Finally. She looked at peace, even happy.

"You do realize that we are married," Cole said.

"Yes – actually – I do realize that," Jewell answered.

"So that entitles us to certain intimacies that were sometimes less appealing when it was ninety-five degrees...at least to you. I was pretty good anytime."

"Maybe," she said, "if you play your cards right. Do you have any cards?" Frankie had settled into her lap with his head resting on her non-wine-drinking hand.

"I got cards you haven't even seen yet," Cole exclaimed.

Janice Dodge

# Chapter 10

June 29th – Saturday – 20 days before the NAMM
show

Jewell was still sleeping when Cole awakened with an epiphany. There was no rhyme or reason why this idea had suddenly come to him, but there it was. He could make an Inflatable that was even lighter than the Despair Sisters, who were already lighter than Desire. He would use Sitka Spruce, which he had formerly eschewed for the more interesting figured-grain woods like curly or flame maple, or the naturally beautiful grain of hardwoods like mahogany, or the exotic padauk, even cherry, with its interesting but tricky mineral streaks and sap pockets. Sitka Spruce wasn't particularly attractive, in that it wasn't distinctive, but it was very light and very strong. And it didn't need to be beautiful, anyway, because no one would see it. The small, central piece of wood that was the mini-body – the heart of the guitar into which he embedded the electronics - had been stained and polished in Desire and Despair to bring out the arresting wood pattern. But for his new model using

Sitka Spruce, he would cover the entire face of an even smaller guitar body with a decorative, plastic pick guard, thus masking the wood entirely while making the guitar even lighter.

He dressed quickly and headed for the basement without stopping to make coffee. From the basement, he heard Jewell's footsteps in the kitchen, and ten minutes later, Jewell appeared at the bottom of the steps. "I made coffee," she said, "looks like….," she abruptly turned and went back upstairs, not a good sign.

Cole had been taking stock of what wood he already had in the basement. No Sitka Spruce, but actually, he could use a two-by-four just to see how his idea would work. It wouldn't be the first time an electric guitar was built from a two-by-four. Les Paul had already demonstrated that an electric guitar could be reduced to its essentials by bolting a guitar neck to a length of two-by-four and installing some pick-ups. That guitar, known as "The Log", was famous - if not popular.

He placed a padlock on a little hinged wood box he had made to enclose and secure the electric plug from the band saw. Let's see Jason try to get into that! He turned the window A/C on high in anticipation of the day's oppressive heat, and then went upstairs for coffee with Jewell.

He poured coffee into a mug and glanced at Jewell, who was sitting by the dining room window looking out over the overgrown back yard. Cole sat across from her. "So, how's it going?" he asked. She didn't answer and he followed her gaze to where the tall grass was moving, pushed by some mysterious unseen force. "What is it?" he asked, truly stumped by what could be rippling the grass.

"Frankie," she said. Interesting how one's entire emotional landscape can be conveyed by one word. Jewell wasn't happy this morning, nor did she seem at peace like yesterday, after she had first returned home to Frankie, air conditioning and two glasses of Prosecco. Either that, or she just hadn't had enough coffee to complete the transition from peaceful slumber to fully awake with moving parts.

Cole looked at the clock. He was expected at Richard's shop – open half a day on Saturdays – and should be there in an hour if he was going to lead the forklift safety training, as he had announced to the shop guys midweek. "No one is going to operate the forklift until they have completed the training."

"Will there be a test?" sniggered one young man. He was the one who always came in late and spent half an hour in the bathroom before starting work.

"Absolutely," Cole said. Although he hadn't really thought about a test, now he would. "Good idea," he said, and all seven guys groaned.

But in the kitchen, standing next to Jewell and watching the unseen Frankie bounding through the grass, Cole knew that whatever was said next, and wherever it led…that was more important than forklift safety training. Richard's shop guys had managed to stay alive without training… so far.

Cole silently ran through some of his favorite Shakespeare quotes: '*Teach not thy lip such scorn, for it was made for kissing, lady, and not for such contempt.*' To which she might reply, '*A fool thinks himself to be wise, but a wise man knows himself to be a fool.*'

Sensing a certain grumpiness in her reply, he might offer: "*The course of true love never did run smooth,*" but she would surely rebut him with "*Love is a smoke made with the fume of sighs.*"
The silent discourse carried forth in his brain:

Cole - "*'tis better to bear the ills we have than to fly to others we know not of.*"

Jewell - "*Having nothing, nothing he can lose.*"

Cole - "*It is not in the stars to hold our destiny, but in ourselves.*"

Jewell - "*Words without thoughts never to heaven go.*"

Perhaps Cole could offer this gem - "*I give unto my wife the second-best bed with the furniture.*"

But she might miss the humor and thus reply - "*No legacy is as rich as honesty.*"

Cole finally remembered this bit of wisdom - "*When words are scarce, they are seldom spent in vain,*" and so he said nothing while they drank coffee and watched Frankie's uneven progress through the grass back to the house.

Frankie emerged from the grass and bounded up the steps to the kitchen door, and Jewell got up and let him in. "Good boy," she said, and dropped a pinch of toast, which he caught in mid-air and gulped without tasting.

"You could lose a finger if you're not careful," Cole said. "Frankie is all business when it comes to food."

Jewell scooped up Frankie and pressed him to her neck, then kissed him on the top of his head. "He's my baby," she crooned. "I'm taking him with me to Miami."

"What!" Cole exclaimed. "What are you talking about?"

Jewell walked slowly from the sink to the refrigerator, cradling Frankie against her like a small child. "To my folks. Jasmine is going to Miami for a conference this weekend. She said that Constantine can't go, and she wanted a companion. She has a paper or poster or something she's supposed to present on Monday and asked if I wanted to ride with her. Keep her company." Jewell kissed the top of Frankie's head again.

Cole was momentarily speechless. How in the hell did Jewell and Jasmine get so chummy? And when would they have cooked up this plan? Cole knew that Jasmine was trouble…this just confirmed it.

"So Jasmine is going to some Biology conference in Miami and said to herself," Cole said with forced calm, "I wonder if Jewell – whom I barely know – would like to go to Miami with me.'"

"Sort of," Jewell said. "Doubt she would say 'whom.'" Cole shifted in his chair and pointedly stared at her. "She came by the Edna P. Slate Center with Constantine just to say 'hello' and 'I hope you're doing ok'. If you'd been there during afternoon visiting hours, you would have seen them…or run smack into them on your way out, since you probably would have had to rush home and glue something." Strident again, Cole thought, but he was feeling pretty strident himself.

"How long are you planning to stay?" He wondered about her work, where they were perpetually shorthanded and had always been so stingy about granting vacation time.

"I don't know yet. I just spoke with Jasmine, and she asked me if I wanted to go, and I haven't planned any more than that. I thought it was nice of her to ask."

Cole did not really want to argue about Jasmine, but he couldn't feel good about Jewell hitching a ride with her, either. And he really, really did not feel good about her taking Frankie. "Maybe Frankie doesn't want to go," Cole asserted. "It's not like he knows your parents all that well. Strange people, strange house, really strange cat."

"Yeah, well, he does want to go."

Cole set his coffee mug on the table a little too hard. "He has a perfectly good life right here. No stress." That wasn't exactly true. Cole remembered the evenings when Jewell was gone that Frankie had been shut up in the house alone until Cole came home from Constantine's, and there was the torn-to-smithereens stuffed squeak toy. But anything had to be better than Frankie having to constantly be on the look-out for Jewell's parents' aloof and nasty-tempered cat. "He likes to hang out in the shop," which was true, although it was also true that Frankie liked to hang out anywhere human beings were present. "He LOVES hanging out in the shop, where we can talk, man-to-man."

Just at that moment Frankie yawned, turned his head toward Cole and said, very conversationally,

"Raaaoh." It was uncanny how like human speech it seemed.

"See what I'm saying? He just agreed with me."

"Well, now you've got Jason for your manly talks," Jewell said.

"You try talking to Jason," Cole said. "It gets complicated fast." Cole tapped at the small divot in the tabletop, then covered it with his hand. "I'll take Frankie any day."

"No. I'm taking Frankie." She was strident again. "What would you do with him, anyway, when you're at the NAMM show?" There was nothing Cole could say to that. He could ask Maureen to come over while he was gone – but she would have to come twice a day so Frankie could eat and go outside, and Frankie would get about fifteen minutes of playtime and get fed and patted on the head for ten seconds, and that would be it. Neither Maureen nor Frankie would be happy.

God, he would miss Frankie. And of course, he would miss Jewell, but she must know that. "So, when are you coming back? Don't they need you back at work?"

She stopped walking with Frankie and leaned against the sink. "Not everything is about money," she said. Her words were clipped, acerbic. She put

Frankie down and leaned back against the sink, folding her arms. "It's all I'm saying."

He didn't really know what she was saying. How did asking when she would return from Miami become about money? "So, if you take Frankie," Cole had already conceded that Frankie would go with Jewell, "if you take Frankie, you have to come back by car. Should I come get you, like…after the NAMM show?"

"I don't know," she paused. "Maybe Jasmine can pick me up."

"Really? What the hell is up with you and Jasmine?" This was truly maddening. "I just really want to know because I…your husband…am offering to come get you. And you'd rather get this near stranger to drive all the way to Miami to retrieve you instead?"

"I like her," Jewell said.

"Well, I don't!" Cole nearly shouted.

"Well, she's not taking *you* to Miami, so why do you care?"

Cole did care. Jasmine was not to be trusted. How was it that Jewell and Constantine did not realize that Jasmine was not to be trusted? She played them, and they let her. That was the only explanation. "You remember that time we were over at Constantine's and the cops came?" Cole asked. Jewell couldn't possibly forget that. It was the last time she had gone over to Constantine's, and she only went that time because Constantine had power – lights, air conditioning and a refrigerator. It wasn't that she didn't like Constantine, but she just preferred to have some time alone at home while Cole was out. Since he started working full time building guitars, Cole was always home. Jewell just enjoyed coming home from work to utter silence, just once in a while, she said.

One Saturday, several months ago, Jewell had gone with Cole over to Constantine's. It was mid-afternoon and already nearly ninety degrees out, when a policeman knocked on Constantine's front door. As Jewell had recounted on the ride home that day, she had been stretched out on the sofa, reading and luxuriating in Constantine's air-conditioned living room while Constantine, Cole, Fabian and their friend, Dan, played music out in the garage.

Apparently, a policeman had come to the door, and stated there had been a noise complaint. Jewell could hardly hear him over Fabian's drums, Cole's rhythm guitar, Constantine's bass guitar, and Dan's lead guitar…soul-penetrating sounds that emanated from Constantine's garage, vibrated the kitchen cabinet doors and the crystal candlesticks on the back of the kitchen counter, rattled the rarely used silver, and resonated in the oak floors. Jewell wasn't quite sure what, exactly, was vibrating, but if you walked around barefoot, you felt the music from the soles of your feet to the top of your head. Even Frankie lay on the floor near Jewell, his eyebrows twitching and his worried eyes open wide, not really enjoying his rare outing. Jewell opened the front door wider, stepped outside onto the patio, and squinted at the policeman, wondering if he could detect the odor of pot. When they smoked it, which seemed a necessary component of their jam session, the rule was 'only in the garage'. One had to exhibit a little caution, so that when a police person arrives on the front patio, calmly instructing them – via shouting - to turn down the stereo, they were not hauled off in handcuffs.

"Yes, we'll turn it down. Definitely," Jewell had told the policeman. "We were just celebrating a birthday," she said, as if this would matter to the police. Actually, Dan was taking Desire on a test drive, and everyone else was along for the ride. "I'll just go tell my husband," Jewell continued. She stepped back inside. "He definitely does not want to bother the neighbors," she said as she backed up and closed the heavy wood door. She watched through the front window as the policeman walked back to his cruiser and got into the driver's seat, then she dashed through the kitchen toward the door to the garage with Frankie close behind.

"The police are here!" she shouted as Frankie ran around the garage, up and down and in a circle around Cole, just for the sheer joy of running. The music had stopped, and four surprised faces glanced at Frankie, and then turned toward Jewell. "There's been a noise complaint," she said as she walked to the far side of the garage and closed the door to the outside utility room. "Turn on the A/C! And keep the windows closed." She reached past Cole and turned on the window air conditioner behind him, then shut the windows in the back near the washer and dryer. They hated the hum of the A/C unit. Rather than put up with its heavy, droning din, they had been willing to swelter with the soft whir of two box fans. "Someone complained," Jewell explained. She expected Cole to go off on a diatribe about the complaining neighbor – probably Russian - but they all remained quiet. They were waiting for her to leave. She had disturbed the continuity of the universe and disrupted a pure and intense musical journey.

"Of course, I remember when the cops came," Jewell said. "Jasmine wasn't even there, so I don't understand your point."

"That is my point!" Cole exclaimed. "She later claimed that she'd been invited – ok, that's true – but she said that she knew that the cops would come. I mean, seriously? She knew the cops would come? When they never came before that? We didn't know her well, so I just let it go."

"As opposed to what?" Jewell put Frankie on the floor. "What are you saying? That she called the cops? Or are you just calling her a liar? Some people can intuit things."

"Some people just make shit up!"

Cole could not see a good way to end this. He wanted to go down to the basement, back to his new design for the two-by-four guitar. He should try to bring this discussion, if you could call it that, to a healthy resolution. No one should walk away angry, Cole believed, although it was so much harder to put in practice than to believe it. In fact, he *should* be at Richard's shop, where they were expecting him to train them not to kill themselves. But he didn't know how to end the discussion well, and despite his semi-good supervisory intentions, he didn't want to go to Richard's shop on a Saturday morning after a week of frustration and setbacks, when he had this really good idea and he needed to see how well it would work. He sat at the table cupping one hand around his empty coffee cup and staring out the window at the tall grass speckled with dandelion blooms and pale blue flowers.

# Chapter 11

June 30<sup>th</sup> – Sunday
19 days before the NAMM show

At nine o'clock on Sunday morning, Jewell placed her suitcase and Frankie's bowl, chow, and bed behind the bench seat of Jasmine's beat-up green truck. Jasmine had parked in the driveway and tapped the horn to summon Jewell from the house. As Cole and Jewell stood outside the truck talking quietly, Jasmine drummed on the steering wheel and sighed. Cole looked at Jasmine and held up one finger…just a minute.

Despite the sighing and drumming, it was only a minute or two, maybe five, that he and Jewell discussed how to protect Frankie from the mentally ill cat; what bills had been paid; a tropical storm that was forming in the eastern Caribbean; and finally, a reminder that Jewell would call when she arrived at her parent's house. Jewell got in the truck and positioned Frankie on a cushion next to her on the seat and rolled down the window to say a final goodbye. Jasmine complained about the late start and the long drive and segued into a monologue about imaginary traffic headaches on I-75, a sure sign to Cole that she was over-caffeinated and everyone in the truck cab would do well to just to listen to her rattle on without interruption regarding future events about which she knew nothing.

Cole's heart sank as he watched them drive away, with the top of Frankie's head and his tented ears just visible through the back window. They had traveled only a short distance when Frankie's small face appeared in the back window, always so hopeful. Cole knew that Frankie's tail would be wagging slowly. Frankie didn't understand what was going on. Neither did Cole.

Early on Monday morning, Cole drove to Richard's shop. Richard had already arrived with three dozen donuts and a carton of brewed coffee, a bribe to entice the shop guys to arrive on time for the forklift training. Five of the seven were present, because, of course, bathroom-guy hadn't arrived yet and one other had called in sick.

"Are you serious about giving a test?" one guy mumbled while chewing.

"Yes, I'm serious," Cole said. "You're going to drive this thing and show me how careful you can be." Cole reached for a donut. "But we're going to go over some safety rules first, right Richard?" Richard nodded.

By noon, each of the guys had passed the test – reciting to Cole the safety rules and slowly driving the forklift to the storage shed and moving a pallet of materials to the opposite side of the yard. Before he let them leave, Cole showed them an OSHA video that depicted investigations of several deaths from falling granite slabs, and another that depicted accidents resulting from spectacularly idiotic use of forklifts.

Cole had shut down the video and was about to hand over the forklift keys to Mr. Bean when Richard showed up for the test.

"You sure?" Cole asked, wondering why Richard hadn't stayed for the actual training.

"Doesn't look too hard," Richard said. Cole cringed. Wasn't this the same Richard who had once let one of his guys stand on the forks holding a ladder, and had watched as the man and ladder were raised as high as the forks would go, who then kept watching as his employee balanced the ladder on the forks and climbed four rungs high so as to hang a large box fan over his workstation? Maybe Richard and his shop could be featured in the next OSHA video about idiotic uses of the forklift. And how did it look that Richard could skip the training and just take a fifteen-minute test?

Cole put the keys in his pocket. "Okay, name the eight safety rules."

Richard stared at Cole for a few seconds, then turned and walked back to his office.

Cole had hoped to have lunch with Richard and iron out some of the details of going to NAMM, less than three weeks away, but this probably wouldn't be a good time. There also another light bill that had come in the mail two days before and now was propped up on the small kitchen table between the salt and pepper shakers. He would have to move that out of view so he could eat in peace. He headed out to pick up Jason, hoping Jason was already awake and ready to go.

Maureen opened the door as Cole was walking up the steps to the front porch. "I'm glad you're here because we have to talk." She ushered him into the living room, where stacks of folded laundry occupied the sofa. She motioned for Cole to sit on the loveseat, and she sat in a narrow space amidst a tower of folded towels, one of jeans, and another of t-shirts. "I have to go to Pensacola. It's Mom and Dad. Don't worry, they're okay. Basically okay. Just that Mom called this morning saying that Dad fell off the roof yesterday and broke his hip and bruised his ribs."

"What the hell was he doing on the roof?" Cole asked.

"Does it really matter?" Maureen said, exasperated. "Don't you ever go up on the roof, to clear the gutters or something?"

"Not if I can help it."

"Well, maybe you should," Maureen said. She hesitated, and Cole could see that she wanted to say something more, but she continued, "Anyway, they are doing surgery on Dad's hip, but when he gets out of the hospital, Mom will need some help. You know how he can be." She meant stubborn, or using Dad's preferred terms - independent, not just one of the sheep.

Cole waited. Should he offer to go? Would his help even help? Maureen was better at these kinds of things, cajoling a person to walk when that person said it was too painful; helping to gently move limbs into sleeves and pant legs; coaxing him to take his medicine before the current dose wore off; cooking and washing dishes…just keeping a grumpy old man company and making him laugh. Cole waited.

"You could go with me, but it would really help if you could stay here to help Richard. Especially with Jason. I'm taking CJ and Chrissy with me."

He tried not to sound as relieved as he felt. "You'll let me know if something happens?"

"I'll let you know. And I'll call Richard tomorrow night. He can fill you in."

"Okay, good. That's good." Cole hadn't visited his parents in nearly ten months, since before Gary and Peter had stopped the trickling flow of funds. And he had seen them infrequently in the preceding years as mounting hardships had piled up while he struggled to get his guitars perfected and out in the world and had built countertops by day and guitars at night and on weekends. He had kept most of his worries to himself in those years. His parents would have tried to help, and perhaps could have even scraped together a little money if they had known Cole and Jewell's recent dire circumstances. But his father had hurt his back in a shop accident four years ago, was out of work for six months, and then shortly after returning to work, he had wrenched his back again, and was out for two more months, and then he was laid off. He continued to suffer bouts of disabling pain. His mother had continued to work, but she increasingly suffered from arthritis in her back and hands and had retired as soon as she had turned sixty-two last Fall. After thirty years working at the community college, she could collect a small pension, and they both could collect social security. Neither one of them was in very good shape. "He should have called me to help with the roof," Cole said.

"Really? You could help," Maureen said flatly. "Maybe they would have called," she went on, "but you need a phone on your end that works, and someone who actually answers." She didn't sound hostile, just tired.

"I can go if you think I could help," Cole said, and for that moment, he really wanted to go.

"I think it's better if I go," Maureen said. "I'll call you."

For the next two weeks running up to the NAMM show, Cole planned to work at Richard's shop in the morning, pick up Jason at lunchtime, maybe show Jason a new pick-strum or chord progression to practice while Cole worked on the two-by-four design, which he had named Diva, and called out encouragement to Jason from across the basement. He would interrupt Jason's music practice to show him each step of guitar building as he worked to bring Diva from a pencil sketch into the flesh and blood of a real instrument. Diva would be ready, along with the polished-to-perfection models of Despair and Desire, to pack up and travel to Nashville.

Cole worried about Jewell and her need for this time away. They'd had troubles before - three failed pregnancies, difficult work situations, too little money, but they had always gotten through it together – this was different. He could go to Miami and talk it out with Jewell, come back with her and go to work for Richard, and in six months or a year, perhaps they could regain the ground that had been lost in their relationship…if ground had been lost. He could give up on the NAMM show – anyone with a modicum of normal intelligence would assess his chances of success as modest, very modest. He could go back to work for Richard. Jewell would go back to work at the university…he and Jewell would again come home from work every day and cook dinner together and Frankie would race around the house with his floppy ears flying and joy on his face and make them laugh.

And what about his parents? When had they transformed from the indefatigable couple who worked Monday through Friday at their outside jobs, and on the weekends endlessly remodeled their small house or traveled to music festivals where they camped and visited with friends - to become a woman whose hands were deformed with arthritis and a man who limped when he walked and grimaced when he climbed into the driver's seat of his faded black Ford truck? Cole should have been driving to Pensacola every month or so to clean out the gutters and sweep off the roof, to help his mother plant the garden she kept talking about and get his father out of the house, maybe take him fishing or to a baseball game.

But in just over two weeks, he would be driving to the NAMM show – a mere five or six day pause in the spin of the earth - and when he returned, he had to believe that life would be forever changed for the better. Lucky breaks do happen. Lucky breaks or who-you-know…take your pick. That's how to achieve the American dream. Cole liked Richard – he loved Richard - but he didn't want to work for him, and after the NAMM show, it would be abundantly clear to everyone that he wouldn't need to.

Every day, Cole showed up at Richard's shop at eight a.m., commiserated with Richard over coffee about being abandoned by their wives, and then headed out before lunch time to get Jason out of bed and out of the house, take him home and show him a few blues licks to practice or show him how to wire up pickups and potentiometers. On Thursday afternoon, July 4th, Richard had closed the shop, and Cole went over to Richard's house to grill hot dogs and talk about what they thought Maureen and the kids, Jewell and Frankie would be doing – definitely not eating the hot dogs that were the epicurean delight Cole had picked up from Bradley's Country Store. They sat on the edge of the pool with their feet in the water, drinking Richard's rum cocktails and listening to Jason and his friends shouting and laughing in the den where they were playing video games. "Don't they want to swim?" Cole asked.

"Too hot," Richard replied. "They're delicate fucking flowers."

Cole didn't know what to say to that. Maureen had convinced them when Jason was a toddler to clean up their language, so to hear Richard use the "F" word was...Cole didn't know. Maybe shocking was too strong, but startling might describe it.

There was another burst of laughter.

"Do they sound like they're having too much fun?" Cole asked. "You know." He mimed taking a toke.

"Nah, they're ok," Richard said. He sighed and held the ice-cold glass to his unshaved cheek.

"You're working too much," Cole said.

"Like you can talk," Richard replied. "I thought you musicians were all about having fun."

"Yeah, that's what I thought, too."

Richard lay back on the hot cement pool deck and rested his drink on his stomach and stared at the clouds. Cole followed suit. "Frankie sure would have loved one of those hot dogs."

Richard didn't say anything. Cole looked over and saw that Richard's eyes were closed, but he couldn't be asleep. No one could go to sleep on a hot cement slab, could they?

They had planned on lighting the bottle rockets and firecrackers just after dark. They had looked forward to it all week. Maureen never allowed fireworks because they so terrified Chrissy. Frankie wasn't on board with them either. But long before dark they shut down the grill and washed up the dishes, and Cole headed home while Richard drove Jason's friends home.

The next day was Friday. Cole went to work in Richard's shop in the morning and picked up Jason just before lunch and headed home. Cole handed Jason the telecaster knock-off he had built in high school, the main reason that high school had been bearable. He had unearthed it when he was looking at the guitars he had in storage to see if there were any more electronics he could cannibalize for Diva. He didn't know why he had kept it all these years…must've been so he could give it to the budding luthier that Jason might yet prove to be. It had rusty strings and old electronics that needed debugging, and one of the tuners needed to be replaced – tasks that would have filled Cole's heart with joy at Jason's age. "I made this guitar in woodshop when I was just a few years older than you." He took it back from Jason to show him the tuner gears that had stripped. "I have some tuners downstairs. And if I remember correctly, the electronics can use some work. You fix it, it's yours." Cole plugged it in to the small amp he kept in the living room and played a few scratchy notes. "See what I mean? Something's loose. Check it out and then come on down when you want to work on it." Cole left him in the living room and went downstairs to work on the incredibly light and delightful Diva. He had just finished screwing on the pick guard when Jason appeared at the bottom of the stairs.

"How's it going?" Cole asked. Could Jason already be bored from twenty minutes with nothing to do but mess around with the guitar?

"Some guy called," Jason said. "I think he was calling for someone else in his band. Daniels."

"You mean my friend Dan. You've met him. Really good guitar player. Tall black guy. You said you liked him."

"No, the *last* name was 'Daniels'. 'Charlie Daniels'. Something like that."

"What?"

"I told him you were busy and to call back." Jason was pretty proud of himself. He had that cocky thrust of his chin that was so like Richard, and eyebrows raised in self-congratulation that was so like Maureen.

Cole was momentarily speechless. "Charlie Daniels Band? Did he say Charlie Daniels Band?"

"I dunno," Jason mumbled. "Could be."

Cole put his hands on his head. "Did you get a phone number?" he croaked. Jason looked at the floor. Cole sighed, wanted to scream – not so much at Jason – just at the world, at God, at every single thing that went wrong…years of brushing up against well-known musicians but not being able to get his guitars into their hands. There had been lots of pats-on-the-back by family and friends and friends-of-friends, and "that's-so-cool" by music store managers with tight budgets. There were up-and-coming local musicians who scored his guitars for free and then faded into obscurity. There was the guitar raffle that was supposed to generate some badly needed publicity for which the ad played on the local rock station the day after the raffle drawing. There were Gary and Peter, the investors…so confident that they knew exactly how things should go, and who had cash and connections but who were mysteriously out of touch when he was nearly at the finish line. And there was the wear-and-tear on Cole and Jewell's marriage and the guilt about Cole's parents.

So maybe he *was* just a little bit mad at Jason, but not really. Cole stood motionless for a full ten seconds, then slowly let his arms hang at his sides. "Ok," Cole said, almost a whisper. "It'll be ok. He'll call back, like you said."

Jason trudged back upstairs. Cole returned to his workbench where Diva rested peacefully, surrounded by small screws, pieces of plastic pick guard scraps, and a number of small pliers and screwdrivers. He leaned on the bench, pressing the flesh of his arms into the loose screws and plastic and tools, rested his forehead on his closed fists, and moaned quietly so as not to be overheard by Jason, whom he could hear walking around the kitchen. Charlie Daniels. Why couldn't it have just been a call from his friend, Dan? Wouldn't it have been kinder if Jason had reported that Dan had called, and Jason had told Dan to call back? An afternoon spent making progress on Diva should have uplifted Cole and would have. In reality, nothing was really different now than when he had left his battered tele in Jason's hands and walked down the basement stairs…the world as he knew it – his own situation - was exactly the same as it had been an hour before. Except that now the sack of cement that rested in Cole's stomach every time another opportunity slipped through his hands had taken up residence again. Just like the time late last year, when Jewell had fielded a call from the manager of the Bee Gees, and she rattled off her favorite Bee Gees songs, which she later recounted to Cole…and he had realized with horror that all of them were Eagles tunes.

Charlie Daniels band.

Suddenly, Cole was taken up with the idea that he should contact Dan, his friend, Dan. It had been Dan who had originally talked to a roadie for the Charlie Daniels band to check out their interest in having an Inflatable to take on their next tour. Dan had some connection to the roadie through a college buddy. Maybe he still had the phone number, or he could contact his college buddy to get it.

Cole stood up and carefully picked off the tiny screws and pieces of plastic that had stuck to his skin. He walked upstairs where Jason was sitting in the living room eating grapes with a glum expression.

"Cheer up," Cole said. "My friend Dan is gonna' smooth this whole thing out."

Jason looked up…a faint trace of a smile . "Wish I could play like him," Jason said quietly.

"Don't we all," Cole said, and picked up the tele and played the notes to an out-of-tune "Popeye, the Sailor Man." When Jason was small, he would laugh whenever Cole played it, but the teenager who slouched on the sofa eating grapes was about as interested as a rock.

"Hey, did I ever tell you how I met Dan?" Cole asked.

A flicker of interest crossed Jason's face.

"Actually, it was Jewell who met him first. At work."

"You mean at FSU?" Jason asked. Jason was a Seminole fan – like half of the city's population.

"Yeah. At FSU."

For most of the years that Cole and Jewell had been married, Jewell had worked at the Florida State University, first as an Administrative Assistant in the Biology Department, and in the last three years as Assistant to the Chairman of the Chemistry Department.

The timing was sheer luck, or perhaps it was cosmic design, when Jewell had moved from Biology into her new job, where it seemed one of her main duties was to forge the Chairman's signature when he was out of town or in a meeting. Had she not been hired there, she would not have met Dan, a biochemistry graduate student, whom she encountered on her third day of sitting in her new office and reading through the chairman's notes and requests. Dan was making the rounds of the Chemistry Department labs and offices, eager to show off the photos of his infant son. One such photo image was imprinted on Dan's light blue t-shirt. Jewell learned that Dan had been in the army during the first Iraq war, where he had been assigned to an army rock band that played for the troops. Through his four years of service in the army, Dan had played electric guitar - rock 'n' roll, some blues, and a little country.

"So, I told him that my husband plays the guitar, as well," Jewell had later recounted to Cole. "And that you had this crazy kind of electric guitar design. I didn't have to say anything more. Dan just cocked his head and smiled. He had the sweetest smile that sort of crinkled the outside corners of his eyes, just like the baby in the photo on his t-shirt. I asked him if he would like to come over some time and see your guitars, but I already knew. There he stood in his dreadlocks and his jeans and his new-baby t-shirt like any chemistry graduate student goofing off for a few minutes. It was too obvious. Dan might have a scientist's mind and maybe a researcher's ambition and life plan, but he has a musician's heart."

It was the Saturday following Jewell's first encounter with Dan, mid-afternoon and already ninety degrees out, when the policeman had knocked on the front screen door and announced that there had been a noise complaint.

A week later, Dan was back with a proposition. Everyone needs a website," Dan told Cole. "It's the phone book of the new millennium. It's better than the phone book. They can find you from China." It was decided. Cole would build a custom Inflatable for Dan in exchange for the guitar website that Dan would design and maintain for the years he lived in Tallahassee while pursuing his PhD in Biochemistry.

Cole would call Dan to feel him out on the Charlie Daniels Band connection. He picked up the phone and dialed Dan's number, let it ring until the answering machine picked up. He hesitated, then left a brief message, "Hey, Dan. It's Cole. Give me a call when you get in." He hung up the phone, hoping that he hadn't sounded too intense.

Jason had finished his handful of grapes and had been watching Cole with a frown. "He'll call back," Cole said. He lightly punched Jason's shoulder and went downstairs to guitar heaven, or hell, or both, depending on the time and day.

Cole held up Diva to assess her feather weight and small stature, and suddenly remembered that the guitar cases – really soft canvas gig bags – that he had purchased last year custom-made for Desire, and that were a little oversized – but acceptable for Despair – would be much too large for Diva. He carefully laid Diva on her back and climbed the stairs to give Jason his first important mission for Heartbreak Guitars – find a cheap, small carry bag they could use as an instrument case for Diva. Cole entered the kitchen and walked through the dining room into the living room. The tele had been placed upright on the love seat, but Jason was not in the room. He wasn't in any room. Cole returned to the basement, just in case. No Jason.

# Chapter 12

July 8th – Monday afternoon
11 days before the NAMM show

Cole waited a couple of hours for Jason to return. He called Richard and Maureen's house three or four times to see if Jason was at home. Jason was nearly fifteen, so a few hours off everyone's radar should be no big deal, right? Cole and Maureen at that age spent most of their summer days out in the neighborhood, riding their bikes, smoking cigarettes with friends, or looking for change among the sofa cushions to take a bus to the mall. Their parents rarely asked where they would be, and just seemed happy that they were out of the house. But there was a reason Maureen had asked Cole to take Jason on as an apprentice. He was not a happy kid, and she was worried what that might lead him to do. By mid-afternoon, Cole had waited long enough. He spent an hour and a half driving through the neighborhood, then all the way to Richard and Maureen's house, and back through his own neighborhood looking for a gangly teenager wearing a rumpled black t-shirt, a garnet baseball hat, baggy jeans, and unlaced black tennis shoes…a teenager with uncombed hair who would be plodding slowly on leaden feet. No luck. Time to call Richard.

"Don't worry," Richard said. "I'll call some of his friends. Just have to go home and get the phone numbers. Or I could call Maureen for them." Maureen was still in Pensacola.

"Would that be a good idea? Calling Maureen, I mean?" Surely, that should be the action of last resort. Richard had already reported that during his nightly conversations with Maureen over the last week, her sighs had become more frequent. "I don't know," she would say. "I just don't." She could be referring to her father's prognosis, or her mother's ability to cope if Maureen were to leave, or even whether she should allow CJ and Chrissy to play on the neighbor's trampoline, or what they would be having for dinner, but some of those sighs had to be about Jason. Still, shouldn't two grown men be able to deal with one sullen 14-year-old trying to make a point? At least that is what Richard said he was hoping for…finding Jason and having a serious talk, learning what in Jason's life could possibly be so upsetting, figuring out what to do, and then doing it. Maureen might not even need to know. A minor and not-worth-mentioning ripple in their day.

"Let me call you back," Richard said.

Cole paced the upstairs, went into the front yard to look down the street, and then returned to the living room to be near the phone. There was a phone in the basement now, which is where he should be every waking minute, but he couldn't concentrate. Jason would turn up soon and have a not-too-crazy explanation of where he had gone and why, and a possibly less solid explanation of why he hadn't let anyone know. Jason would be dismayed that anyone had worried about him, and a little angry, considering his advanced years and worldly wisdom which he would sum up in one derisive comment: "I'm not stupid, you know."

An hour later, Richard called. "Negative. They haven't seen him."

"Do you know if he had any money?" Cole asked.

"Ten bucks. I left it on the table next to the cereal. He was still in bed when I left."

"He was still in bed when I got there at lunchtime to pick him up," Cole said. "I didn't notice any money."

"Hold on." Richard put the phone down with a clunk. Thirty seconds later he was back. "Yep. It's still here."

"Well, he can't get into much trouble without money," Cole said, but he was thinking – he can't get himself out of it either. The mind of a fourteen-year-old…anything can happen in there.

Richard and Cole agreed that they would not call Maureen unless Jason had not appeared by dark. That would be around 9:00 p.m. Jason would be hungry, and that fact gave them comfort. That kid could put away some food.

At seven, Cole called Richard and said he would be away from the phone. "Just thought I would ask a few of the neighbors if they saw him and which way he went."

"But you don't know any neighbors."

Cole and Jewell knew their neighbors by sight and had chatted with a few of them when re-delivering mis-delivered mail or giving a ride to some young father walking down the street under the blazing sun with his toddler on his shoulders and carrying a gas can, or by signing a petition for traffic calming signs or buying a candy bar for school band uniforms.

"Yeah, I don't really know them, but we've waved a few times."

Cole wondered if he had a photo of Jason. Probably nothing recent, unless there was a guitar in it, and it would be a close-up shot of the guitar and

Jason's hands. Cole had taken rolls and rolls of photos of guitars for potential promo materials, until the promotional endeavors had fallen on the hard times that were all too familiar. Richard was quiet, so Cole said, "I'll call you back soon," and hung up the phone.

Cole locked the backdoor, then left via the front door and locked it, thought better of it, and unlocked it, just in case Jason returned while he was gone. He'd left a note taped to the telecaster that read, "Be right back. Don't go anywhere!"

One of the college-age renters across the street was standing on his porch smoking a cigarette and letting the ashes drop onto the front of his Ghostbusters t-shirt. As good a place as any to start. Cole walked up their driveway.

"Hey, I'm just looking for my nephew. He left the house this afternoon without his medicine." Cole didn't know why he said that, maybe just to make the whole thing sound innocent but urgent, which in fact, it was. "Fourteen, head-in the-clouds."

The young man smiled, if one could call it that, an apathetic upturn of the corners of his mouth. Cole was pretty sure this guy was stoned. Ghostbuster was too energetic a calling for him. He leaned back through the open door and yelled, "Karl, you seen some young dude with his head-up-his-ass come by earlier?" Cole instantly did not like him and was pretty sure Ghostbusters-guy was in a fraternity. No, he'd probably been kicked out of his fraternity. Now *that* is serious. The guy continued to lean backwards and nearly lost his balance, but he waited to convey Karl's answer. Negative. Cole waved and turned to go. "Wait," frat-boy said. "Some guy and a girl were walking that way earlier." He pointed toward the highway, U.S. 27. Cole's spirits sank. From U.S. 27, you could either go south to head into town, or north to the small town of Havana and further north into rural Georgia. Jason would go south into town, maybe home, or to a friend's house.

"Ok, thanks man," Cole said. A 'guy and a girl' wasn't much to go on, and Cole hadn't paid attention to the teenagers who got off the school bus in front of college boy's house every afternoon and dispersed in all directions. The only house with a teenaged girl that he could pinpoint was Martina's. He'd never thought about it before, but Martina either must have had a daughter late in her childbearing years or she was raising her granddaughter.

Cole knocked on Martina's door, hoping that her husband would answer, or maybe the daughter. Did they have other kids? Cole thought so…a son…somewhat older. Drove their massive Oldsmobile ten miles-per-hour below the speed limit like his old man. Rather suspicious. What red-blooded American teenager would drive like that?

Martina opened the door and then, seeing Cole, stepped back quickly and crossed her arms on her pendulous breasts. She raised one eyebrow.

Cole produced a friendly smile – Jewell would have called it his shit-eating grin. "Hi. Good evening." Cole wondered why Martina was not sitting on the porch sipping vodka on this relatively mild summer evening, at least compared to the blistering heat of the afternoon. The aroma of rosemary, garlic and roasted pork washed over him. "I won't keep you from your dinner. I'm just looking for my nephew. He's fourteen. Wondered if you saw him earlier."

"His name is Jason? Your nephew?"

"Yeah, yes. You saw him?"

Martina fired some Russian over her shoulder toward the dining room. Cole could see a portion of the dining room from the small living room where he and Martina stood just inside the front doorway. The living room was overfilled with furniture: a plush red sofa and loveseat, a rocking chair, and under the window a baby grand piano. A chair was pushed back from the near end of the dining room table where there was a place setting. It was clear that Cole had interrupted their dinner. The plate had scraps of food and half a bread roll.

A moment later Jason emerged followed by a tall girl with long brown hair. "Come here," Martina said to Jason. "You said you would call home," she accused him, clucking her tongue. "You can come back tomorrow for piano lesson, but only if your parents – or your uncle – can know." With one eyebrow still raised, she squinted at Cole with what could only be called The Evil Eye. The next moment, she ruffled Jason's hair as he walked slowly by her like a man to his own hanging.

Jason stared at the roadway as he plodded next to Cole on the short walk back to Cole's house. Cole half-expected to see Frankie leaping for joy at their return…but then he remembered. It was like a punch in the stomach. They entered the quiet, empty house.

"First call your dad," Cole said, "then we'll talk."

"Why can't you call him?"

"Seriously?" Cole said. "I mean seriously?" He handed Jason the phone.

Jason dialed, then mumbled, "Hey, Dad."

Cole could hear Richard from across the room. "Where the hell are you?"

"I'm at Cole's." At least Jason sounded contrite.

Silence and then at high volume, "Well are you going to tell me where you were, and why you thought it was ok to just let us wonder? I called everywhere. We looked everywhere. Next on my list would have been the police."

"Sorry," Jason mumbled. "Martina was just showing me stuff on the piano. Cole *knows* her."

"Let me talk to Cole," Richard said. Jason handed over the phone.

"I don't exactly know her," Cole said. "Martina. We've had a few words." Cole didn't say *which* words. "She said she thought he had called home."

Richard sighed. "I'm going to kill that kid," he said softly.

"I know," Cole said gently. "Do you want me to talk to him or do you want him home or what?"

There was a pause, and then Richard said, "I'll come get him. We'll talk to him together."

"Okay, good idea." But was this really a good idea? Surely it would be more productive to talk to Jason one-on-one, but Richard had been at it a long time with three kids, so he should know.

"I'll bring a six-pack," Richard said. "I could use a cold one."

"And bring some hot dogs if you have any left," Cole said. "Jason ate dinner but…"

"Sure," Richard said. He was already losing some of his worry and starting to relax. That would be better for any planned discussion with Jason. A cold beer first.

"And pick up some soda, or whatever Jason drinks. We don't have anything here."

Cole sipped his beer while Richard lectured Jason about parental worry and listed work-related stressors and recent events that he had had to deal with…all in all, a pretty good guilt trip. There wasn't much for Cole to add, and as Jason sat on the loveseat, glumly staring at his knees, Cole realized that Jason wasn't going to understand Richard's heavy burdens, and neither would Jason share his own.

When Richard momentarily fell silent, Jason asked, "Can I go now?"

"Go where?"

"I'm just going to take a shower. You know, soap and water?" Cole guessed that Jason was after any excuse to leave the room.

Richard closed his eyes and pinched the bridge of his nose. "Yeah," he sighed. "Go take a shower."

Jason got up and walked down the hallway.

"Did I say I want to kill that kid?" Richard asked. He stood up and leaned back while pressing his fists into his lower back, grunted, then headed into the kitchen.

Cole looked through CD's, put on one of Jewell's favorites, Blue Kentucky Girl, and sat back on the loveseat, slumped down with his head back and closed his eyes. He felt something brush his knee…Frankie? He opened his eyes. Richard was sitting across from him on the sofa. "Beer?" Richard held out a Heineken.

Cole took his beer and sat back in the loveseat. "For a second I thought you were Frankie."

"Yeah," Richard said. "I get it."

Cole was glad Richard hadn't said more. "I get it." *It* was painfully evident. No Frankie, no Jewell, no Maureen, Chrissy or CJ. They drank and listened to Emmy Lou.

"Remember Y2K?" Richard said.

Cole remembered. Who could forget? The world as everyone knew it was predicted to come to sudden standstill. No computers, no lights, no operational ATM's, no gas pumps, no telephones, no communication, no anything. Want the weather? Go outside and look at the sky. Want some food? Hope you have a can opener cause everything fresh will be spoiled. That's if you can get the money to buy the canned food and find a store that will take cash. Want to contact your family? Lucky…you get to see them face-to-face…better start walking. Y2K had been a worldwide anxiety trip about a computer code meltdown that had never happened. No operational computers would have meant no functioning computer driven systems…no trappings of a modern lifestyle. Jewell and Cole had been living it for the last six months. It wasn't impossible to survive it, perhaps, if your fellow man with more resources took pity on you, but your marriage might not make it. "Yeah," Cole said. "Don't want to talk about it."

"Barely got over that," Richard continued, "and then…wham… it's the presidential election debacle of the millennium. And before we could get over that…nine-eleven. Jesus!" Was this Richard's way of taking his mind off his own troubles? Cole noticed that Richard was drinking something dark and bubbly from a crystal tumbler. A coke. Then he knew…rum and coke. Rum was not Richard's best friend. Was it anyone's? It was just a few days ago, July 4th, that Richard and Cole had last drunk rum and ended up lying on a hot pool deck, filled with longing for their missing spouses and kids and canine. Before Richard had come over tonight, he had probably been hanging out at home hoping that Jason would call, drinking rum and coke, looking around at his empty living room and through the sliding glass doors at the pool from which he needed to net a few dead frogs, and at the overgrown grass now seasoned with purple flowering weeds, and listening to the din of the cicadas. He wouldn't have noticed cicadas when Maureen was bustling around in the kitchen or CJ was heading off intruders on his video game or Chrissy was asking him to read a story.

"Y2K...hanging chads, Nine-eleven," Cole said. ""*When sorrows come, they come not single spies, but in battalions.*' That's a Shakespeare thing. You can learn a lot from Shakespeare."

Richard picked his head up and looked at Cole, then slumped back against the sofa. "Did he have any kids?"

Cole quoted, "*There was never yet a philosopher who could endure the toothache patiently.*'" Cole wondered if he should find Richard's rum and check out how much had been drunk. Better idea..."You want to stay over tonight?" Cole asked. "You and Jason can have the bed...king size, man." Then as an afterthought, thinking Richard's mood might have lightened, "*Misery acquaints a man with strange bedfellows.*"

"What strange bedfellows." Jason was standing in the living room, his wet hair dripping onto his black t-shirt.

"You, Bud," Cole said. "Let me find you some clean clothes." How ironic. Cole had spent half of the last five months wearing mostly the same

147

clothes day after day, dreading the days that Jewell would object and enlist him in the bathtub clothes-stomping-wringing-draping laundry routine they had both come to abhor. It could easily come to that again. A new electric bill was waiting pristinely in its envelope in the kitchen odd-and-ends drawer, as if not opening it would delay the due date. The new billing cycle must have started just after Cole had paid the prior overdue charges to get the lights back on. Richard would not have seen it, and now was probably not the time to discuss it. Anyway, Cole only needed the electric for another eleven days, so he wasn't going to worry about it, or even mention it to Richard. He needed so little… some gas and some food for just over a week, enough to get him to the NAMM show. And then, of course, some travel and show expenses. He ushered Jason into the bedroom and pulled out some t-shirts and a pair of sweatpants. The sweatpants were Jewell's, but they were gray and baggy, so who would know? "If you find anything better, help yourself," Cole said. "I think you guys are spending the night."

"Where?"

"Here," Cole said. "Look, you got your own TV." Cole indicated the TV on the dresser directly opposite the bed. Jewell had draped a shawl over the face of it to block whatever radiation she believed would come out of a TV at night when all was dark.

Cole peeled back the shawl, and punched the power button, and returned to the living room.

"Turn down the TV," Richard yelled toward the bedroom. "Jesus, kids," he muttered.

"So, Richard," Cole began. "The NAMM show starts in eleven days. Gotta leave in just over a week. Takes one long day to get there, but splitting the drive in two might be better, and we're supposed to actually be there at least the day before the show starts to set everything up."

Richard had not yet committed to coming to NAMM. And it was Maureen who had said they would finance it. Cole was pretty sure that Richard was on board, but would he remember, given his own headaches?

"Okay, man. We'll be ready," Richard said. "Jason is coming. You get that, right?"

Oh, yeah. Jason. They couldn't just leave him at home. Well, they could...Cole's parents would have, but...that was different times. "Sure. Of course," Cole said. What the hell.

# Chapter 13

July 9, Tuesday morning
Ten days before the NAMM show

Cole and Richard sat across from each other at the dining room table, sipping coffee from oversized mugs Jewell had made in a pottery class. "Let's not do that again," Richard mumbled. Cole hesitated to say anything, unsure if Richard meant the staying up until two a.m. drinking beer and rum or forming a new – and Cole hoped soon to disband - rock band. Cole, Richard, and Jason were now "The Solid Surface Men." They had headed into the basement in the middle of the night, initially so that Cole could show off Diva, but one thing had led to another, though Cole didn't remember exactly how.

Cole had played lead on the ruby-throated Desire; Jason played rhythm guitar, dragging just a little behind the rhythm so that their songs got slower and slower as Cole and Richard tried to match him. Richard played the air drums until he spotted some dowels and then began enthusiastically drumming on every dusty surface he spotted, delighted when he discovered the marine buoy-like clanking of the circular saw housing. Cole remembered that they had rigged up a mic on a stand within inches of the circular saw, transformed into a drum, and dialed in some reverb, and cranked up the volume.

"Yeah, let's not."

Richard looked at his watch. "Late for work. Slept in."

Cole looked at Richard. Even wearing yesterday's clothing, having uncombed hair, and sporting dark, burgeoning facial hair, Richard looked pretty well put together. The clue that he was suffering hang-over misery was this communication using as few words as possible, not Richard's usual early-riser, burst of new day style.

"What time do you have?" Cole asked. There was a weak light in the east, and even with the window blinds all the way up, which they clearly hadn't remembered to close last night, the dining room was lit by a soft gray light.

"6:42. Slept in."

"Really? What time do you usually get up?"

"6:25."

"So then. Glad you got all that extra sleep."

Richard put down his coffee mug and stood, ran his fingers through his hair and then stroked his dark stubble. "Got a razor in my office," he said. "And a toothbrush. And a clean undershirt. See you

151

in a few?" He didn't wait for an answer, just nodded and started toward the front door.

"Wait, what about Jason?" Cole asked.

Richard stopped with his hand on the doorknob, turned toward Cole. "Honestly? If sleep were an Olympic sport, he'd take the gold." Richard was right. Jason wasn't likely to be upright and talking for many hours. And *that* would be a good thing. *Where unbruised youth with unstuff'd brain doth couch his limbs, there golden sleep doth reign.*

At Richard's shop, Cole parked in the crabgrass under a massive oak tree, next to Mr. Bean's shiny, red F-250. It was eerily quiet. No saws, no sanders, no whine of the forklift, no hurled insults, no clatter from scrap pieces being flung into the dumpster…just the whir of the large fans and a faintly heard Garth Brooks tune emanating from the open roll-up doors. It was very weird. Cole noted a clot of people at the far end of the grassy parking lot nearest to a pair of storage sheds, and he headed that way at a trot. Richard and Delroyce, one of the new guys, cousin to bathroom-dude, were crouched and leaning over someone whose long legs lay motionless, and whose polished boots were splayed…Mr. Bean. Cole stood at the edge of the group of men who silently waited for Richard to tell them something hopeful. Finally, Richard looked up at them and said, "Well, he's breathing." All heads swiveled toward the entrance gates as they heard the siren of the approaching ambulance, which abruptly quit as it rolled into the sand and grass parking lot.

"Do you know what happened?" Cole asked the guy standing next to him. James somebody. James Henry.

The guy shrugged, and then said, "He just went down. No one knows why."

Later they learned that Mr. Bean was a diabetic who injected insulin after every meal. That explained why he always ate lunch in his truck…that, and maybe the air-conditioning and the peace-and-quiet and the solitude. Mr. Bean kept to himself, and even Richard hadn't known until visiting him in the hospital that afternoon that Mr. Bean's daughter had died last month in a field hospital in Burundi where she had gone with their church to help fight a cholera outbreak. She had been there for less than two months when she had also succumbed to cholera, or rather…to an allergic reaction from the antibiotic treatment. Mr. Bean's wife explained that he had taken insulin sporadically in recent days, mainly when she asked him about it. She wondered if he was just waiting for his heart to break open and put him out of his misery.

That afternoon, Cole worked in Richard's shop, trying to fill in for both Richard and Mr. Bean.

Right off the bat, the sales guy, a beefy man with a chronically ego-inflated smirk, argued with Cole about the estimate he was working on for countertops that would go into a large kitchen in Killearn Estates. It was from this exchange that Cole learned that they charged customers for the square foot dimensions of the countertop surface, regardless of the number of sheets they had to order for the job. Cole was pretty sure that this guy had it wrong. Richard would not have approved of this underpricing of material costs. That wasn't the way they did things when Cole still owned the shop and Richard worked for him in sales, so Cole was confident he could set this guy straight and help Richard's bottom line. They were standing in Richard's air-conditioned office, where Cole had shown the sales guy an invoice that indicated the sheet price of Alpine White, one of the most popular countertop colors. Then he motioned for the sales guy to follow him outside, and they marched through the shop to the dumpster, where Cole peered over the top. "Yep, look at all that money that is literally just going into the trash."

"Not the way I learned it," sales guy said flatly. Laney, that was his name. Maybe Laney's method would work with finished products that are purchased wholesale and marked up for retail, but products like countertops had to be priced to pay for the materials, labor costs, the shop lights, equipment repairs, the insurance, the shop vehicles and gas, disposal fees, business licenses, on and on. You can't just add up employee hours to the square footage cost of the countertop material and be done.

"I can beat any other price in town," Laney said. He was practically strutting – if one can strut while standing in place with arms crossed and shifting one's weight from one leg to the other. "Customers are happy."

"Customers are happy," Cole repeated. "The shop might go broke, close down, and everyone get laid off, but you can feel pretty good that we provided a gift countertop to every customer...whoopee!" Laney donned his sunglasses, took a good look at Cole over the top of them, then turned and walked back through the shop into the office.

Cole looked at the clock, wondered again when Richard would return. He hadn't intended to stay at the shop all day. It was ten days before the NAMM show. They would have to leave in eight days: one very long day driving and one day to set-up. Eight days left to get ready. Of that, Cole was painfully aware.

Cole walked out of the office, through the shop and into the parking lot. Mr. Bean's red truck was still there, of course, but not Richard's. The new kid, Delroyce, drove by on the forklift with a few flattened cardboard boxes bouncing up and down on the forks. Seriously? They couldn't carry a few boxes to the recycle? And Delroyce had not even been in the forklift training! "Hey!" Cole shouted as it turned the corner of the building and disappeared. "Jesus!" he mumbled and walked back through the roll-up doors, waved as he passed the only female shop employee, a new hire, and walked into the office.

Cole looked at the wall clock again. Two o'clock already? He dialed home and imagined a sleepy Jason sitting in a stupor on the sofa tossing bits of left-over hot dog to Frankie. Only Frankie wasn't there. It hurt every time Cole remembered it, a leaden heaviness in his chest, missing Frankie, and even more, missing Jewell. He hadn't called Jewell in a couple of nights, but definitely would call tonight. And maybe Maureen as well since Richard was so distracted. Where was he anyway? He'd been at the hospital all morning. Cole realized that Richard had been fraying at the edges even before this thing with Mr. Bean. Richard just didn't do well without Maureen and the kids. It was taking a toll. Just about when Cole was going to hang up the phone, the ringing stopped abruptly, and he heard Jason's flat affect. "Heartbreak Guitars, where dreams come to die."

"Very funny," Cole said. "That is really, really helpful."

"What? I recognized the number. I thought it was my dad."

"We don't have Caller ID," Cole said. "We have an answering machine, remember?"

"Okay. But I knew it would be my dad, or Mom. Nobody else calls here."

The truth hurt. It hadn't helped that they had gone months without a working phone. At first, Cole had been gleeful to be working in the shop without having to haggle on the phone with Gary over the price of every box of tiny screws, or the costs of mother-of-pearl pick guard material. Gary and Peter saw gigantic dollar signs everywhere they went. Cole could appreciate that. He had just chewed out and probably deeply offended Richard's sales guy over this very concern. But the solid surface shop had already done its research and development. He had done most of it himself and had handed it over to Richard to build upon and expand. The guitar business was a whole different animal. It was still an experiment, and ironically, it was Diva that would enable that low – practically give it away – price option that Gary and Peter, mostly Peter, thought they could churn out by the hundreds a month...and since they had fallen into radio silence, they didn't even know about Diva. So, for all their talk, Gary and Peter sucked at this whole business thing. That was one of the things that Cole and Richard had concluded last night.

"Jason, listen. The reason I'm calling is just to let you know why I haven't come home yet. Mr. Bean is in the hospital, went there in an ambulance, and your dad is there to check on him, so I had to stay at the shop." Quiet. "You still there?"

"Is Mr. Bean okay?" Jason asked. Despite his studied aloofness, Jason had a big heart.

"Yeah, I'm pretty sure. Hey, you hungry? Your dad brought over hot dogs last night. Breakfast of champions." Their diet was not among the topics Cole meant to discuss with Maureen.

"Yeah, probably. I'll find something."

Cole let it go. Jason did not realize the depth of food depletion in Cole and Jewell's fridge and pantry. Jason was used to living in a house jam packed with all kinds of edibles, and with Maureen there to police the scene so that they didn't sit in front of the open refrigerator stuffing themselves all day. Cole did Jason one better than that…no food in the pantry, so no stuffing.

"Okay, so here's the deal. I'll try to get there as soon as I can, but just stay put." No answer. "I can't seem to hear you," Cole said.

"You didn't ask a question," Jason said.

"Will you," Cole spoke slowly, enunciating every word, "Please. Stay. Put?"

"What if I just go over to Laura's?"

"Laura?"

"Martina's daughter," Jason said. "And Martina can give me a piano lesson. And I think they actually eat real food."

"A hot dog was good enough last night, I seem to remember," Cole said. "And that was after you already ate dinner at Martina's."

"By the way, I told Laura about your guitars. She thinks you should make one with a hot pink inflatable body and a neck that looks like the head of a flamingo."

"Jewell would approve of this girl," Cole said. "Yes, you can go there, but nowhere else. So, can you affirm that you will stay where you are, right now, to be precise, or only go to Laura's?"

"I. Can. Affirm." Jason said and hung up the phone.

# Chapter 14

Where the hell was Richard? Had things gone badly for Mr. Bean? Cole had tried to get Richard a few times on his cell phone, but no answer. It was late in the afternoon, forty-five minutes 'til quitting time, and apparently Richard was still at the hospital. Laney had left early, saying he had a job to look at on the other side of town and would just go home from there. Two of the shop guys left early, saying they had come in early, and that Richard let them work earlier hours. Catherine had disappeared.

Cole had meant to have gone home hours ago, but Richard had not returned to supervise or to let them know Mr. Bean's status. Cole looked through the floor-to-ceiling glass wall that separated the office from the shop. People were busy, mostly, although bathroom guy was nowhere in view. Forty-five minutes 'til quitting time. OK. Cole would let them go home early, a small gesture of solidarity considering the worries of the day.

Cole tried Richard's cell one more time. Richard picked up after the first ring. "Hey buddy, what happened?" Cole asked. "I've been calling all day."

"Sorry," Richard said. "I came home to shower and change, just wanted to shut my eyes for a minute, and then…dead to the world."

"Mr. Bean. How's he doing?"

"Better. I think he'll be ok, but probably not back at work for a while, a few days at least. But losing his daughter…"

"Yeah," Cole agreed.

Richard sighed.

"So," Cole began. "Are you okay?"

"Yeah, but I was wondering. Can Jason stay over there one more night?"

"Sure," Cole said, but he wasn't feeling it. He could work on Diva with Jason there - but it was just different. Sometimes it was just easier when he was alone.

There was a tap on the door, and Cassandra, the new employee, stuck her head in. She was small and compact, with short blonde hair, wiry and thick, too wiry and thick to be real? Cole wondered if she was from the islands like Mr. Bean, although her skin color was much lighter than Mr. Bean's…teak, or a light walnut.

Cole motioned for her to come inside. "Gotta go," Cole said to Richard. "See you in the morning." He hung up the phone and indicated the chair across from the desk. Cassandra sat, straight backed, on the front half of the chair.

"That was Richard," Cole said. "Mr. Bean is better…gonna take a few days off, I think. So," he waited.

"You know I don't like to complain." Cole didn't know that. "But I can't stand it. We have to share the kitchen, and those boys," she rolled her eyes toward the shop, "they make a mess." Cole waited, thinking it over. They made a mess in the shop: tools not put away; rags on the floor instead of the rag bin; countertop scraps all over, safety glasses sitting in thick dust. So yeah, the kitchen was probably a mess. "They leave dishes in the sink," she continued, "and they boil over things in the microwave and never clean it afterward. They're just thinking I'll clean up after them because I'm a woman." Cole's immediate thought was that she was the only one who noticed the mess because she was a woman, but that was probably sexist.

"Okay, let me…"

"And the bathroom's just as bad," she went on. "The other bathroom has been out of order since I started working here, so we all have to share just one." She wasn't from around here. He tried to place her accent, not from the islands…maybe Spanish, with a dash of the Bronx?

"Ok, I'll talk to Richard. Definitely gotta work on that bathroom. In the meantime, you can use this one in the office." Cole hoped that would satisfy her for now. *"Though she be but little, she is fierce."*

She nodded, and then got up and walked to the door, started to open it, then turned and said, "Richard might want to watch where his tools go, and that's all I'm saying," and then she left.

Cole would talk to Richard tomorrow. The bathroom would be the easy part. The kitchen? Have a heart-to-heart with the guys, but how long would that last? And there were probably only one or two offenders. Richard hated instituting draconian measures for everyone to address the problems caused by a few. Let him decide. But tools going missing, that was serious. Someone needed to be fired.

It was 5:30 by the time Cole had turned off all the lights and locked up. Traffic congestion had peaked, but it was still heavy. Cole arrived on his street just as Jason was plodding toward the house. 'Plodding' was a word that could've been invented with Jason in mind. Cole waved as he passed Jason at the mailbox, turned into the driveway, and got out of the truck.

"Weren't you supposed to be home at five?" Cole realized in that instant that he sounded just like his father, and he envisaged a lumbering old man who was recovering from a broken hip without

Cole's help and knew that he should at least call. Maybe tonight after dinner.

"Noooooo." Jason said.

Cole couldn't actually remember if he they had discussed when to be home, so he handed Jason the Coke he had gotten from the vending machine in Richard's shop and turned to go inside.

"Mr. Bean?" Jason was standing there with his Coke, sounding a little exasperated.

"I think he'll be alright. Needs a few days off. Did I tell you about his daughter?"

Cole and Jason sat in the living room, Cole drinking a beer, Jason his Coke, and talked about Mr. Bean, the dirty dishes in the shop kitchen, the out-of-order bathroom, and the guys leaving early. Cole didn't tell him about the allegation of pilfered shop tools or that Laney was not only an unlikeable, unmanageable self-congratulatory SOB, Laney could not be trusted. Cole had nothing to go on but his instincts, but if he were still in charge, Laney would be gone.

"Call your dad," Cole said, "just to say hello. The day's been a little tough on him."

"I already tried. He didn't answer."

"Did you leave a message? 'Hey Dad, I think you're really great. My life is wonderful and fulfilling because of you'?"

"No…"

"Then call him back."

"I'm not saying all that," Jason said.

"I know, but can you muster a little enthusiasm?"

"Yeah, I can muster it," Jason said slowly in a monotone. But there was a hint of a smile. Good enough.

Cole left Jason in the living room, grabbed another beer and trudged downstairs. He sat for a moment at his electronics bench, sipped his beer, slid one of the pickups into a slot routed in the small guitar body that was Diva, and secured it with tiny screws. By the end of the evening, Diva would be on the verge of completion. In a day or two, he'd be putting on the strings and taking her for a test drive.

He heard slogging footsteps on the stairs, then saw the unlaced black tennis shoes, faded blue jeans, and the familiar black t-shirt. "Did you wash those clothes?" Cole asked. He couldn't help himself. He was transmogrifying into a parent against his will. Kafka could have written a book about it: the horror of waking up one day, looking in the mirror, and seeing a full-blown parent staring back. One who must comment on the appropriateness of every utterance from his child, every exasperated sigh, every less than stellar decision, a parent who would direct every footstep toward a better goal.

"No," Jason said. "I always go over to a girl's house smelling like I work in a basement."

"What do you mean? What smell?"

"You can't smell it?" Jason asked. Sniff, sniff. "Eau de bathroom with notes of mold and a hint of wood dust."

"I fixed the bathroom," Cole said stiffly. "Two days ago."

"Well, it still stinks," Jason said.

"I've been a little busy. Maybe someone I know can help me clean it."

"I'm good." Jason ran his fingers through his hair, tucking it behind his ears. "I was just saying."

"So, did you come down here to tell me the basement stinks?"

"I just thought you might want to watch the news once in a while. There's a hurricane about to hit Florida."

"Where in Florida?" They were already heading up the stairs.

"I don't know. Everywhere." Jason, Jason, Jason.

Jason had been correct, in a way. There was a tropical storm that was likely to strengthen, and it could hit *anywhere*. It was in the Atlantic, more likely to turn north toward the Caribbean and Florida than keep tracking west toward Mexico. But where it would hit Florida was still very uncertain, and it was many days away from Florida, a week or more, and there was no guarantee that it would even turn into a hurricane.

"Did you tell your dad about the storm? You did talk to him, right?"

"No. I mean, 'yes', I talked to him, but 'no' about the storm. He actually watches the news." There was another hint of a smile.

"Well, la di da," Cole said. "Good thing I have you to watch it for me, since I'm still working and all."

"Yeah, you got pretty lucky there," Jason said. He was on a roll.

"Constantine called earlier," Jason said. "A couple of hours ago. You were sanding or something. Making a racket down there. It was hard to hear the TV."

"Oh man, you are pushing your luck, kid. What did he say?"

"He invited us over for dinner tomorrow. I said 'yes.'"

"You said 'yes'. Really. You got your own car now?"

"Well, actually, I said 'probably' and that you would call him back."

"And he invited both of us, you and me?"

"Yeah, both of us," Jason said.

Cole thought that Constantine was just being polite, but he would check with him in the morning to make sure. "Are you sure you want to go?" Cole did not have time for this dinner. Constantine would understand, but here was Jason, wanting to go. "It'll just be two old guys sitting around, eating, talking about the good ole times."

"I'm used to that," Jason said. "I got you and my dad."

"And Constantine teaches high school. Gives out detentions to miscreants all day long. Just so you know."

"You think I'm scared of some teacher talk? I deal with *them* all day long, too."

"Ok, then," Cole couldn't think of anything else to say. He would check with Constantine. If they had both been invited, as it appeared, Cole would go, but they wouldn't stay long. Constantine would understand completely.

In the morning, Cole arrived at the shop early so that he could talk to Richard before Richard was swept up in putting out fires. Richard was sitting at his desk, drinking coffee, and rifling through some paperwork. He was clean-shaven, his hair combed, wearing nicely pressed clothes…all in all…back to normal.

"My dear," Cole began in his Julia Chiles falsetto. "You appear to be in good form this morning. Right then, old boy. Carry on, now."

"You want some coffee?" Richard asked, gesturing with his cup toward the coffee maker that rested on a countertop in the corner.

"No, I already had more than I probably need, but thanks. Hey, but I did want to talk to you about some of the issues that came up yesterday."

"I'm gone one day and there are issues?"

"There are always issues. Some are small, and some are not so small. Which do you want first?"

Richard sighed. "Neither, but okay, gimme what you got."

"First, we need a plumber to fix the toilet in the bathroom. There was a complaint."

"Yeah, I thought I could do it myself. Just haven't had time," Richard said.

"What's wrong with it?"

"Needs a new flush mechanism."

"Alright. Let me see what I can do," Cole said. "Next. The kitchen is a mess…dishes in the sink, baked-on food in the microwave. There was a complaint."

"Cassandra, right? She starts off by saying 'you know I don't complain'."

"Well, if she is right, and it appears she is," Cole said, "then she is a force for good in the world."

"I'll talk to the guys. I'm pretty sure I know who needs the talk," Richard said. "Is that it?"

"No. I'm just warming you up for the serious stuff. First, Laney is practically giving away countertops. He needs retraining on how to estimate a job." Cole stopped short of making further accusations he couldn't back up with evidence. Anyway, Richard already knew that Cole did not like Laney. Cole had told him several times that he could get someone better. But Richard was reluctant to start over with a new sales guy who knew nothing about the business. "I can train him," Cole continued, "but it might be better if it came from you.

"And someone is stealing tools. I don't know who it is, but it explains why the installation trucks are always short. They need to be locked up, and tools signed out for each job. And the fabricators and installers need to have assigned tools…I mean like each have his own. Tools that have unique serial numbers. We just need a log to know which guy has which tool."

"Yeah," Richard sighed. "You want to get that going? Catherine is taking one of her boys to the dentist this morning, but she can help you after lunch." Catherine was Richard's office assistant.

"She wasn't here most of the day yesterday either," Cole said. "Not sure if you knew that."

Richard sighed.

By mid-afternoon, Cole had fixed the bathroom toilet, and had drawn out a matrix for inventorying the tools, including columns for "usernames" and tool "check out" dates, descriptions and serial numbers. He handed his notes for creating a tool inventory form to Catherine, who had arrived well after lunchtime carrying her sandwich and chips and soda, which she placed on her desk next to the newspaper she had opened to look at ads. She slowly ate without looking at her food while she clipped coupons and placed them in a large envelope. No sale would get by her, Cole noted, so perhaps she was just the eagle-eyed employee he could task with jotting down the shop tools on the inventory, along with descriptions and serial numbers. But it looked like she could be clipping coupons until next December. Cole wanted the inventory finished before he left for the NAMM show - it was the least he could do for Richard – and that meant that only one person could "get 'er done." One person with a big-mouthed, young apprentice whose idle hands and empty days signaled that he needed something fulfilling and important to do. Maybe not exactly fulfilling, but it was important.

"Jason, I've got a job for you," Cole spoke into the phone, having called Jason to explain why he would be home later than he had planned. He was always home later than planned. And because of it, every night in the basement, he worked past midnight. He should work even longer, but by then, he was exhausted, and night after night, he stumbled up to bed.

"Great," Jason mumbled.

"Yeah. I'll be home in a bit. You need anything?" This was so reminiscent of when Cole was working for Richard, before abandoning nearly all activities and pursuits for Heartbreak Guitars. Before leaving work, he would check with Jewell to see if he could pick up something for dinner. Here he was again, working for Richard, thrust back into the very situation Jewell had so recently wanted and Cole had resisted. It would only be for a few days, Cole reminded himself. Just a few more days.

"If you need anything, I can pick it up on the way home," he said.

"Like what?" Jason asked.

"What do you mean?"

"You asked me if I needed anything," Jason said.

"Yes. I did ask you that. Usually, the person on your end of the question would figure out *what* he might need and convey the name of that item back to the questioner."

"Okay, I need a car," Jason said. "And a cell phone would be good."

"Be home in a few." Cole hung up.

The front door was ajar, Cole noticed, so he closed it behind him and stood in the living room and listened to the quiet house. No Jewell, no Frankie, and no Jason. He slumped. Not again. But then he heard the shower start up and the shower curtain screech. A few minutes later, Jason came out of the bathroom followed by a cloud of steam. He was wearing a clean t-shirt and relatively clean jeans and was toweling his hair dry.

"Dude," Jason said, "did you forget about dinner?"

Cole just looked at him.

"At Constantine's. Remember? We're 'sposed to be there in thirty-five minutes."

Cole looked at the floor and sighed. "Just gotta jump in the shower," he said glumly. "Did you leave me any hot water?"

"A few molecules." Oh, Jason.

Cole pulled up in front of Constantine's gate and parked the car, only ten minutes late…Tallahassee traffic, even worse in the fall when the college students were back. Fortunately, Cole knew every back road to Constantine's. He would drive on anything – dirt roads, parking lots, driveways - to avoid the congestion on U.S. 27. Before they got to the front door, they could hear Constantine talking with someone, and he clearly was not happy. Cole opened the door and stuck his head in. "We're here," he said. Constantine was on the phone but waved for them to enter.

"I've got to go," Constantine said into the phone "They're here." He placed the phone on the hook and walked into the living room and held out his hand for Jason to shake. "Have we met?" he asked.

Jason was silent at first and then, looking confused and a little hurt, shook Constantine's hand and softly answered, "Yeah. Like a hundred times."

"Oh, man," Constantine said, a smile tugging at the corners of his mouth. "I thought you looked like this kid I know named Jason, but then in walks this tall person looking about ten years older." Jason smiled and put his hands in his pockets, a moment of uncharacteristic shyness.

"Trust me," Cole said. He was going to say, 'same smart-alecky kid', but Jason was enjoying his moment, so Cole said, "he's going to be taller than his Dad soon."

"Are you hungry?" Constantine asked.

"Starving," Jason said. "I mean, pretty hungry."

"Well, you're in luck," Constantine said. "Dinner is ready." They followed him into the dining room, where the table was set with a dark green tablecloth and light green napkins. Constantine lit the tapered red candles he had placed in cut-glass candleholders. Alongside the plates was his mother's silverware engraved on the handles with roses, and delicate wine glasses etched with a frosted rose pattern. That was Constantine...thoughtful as ever. Instead of beer and cola and pizza eaten in the living room, they were honored guests tonight. That was for Jason. Cole groaned inwardly. He would have been fine with pizza or something else casual and quick, knowing that Constantine would understand when Cole brought him up to speed on all he had to do and then dashed out the door.

"Take a seat," Constantine said.

Cole waited for Jason to pick his spot, and then sat down, gratified to see that Jason was opening his napkin to place on his lap.

"I hope you like spaghetti," Constantine said as he poured red wine into Cole's glass and his own. Constantine raised his eyebrows and looked at Jason, then back at Cole. Wine? Cole indicated with his thumb and index finger...about an inch. Jason mimicked him...about four inches. Constantine poured a small amount into Jason's glass, and then disappeared into the kitchen.

"Do you need any help?" Jason called out. Maybe he had metamorphosed during the day, and a new and better Jason had emerged, one who is timely, shy, polite, and helpful.

But during dinner, Cole had to remind Jason to slow down. "Savor the food," Cole said. "One of Constantine's specialties." He refrained from adding, 'Not like beer and pizza.'

"We have plenty for seconds," Constantine said before Cole could hand out any more instructions.

Constantine let them help carry the plates and glasses and silverware to the kitchen and place them next to the sink. "We have dessert," he said. "Key lime pie. You ready now or do you want to let your dinner settle?"

Jason had had two helpings of spaghetti, about half a loaf of Cuban bread with garlic butter, and a salad. "I can wait," he said. "If I have to." He smiled. "Just kidding. I'm pretty stuffed." They moved into the living room. Cole took up his usual place in the chair at the end of the sofa next to the small fridge, and Jason sat at the other end of the sofa from Constantine.

"Where's your girlfriend?" Jason asked. Cole drilled him with a 'don't go there' stare but Jason wasn't looking his way. Surely Jason wouldn't recount the complaints about Jasmine that Cole had hurled into the air every time he got off the phone from talking with Jewell. "She was in Miami, right?" Jason continued. "At a convention or conference or something? I just wondered if she was back." Cole had been wondering that very same thing, hoping that Jasmine was back in Tallahassee so she couldn't be bad mouthing him to Jewell, and wishing she wouldn't come back, so that Constantine would be free to find someone who wouldn't break his heart.

"I was just on the phone with her before you got here. She's at the lab," Constantine said. "She works in a Biology lab at FSU. She studies fruit flies and how they sleep."

Cole could almost hear Jason thinking 'why would anyone care how a fruit fly sleeps', but Jason surprised him and said, "Cool."

"Fruit flies need to sleep like we do…like all animals do," Constantine said. "And if you wake them up during their sleep, and do it often, or if you keep them up all night, they stumble around like they're drunk. It's really just a good way of looking at human sleep without having to wake people up or keep them up all night. Turns out flies need a full night's sleep, just like people do."

Jason looked at Cole. "See? I bet Jasmine wouldn't wake me up at the crack of dawn."

"Right, she wouldn't," Cole said. "But some of us have jobs to do, and anyway, I don't think Jasmine would call noon the crack of dawn."

On the way home, Cole and Jason listened to a CD of Credence Clearwater Revival. They were halfway home when Jason turned down the music and said, "I hope I can take his class next year," and then turned up the music again.

# Chapter 15

July 11, Thursday
Eight days before the NAMM show

In the morning, Cole managed to rouse Jason, steer him into the passenger seat of the truck, and cajole him to put on his seat belt, after which Jason slumped against the door and was asleep within seconds. Cole reached across him to press the door lock button, and they soon headed north on U.S. 27. Cole was thankful that the shop was on the north side of town, in a small enclave of warehouses made into shops: a paint and body shop, cabinet shop, pool supplies store, and Richard's countertop shop. The early daylight revealed the soft, gray landscape as they passed still unlit houses, held by the mist in a slumbering torpor, and the wooden piers and part of a public boat ramp that disappeared in a grey mist that rested on the waters of Lake Jackson. Richard's shop was at the end of a narrow roadway past the other shops. There was the shop, a large warehouse structure surrounded by a grassy field.

Cole parked among the trucks and vans and sedans that were spread out on the expanse of worn-down grass. Some were big, shiny, and expensive. Others wore dents and scratches and smears of Bondo, and one faded brown Honda Civic had a spider-web crack in the windshield and clear plastic instead of window glass on both the driver and passenger sides. He left the sleeping Jason in the truck and walked into the shop through the open warehouse doors and observed a bustle of activity. Some workers were already cutting sheets of Corian, or organizing their work areas, or carrying some sink cut-outs to the sanding area to be polished and provided to customers later for cutting boards.

Cole headed for the office. He could see Richard sitting at his desk listening to Laney, who stood on the opposite side of the desk, gesticulating with his cell phone. Laney hooked the phone onto his belt and stomped out of the office, not speaking to Cole, who had stepped to one side to let him pass.

Cole entered the office and sat across from Richard. "Went pretty well, huh?" he said.

"He'll be all right," Richard said. "Just has to let out a little hot air now and then and join the rest of the team…once he remembers we're on the same team." Richard sipped his coffee. "He's not too fond of you right now."

"Don't care," Cole said. "But you knew that." Suddenly, he realized where Jason got his smirky smile. There sat Richard, feeling good, smirking away. "What?" Cole said.

"I was just thinking that you were always pretty good at sales, and really good at scoping out the jobs and working up the estimates."

"Oh, no," Cole said. "For one, I suck at sales. And at the moment, I should be checking out the ever so lovely inflatables, but here I am fixing toilets and trying to keep your tools from going on vacation, not to mention keeping everyone out of the forklift jaws of death. Maybe after Mr. Bean comes back. How is he, anyway?"

"I'm waiting until after nine to call him. But I talked to his wife yesterday. I think he's better…coming along."

Jason appeared at the office door, rubbing his neck. "Were you just gonna let me suffocate out there in the truck? And I think my neck is broken."

Cole sighed and looked at the smirking Richard, then back at Jason. "Yes, I was just going to let you suffocate in the truck, which I think would take about a thousand years. It looked like you could sleep that long."

Richard swiveled his chair. "C'mere Bud," he said. Jason come closer to Richard's chair, and Richard lightly gripped Jason's shoulders and turned him to face the other way and began massaging his neck.

"Hey Richard," Cole said. "I think my neck is broken, too."

Richard raised an eyebrow and continued to massage Jason's neck.

"*They do not love that do not show their love*," Cole said. "Shakespeare wrote that four hundred years ago. I'm just saying."

Cole and Jason spent the morning writing tool names, descriptions, serial numbers, and locations onto the spreadsheet that Catherine had typed up. Once Cole could see that Jason had learned the names of all the tools and generally had the hang of their mission, he handed him the paperwork and pen. "Gotta go see how much money these guys are costing the business," he said, and turned toward the open warehouse door, where just outside, three of the workers were smoking cigarettes, and one stood a little further away talking on his cell phone.

"Don't I get lunch or something?" Jason complained. "This is child abuse."

Cole turned back to him. "Oh, so now you're a child," he said. "I'll remember that next time someone breaks out the wine at dinner. Lunch? Go talk to your dad."

Jason tucked the papers under his arm and walked toward Richard's office, although it was clear that no one was in there. Cole looked toward the parking area and noted that Richard's truck was gone. He sighed and walked back to catch up with Jason. "Your dad should be back soon." He reached into his pockets and pulled out a small handful of change, barely enough for the vending machine. "I bet he's bringing you some lunch."

"I've got a ten," Jason said. "What would you do without me around to help out?"

"You don't want to know," Cole said. "C'mon. Let's go get something and bring it back so I can babysit the shop guys."

They returned in twenty minutes with chili dogs and fries, a Coke for Jason and an iced tea for Cole. They sat in the cool of the office and looked out over the shop where they could see that Richard had returned and was standing just inside the shop roll-up doors talking again to an agitated Laney.

Cole put his hot dog back in its wrapper and debated whether he should go out and help Richard or stay out of it.

"If you're not going to eat it," Jason said, "I will."

"Go ahead," Cole said. In fact, it had been a mistake to go to The Hungry Dog. The last time he was there was with Richard, and he had saved half of his hot dog for Frankie. He missed Frankie. He missed Jewell. Only his desperation to finish the guitars for the show kept his thoughts busy.

183

Otherwise, he'd have headed to Miami days ago. He was still ready to do that…after the NAMM show.

After lunch, Jason resumed his inventory and Cole walked around the shop to see who needed help. By mid-afternoon a thunderstorm had rolled in, and the power was out. Three of the younger guys stood near the door, watching the roiling clouds and smoking cigarettes.

"Hey guys," Cole shouted. "Haven't you heard that Florida is the lightning capital of the country?" They turned their placid gazes his way but didn't move. "Get back from the door!"

By late afternoon, the electric was back on, and the shop was a symphony of saws, sanders, raised voices, and the high-pitched beep of the forklift backing up. From across the shop, Cole noted that Jason was back in the office, sitting with his feet up on Richard's desk, the chair adjusted so that it tipped back. It looked like his eyes were closed. He held a pencil in one hand and was tapping the eraser against his forehead, his cheeks, and lips. Catherine, who had been missing in action in the morning, was sitting at her desk in the far corner looking through a pile of paperwork, maybe the invoices that Richard had been reviewing before lunch. Catherine unclipped several papers and spread them out on her desk, and then read from them and typed on her keyboard. At least, Cole hoped she was typing from invoices and not from the Piggly Wiggly and Walmart coupons she amassed each week and sorted into piles. He started walking toward the office to check on her when Richard entered the office, stood next to his desk, and tapped on the toe of Jason's tennis shoe. Jason removed his feet from the desk and languidly rose from the chair. A sloth would be envious.

Cole looked at the clock. A quarter after five. Time to call it a day – at least here. Get some dinner and see what progress he could make working in the basement. Eight more days until the NAMM show. In reality, only six more days of preparation.

He entered the office. "You guys ready to go home yet?" Cole sat down in one of the two chairs opposite Richard's desk. Richard sat heavily in his desk chair and sighed. Jason took a seat in the chair next to Cole and stretched his legs out – just like Cole's – and jiggled one leg and tapped his pencil on his thigh – just like Cole. When Cole squinted and hung his tongue out one side of his mouth, Jason did the same. Cole narrowed his eyes and acquired a stern, prim, pressed-lipped frown. Jason did the same.

"You guys having fun?" Richard asked.

Cole sucked in his cheeks, scrunched up his nose and tilted his head to one side. Jason did the same.

"Jesus!" Richard said.

"Hey," Jason said and sat up straight. "Did you see Mr. Bean today?"

"Yeah," Richard said. "They're releasing him this afternoon. I think he'll be back at work soon. He's definitely better. "

"Will he be at work tomorrow?" Jason asked. Just what Cole had been wondering.

"I don't think so, Bud. We'll have to see. Maybe."

"So, we are about half-way through the tool inventory," Cole said. "I mean, Jason is 'bout halfway through." Cole turned to Jason. "Did you give your info to Catherine to type up?"

"Yeeesssss," Jason said and cast Cole a withering look.

Cole turned to Richard. "Any progress with Laney?" he asked.

"It isn't easy talking with Laney," Richard said. "Especially since he knows that I need him. Or need someone. If he leaves, I can do the estimates, but with Mr. Bean out…" he let it drop. "Let's talk about it tomorrow." Richard gathered the papers from his desk into a neat pile, slid them in the top desk drawer, and stood up. "Closing time."

Cole declined the invitation to follow Richard and Jason home for vegetable fettuccini that Maureen had made and frozen. If Cole wanted something quicker, Richard said, he could fire up the grill for burgers. Instead, Cole headed home, thankful he wasn't in the northbound lanes, where cars were headed out of town, moving like sludge. How many times was Cole in that same traffic when leaving Edna P.'s after visiting hours, or winding his way through the back roads after stopping at Constantine's for a beer? Even a beer was hardly worth driving at the snail's pace of U.S. 27 in rush hour. Well, maybe a beer with Constantine when one is penniless, without electricity, and running on fumes…that was worth a lot…and absolutely a visit with Jewell was worth it, even when she was feeling so down that her sentences trailed off before she reached the end. Tonight, Cole would call both Jewell and Maureen, just to hear their voices, and find out how Frankie was faring with his feline nemesis, and how Cole's dad was doing.

The house was eerily quiet. Yes, there was the hum of the air conditioning, but no Frankie, no Jason, no Jewell…not even the once ever-present growling Russian exclamations…only the distant drone of a lawnmower. He looked out the window at his own overgrown yard. Here was an excellent job for Jason. Cole would have to check the lawn mower to see if it would start, or if it even had gas.

He stood in front of the refrigerator with the door open, staring at the mostly empty shelves. In one of the cabinets, there was a can of split pea soup, some linguine, a jar of stewed tomatoes and a package of undoubtedly stale saltine crackers. He took down the can of soup and the crackers, poured the soup into a bowl and heated it in the microwave, and crumbled crackers onto it.

He sat at the dining room table looking out the window at the tangle of tall grass and weeds, thinking about Jewell watching Frankie bound through the same weeds. She couldn't see Frankie, but knew he was there. Cole could sense both Jewell and Frankie acutely. He lowered his spoon to his bowl and watched a gentle breeze riffling the grass.

That evening, Cole spoke first with Jewell and then with Maureen. Jewell assured him that they were watching the tropical storm forecast, and that they were somewhat confident that it would miss them and head further west into the Gulf of Mexico before turning north. However, she claimed she had to stay to help her parents move their boat out of the storm's path if it headed their way. It was still pretty far off, way too soon to worry. Frankie was fine. The cat was fine. Her parents, her brother, Dean, and his family were all fine. She seemed happy, and while Cole fervently wished for her to be happy, it was unsettling that she was so cheerful. "So, you seem happy, or at least content," he said, hoping she would tell him that she was feeling better and wanted him to come and pick her up and bring her home.

"Yeah, it's peaceful here. I forgot how restorative the ocean could be." A moment of silence. "And air conditioning."

"We have air conditioning, too," he said gently. Of course, she knew that. "Apparently you just turn the thermostat and *voilà.* Who knew?"

She didn't answer. Her mother was bringing out a casserole and she had to go. She hadn't asked about guitars, the shop, plans for the show, or even how Cole was doing.

He hung up the phone, but his hand still rested on it, as if to keep the tenuous connection to Jewell that had stirred up a sense of loneliness. Not really loneliness, more like loss, as if hearing Jewell's voice made their separation more real and more troubling. Hearing Jewell's voice only made him miss her more.

Cole sat at the at the dining room table and listened to the kitchen sink faucet drip. He hadn't noticed it before. One more thing to fix, after he had checked on his dad.

189

Maureen was simply tired, she said, but everything was mostly okay, "as well as it can go when Dad keeps trying to get up and do things his hip is not ready for. He honestly thought he could get on a stepstool and change out a light bulb."

"Maybe you can come home, take a break, if he's feeling so spry," Cole said. Maureen would only come home if things were going really well with their parents, and Cole could feel both hugely relieved and less guilty of parent neglect. "Or I can run over there and give a hand for a day? I do know how to change a light bulb."

"No, don't come," she said. "Richard said that things are crazy at work, and that he only was getting by because you're there. Thanks for helping him. I mean it."

"Ok," Cole said, "but if you decide you need anything…"

"I have to go," Maureen exclaimed. "Dad's out in the front yard now and he's…" the phone line went dead. Everything was as unsettled as the week before, and the week before that.

Cole could still decide to forgo the NAMM show and forfeit the registration fee. He could drive over to Pensacola for the weekend, come back and help Richard, and then next week drive to Miami to help move the boat, if they needed to move it. But none of that had been suggested, or even hinted at, and it wasn't clear that he was needed, even a little.

He headed toward the stairs to the basement, but his heart was not in it tonight. For the first time in a long time, he wondered if it was worth it, if he should go to NAMM with but a few tenuous connections, without business cards or a well-placed advertisement or even a plan to scale up production once they secured the sales. Peter and Gary would have had a plan. They would have had a banner for the booth and would have sent out slick post cards to registered attendees that would advertise the product and the booth number. They would have arranged for some meetings with Fender, Paul Reed Smith, Epiphone, Gibson, or Alvarez...just in case there was interest in licensing the patent, a patent they had now apparently abandoned along with the rest of their contract with Cole. They would have figured out how to hire a studio player to do some demos. They were skinflints when it came to building the product, but they sure knew how to market. They were all in for that. Cole wondered if Constantine had been right about them, suggesting that the entirety of their interest might have been to have a business write-off that would allow them to justify flights to New York, London, Madrid, wine and dine their way from San Francisco to Tokyo, and cop some tickets for concerts all over the world. That made the most sense. But what had changed that they had so suddenly bailed? Cole might never know. At least they had backed out before the contract period was up, and therefore had no claim to the patent. That was the only bright spot in the whole investor story. Peter and Gary couldn't hang in there, so it was up to Cole now to take it the rest of the way. They hadn't cared enough, but Cole did. He cared enough for everyone. It was a simple as that.

Cole spent an hour or so putting away tools and lining up guitars for a last assessment, in the morning when the light was better. He took a shower and brushed his teeth, dressed in boxer shorts, locked the front door, turned off the lights, and sat on the bed in the dark strumming the dead strings on Desire. She still needed batteries for tone and amplification, but he picked a dull thwap-thwap melody, then pushed Desire off to the side and settled back against the pillows.

# Chapter 16

July 12, Friday
Seven days before the NAMM show
Five days before departure

Cole drove toward the shop, steering with one hand and holding his coffee cup in the other. He accelerated slowly to steady the hot liquid as it lapped the rim of the cup and splashed onto his hand. By the time he arrived at the shop and parked, coffee was dripping from his hand onto the seat. He wiped his hand with the extra t-shirt he carried behind the seat and sat for a few minutes staring through the large opening of the roll-up shop door into the bright, cavernous space. It appeared that a full crew was already at work. He breathed in the aroma of roasted arabica, and took the first sips of his coffee, holding each small mouthful a few moments, rolling it on his tongue, feeling its warm, velvety smoothness, and letting its invisible energy focus his mind for the day.

It was Friday. He would spend the weekend sound-checking each guitar and ensuring that they were ready to impress. Maybe Mr. Bean would be back on Monday, and Cole would not be needed in the shop next week. Free from shop oversight he could pack for the show and make sure everything could fit in the back of Richard's truck and leave room for their travel bags, that is if Richard was still on board. But he had to be. They would leave town early on Wednesday, get most of the way to Nashville that night and drive the last leg on Thursday morning. They had to be there Thursday to set up the booth. The show would start on Friday for three full days of product display, luring manufacturers and players to their booth where they would be captured by the voluptuous Desire, the beguiling Despair sisters, and the arresting Diva.

On Sunday by 6 p.m., the show would come down, and on Monday they would pack their bags, drive all day, and arrive home by dinnertime. He and Richard would be away for four business days plus the weekend, after which Cole would return and help Richard find a new salesman, hand over the keys to the shop, and focus on getting his guitars built and out the door. He prayed that Mr. Bean was well again, in heart and body – or as well as he could be given his terrible loss - and that he would be able to supervise the shop while they were gone, and of course later, continue to run the shop after they returned, when Cole would be knee deep in guitar orders and ready to partner with a larger shop to have the guitars built. Richard held Mr. Bean in high regard, and Cole hoped that was reflected in his paycheck. Respect and "atta boys" would not pay the bills. Cole knew all about that. He finished his coffee, exited the car, and headed for the shop doors.

The shop was filled with a quiet energy typical of a Friday, when everyone just wanted to get the work done and go home, where they might be treated to the aroma of country fried steak before getting halfway to the front door. Or they would fire up the grill for chicken and burgers or stop by the Pastime bar first for a few beers and a game of pool. Once Cole would have been happy to have a few beers and shoot some pool, but they didn't invite him anymore, even those who had known him before he had quit working for Richard. You can only say "no" so many times and then rush home to work in the basement before the invitations ceased.

Cole could see through the glass wall that Richard was sitting at his desk, studying some paperwork. Cole entered the office, took the seat across from Richard, and waited for Richard to look up.

Richard frowned, slumped his shoulders and sighed, and then sat back in his seat, but remained quiet.

"Bad news?" Cole asked.

"It's not good," Richard said. "We're apparently turning into a non-profit organization."

Cole glanced at the door to the back that led to Laney's small office. He didn't say anything, however. Richard knew.

"I talked to him," Richard said. "He's stewing right now. If I push him any harder, I'm afraid he might quit." Cole didn't say anything. Richard continued, "Don't say it, unless you know of someone else I can get in here and get trained by Monday...or you want to take it on yourself." Richard must have seen Cole's horrified expression, and he laughed. "You see my problem."

"I can help you interview after the NAMM show," Cole offered. "You can tell Laney I suggested that. Maybe he'll rise to the challenge." Before Richard could reply, Cole continued, "But it's not just Laney. The shop guys have to work smarter...quit making stupid mistakes. And some of them do everything they possibly can think of to be away from the job. They're just dead weight on the ledger. Maybe they were better when Mr. Bean was here. Did you hear anything?""

"Nothing definite," Richard groaned. "I'm hoping he'll be back sometime next week. It's not the kind of thing I can push, you know?"

"Yeah," Cole said, "I know." He looked down at his shoes and stared at a small hole in the toe of the right shoe. The shoes weren't new, but not *that* old. Or maybe they were. The shoelaces were fraying, and anyway, resin had dripped across the tops of both shoes and left dark greasy-looking spots. He couldn't wear those out of town. He looked at Richard. "You know the NAMM show is next weekend. It's a long drive and it means leaving next Wednesday. We need to have the product display set up Thursday by five or so."

Richard looked out over the shop. "I can't go. You know that don't you?"

Cole felt his heart sink. He sat perfectly still, looking down again at his tennis shoes, absorbing the blow. It wasn't Richard's fault. The forces of the universe had conspired to create this moment, had placed before him obstacle after obstacle to deflate his spirit – but somehow, each time, he had figured out a solution or one had come his way so that he was re-energized, elated, and confident that the torch that burned in his heart would be carried across the finish line. But this...so close to the show? What the hell?

"So, I can still help you out financially," Richard said, "if you can make another plan. You can take my credit card." Richard pulled his wallet out of his back pocket and flipped through three or four credit cards, selected one, and handed it over to Cole. "There's about eight or nine hundred on this one. Should be enough, right?"

Cole honestly didn't know, but it seemed low. He needed to pay back Constantine, who had fronted Cole the money to register for a booth at the show. It was either that or show the one Inflatable he had been invited to display for free in the Sound Bridges booth if he used their bridge in his guitar. The bridges would be featured in the Sound Bridges literature but showcased in the Inflatable and probably a dozen other guitars by more well-known manufacturers. They were beautiful bridges, well made, and would have been totally out of Cole's price range – maybe out of anyone's price range - if not provided to him for free. A good product, but still, they were just bridges. They didn't have superpowers. They wouldn't invent new soundwaves or spit out original music while one is sleeping or float a guitar to the ceiling and fly around the room. But an Inflatable could do that...fly around the room...possibly...if filled with helium. That would be worth displaying at the NAMM show someday. At any rate, Cole needed his own booth, Constantine had offered to help, and Cole had let him. If it meant that Cole had to sell the Mustang, he would pay back the money. But that wouldn't be necessary. After the show, everything would be different. *"Our doubts are traitors and make us lose the good we oft might win by fearing to attempt,"* Cole said.

"Say again?" Richard commented.

"Nothing. Just Shakespeare thinking out loud," Cole answered.

Cole still needed to book a room somewhere in the vicinity of Nashville, but he could go cheap. And he could go low on meals, peanut butter sandwiches low. But he'd have to get his hands on a small cargo trailer he could pull behind the Mustang. He suddenly was tired, despite the coffee. He was tired of thinking, and his gut felt like a sack of wet concrete. "Hey, thanks man," Cole said, "If you're sure."

"Yeah, a drop in a leaky bucket," Richard said, worry lines pinching his eyebrows.

Cole thought it over.

"One more thing," Richard said. "Jason is really looking forward to going."

Cole looked up in surprise. Jason. In Nashville. "I'm surprised. It's not really a kid's thing." he said, a sack of wet concrete shifted in his belly as he sank lower in his seat. Of course, Jason would want to go to Nashville, get out of town, experience something new, check out some guitars, escape from parental control for a few days. Which was exactly the problem, Jason would be a heavy weight, one more worry. Maybe Richard would reconsider. "I get it that he wants to go," Cole said, "but Nashville is a big city. Ten hours away. I mean, if he needed you." Richard raised one eyebrow, but otherwise had perhaps not absorbed the gravity of what Cole was saying, of what Cole was imagining.

199

There was another argument in his favor…his ace-in-the-hole. He didn't like to use it with Richard, but… "You think Maureen would be on board?" Maureen would definitely not be on board.

"I already talked with her." Richard sat back in his chair. "We both really appreciate what you're doing. I mean with the guitars and the show. Takes a lot of heart. And Jason can have his head in the clouds, we know that. But we think it will be good for him to go. Just give him something to be responsible for. Make him work for his fun."

Cole looked at his shoes, at the ragged hole in the toe, and the dull shine of the nail of his big toe. The show, his success there, was as ephemeral as the early morning mist that lay heavy on Lake Jackson. It was almost tangible, but not quite. It could evaporate at any time, and whether it did or not seemed completely out of his control. Would he have been better off if Gary and Peter were still part of the enterprise? Hard to believe, given their increasing lack of enthusiasm, but they did know how to sell, and they could problem-solve, as long as the solution was cheap. Everything cheap, peanut butter sandwich cheap. So no, he would have been no better off. "Where is Jason, anyway?"

"He's out back taking inventory on the service vehicles." Richard looked out over the shop and back at Cole. "Maybe he can be helpful to you at

NAMM, watch your inventory. He has experience."
Richard meant it to be light, but nothing in his face
conveyed light. Always handsome, his forehead was
pulled into vertical furrows, and the corners of his
mouth were turned down. This was becoming his
"usual look".

Just after lunch, the universe sent Mr. Bean.
A gift to Cole, to Richard, to everyone in the shop,
he appeared out of nowhere and started sorting
through the current job orders. Cole was elated. Here
was one good thing…one lucky pool shot that broke
the right way. He watched from the office as Mr.
Bean walked from one work bench to the next and
spoke to the shop crew, and then let out a piercing
whistle aimed at the two guys near the bathroom who
looked up from their phones with surprise as he
motioned them over to where he stood near their
work benches with his arms crossed.

Sometimes you see only what you need to
see. Cole saw a tall, thin man in blue jeans, a bright
white t-shirt neatly tucked into his waist band, and
work boots. With the self-assurance and elegance of
a symphony conductor, Mr. Bean was making the
rounds…now leaning past his coworker, whose
name was Alfonso but was known as Alfie. Mr. Bean
quietly organized Alfie's workspace while he talked,
placing screwdrivers and pliers and clamps into the

bins built into the work cabinet, motioning for Alfie to pick up the soft-bristled brush and sweep the area so that they could properly place the solid surface pieces onto a smooth and uncluttered worktable. At that moment, five days from departure for the NAMM show, Cole observed a group of men at their work benches take hold of their clamps, glues, templates, saws, or sanders…a small, inchoate orchestra, the musicians taking their places and tuning their instruments. Or perhaps it was more like a cover-playing country-rock band that one minute was generating discordant noise, and a few minutes later was sending up some sweet sound. *I never heard so musical a discord, such sweet thunder.*

With Mr. Bean in the shop, with the air just a little lighter and more breathable, Cole headed outside to check on Jason, survey the state of the installation trucks, and take a look in the dumpster where solid surface scraps were discarded and where Cole suspected a lot of usable material was deposited. Jason was dangling his long legs from the back of one of the installation trucks - a big, yellow box on wheels, a hard-to-maintain, leave-you-stranded by the side of the road, gas hog, piece-of-junk that somehow Richard had been sweet-talked and wined-and-dined into purchasing – three of them - and that he had regretted ever since. Richard was a pretty good salesman himself, knew all the sales methods, and should have known better.

Jason was nodding his head to the drumbeat blasting from earphones connected to a small Walkman in his pocket. There was a clipboard in his lap that he – or someone – had made by using a small clamp taken from the shop and using it to pinch the pages of the tool inventory onto a sturdy slab of cardboard. With his eyes closed, oblivious to the mosquitoes swarming around his face and neck, Jason tapped on the papers with a pencil and nodded his head to a drumbeat that blasted past his ears and filled the humid morning air. Cole tapped Jason's thigh. Jason's eyes flew open, and he yanked the headphones off. "Man, you scared me," he said.

Cole nodded at the clipboard. "Nice clipboard you got there." Jason's mouth upturned ever so slightly. "So, what's the word on the inventory?" Cole asked.

"I'm almost done," Jason said, "and I'm ready for my check. Cash would be better."

"Talk to your dad…just go easy on him," Cole said. "Let me have a look at that before you put it on Catherine's desk."

"What? You don't think it's any good?"

"No, man," Cole replied. "I just never know what Catherine is doing, or if she'll be here to type it up." Cole glanced inside the truck. "And I don't want

Janice Dodge

to wait until I get back – I mean, until *we* get back
from the NAMM show to see how many tools we're
short." Cole climbed into the back of the truck. Not
too bad, not as disorganized as the shop: lumber, a
compressor, toolboxes, sanders, boxes of sanding
paper, joint adhesive and caulking, gallon cans of
denatured alcohol, extension cords, Corian and wood
scraps, all of it mostly held in bins or behind bungee
cords. On the truck floor were a hundred black boot
prints. Cole remembered the Midnight Black
countertops that had gone out recently to be installed
in a coffee shop in Quincy. He hated black, at least
in countertops. It took hours of sanding, using
sequentially more fine-grained sandpaper to bring
out a high gloss that customers loved, but that
showed any scratch or ding. If you never put
anything down on the countertop, they were great,
beautiful, elegant, but with normal use, especially in
a high traffic area like a coffee shop, they would look
dull and gritty in no time. It was hard to convince a
customer of that, but that was Laney's job. Laney had
never built anything in his life and hadn't bothered to
learn how countertops were built just a few yards on
the other side of the wall from his desk, where they
started off as big, heavy rectangles of materials, and
were cut and shaped and seamed and sanded within
an inch of their lives. He would not have priced in
the extra hours of work it took to achieve that

Midnight Black high gloss. He wasn't even that good a salesman if he had to practically give away countertops to ring up a sale. When Cole returned from Nashville, he would find a real salesman for Richard. And if he had to train the new guy himself, so be it.

At noon, Cole saw Mr. Bean sitting in the parking lot in his big truck with the air conditioner running, eating his lunch. Mr. Bean was back, and it appeared he was well, or at least he appeared as cool and collected as always, even if it was only a façade for the outside world. With Mr. Bean on board, Cole saw his opportunity to call it a day, go home and work out how he was going to transport his guitars and accessories in the back of the Mustang. He currently needed to pack guitars, an amp, a small electric pump, some tools (just in case), electric cords, and leave space for two suitcases and a cooler, or at least room for a box of bread, peanut butter, snacks and utensils. Could it possibly fit? They were inflatables, after all, and one of the top selling points was their compact portability.

If Jewell had not taken the camera, he would photograph the packing. Maybe someday, he would photograph a whole band's worth of guitars in their slim-jim gig bags - yet to be acquired - miraculously extracted from the trunk of a Triumph Spitfire like a dozen clowns unpacked from the passenger compartment of a Volkswagen Bug. With careful packing, he wouldn't need to rent a cargo trailer, for which he would have to purchase or rent a trailer hitch and have it mounted on the back of the Mustang.

Cole headed for Richard's office to let him know that he was leaving. He opened the door just as Richard and Jason were approaching from the other side. "Well thank you, good sir," Richard said as Cole held the door, and they passed through into the shop. "Care to join us for lunch?"

"Just tell him you want to go to The Hungry Dog," Jason interjected. "For some strange reason, he thinks we're going to Wendy's." Cole let go of the door, and it slowly swung shut with a faint hiss.

"For some strange reason," Richard said, dangling the keys in the air. "Need I say more?"

"So actually, I was about to leave," Cole said. "Still got a lot to do to get ready."

"Wait a sec," Richard said. "What about the Grady job?" Then he frowned. "Did I talk to you about the Grady job?"

Cole shook his head slowly, looked at the ground, shook his head again. "First I've heard." He wanted to object – no way did he have time to build a countertop or rather, fix a job that someone in the shop had botched. That was more likely. Richard probably wouldn't be asking Cole to build a new countertop this late in the game. But there were only two people who could fix the screw-ups. Cole didn't have time for this, but Richard had just given him his credit card. There was nothing to say.

"Come have lunch with us and I'll fill you in," Richard said and started walking toward his truck.

Jason gave a sympathetic shrug and raised his eyebrows. He didn't say anything. Sometimes he was smarter than he looked.


The Wendy's on this side of town was usually packed, but today it was half empty, which meant that the students were taking final exams, or maybe they were already out of town on summer break. They took their food to a table in the corner, spread out their feast and dug in. "Is that all you're eating?" Richard nodded at Cole's chocolate Frosty and fries.

"Not that hungry today," Cole said. It wasn't just the heavy feeling in his stomach, or the unpalatable greasy sheen on the fries, or the brain freeze that manifested after a few bites of the Frosty. He was overtaken by a sense of futility. The obstacles to success at NAMM and beyond were insurmountable. And it was costing too much. His life was a lonely stream of days, all of them filled with work, which he would be okay with – he didn't mind working hard – but there was nothing at the end. His wife was off having a good time without him and seemingly with no urgent plans to return; his dog was off on an endless vacation as well – at least he hoped that was how Frankie felt – and he was subsisting only because of the kindness of his brother-in-law…and his sister. He needed them, all of them, but he was not needed. Actually, Richard and Jason needed him. That was something. But Jewell and Frankie...

"Earth to Cole," Jason said. Cole realized that Jason had asked him something.

"Sorry, what did you say?" Cole asked.

"I said," Jason dragged it out, "or rather, I asked if you needed help in the shop this weekend. You know, the shop, where you put together funny looking guitars and say a lot of four-letter words to yourself that you think no one else can hear."

"What do you mean funny looking?" Cole asked, bewildered and a little miffed. "And anyway, I don't swear," he said, glancing at Richard. "At least not very often." Cole thought about it - a long ago promise to Maureen that he wouldn't curse around the kids. Sometimes a well-placed curse word was just what the soul needed, however. Maybe even Maureen had discovered that.

Richard interjected, "What he meant to say is 'different.' The Inflatables are just different."

Richard was smooth, with the attributes of a true salesman.

"Yeah, that's what I meant," Jason said. "Just different. Don't get all..." he paused. "Anyway...just offering."

"Thanks, but I guess not," Cole said. He didn't have the energy to accommodate Jason, to come up with jobs that he thought Jason could do, or ones that would be essentially busy-work, or show him guitar chords or finger picking, or explain anything about anything. He picked up a fry, dipped it in catsup, and put it back on the greasy paper, and looked up at the crestfallen Jason. "Hey, you did a great job on that inventory. Don't think I told you that yet."

"Thanks," Jason mumbled.

"Thanks, Bud," Richard said. He pulled out his wallet and fished out two twenties and handed them to Jason. "Really, thanks."

"Cool," Jason leaned to the side so that he could stuff the money into his front jeans pocket.

Richard pulled out a couple more twenties and handed them to Cole. "This is for a haircut, if you were planning on that." Jason sank lower in his seat, obviously hoping he wouldn't be expected to spend *his* money on a haircut. Cole reached up to pat his hat. He had worn a hat, hadn't he? No. Just his untamable fluffy mane. Richard was probably right. Cole should get a haircut before the show.

"We'll settle up some other stuff before you leave," Richard said. "And by the way, I can put Mr. Bean on the Grady job next week." He hesitated, leaned forward slightly, wanting to say more it seemed, but then he relaxed against the seat back and started gathering the lunch debris onto a plastic tray. "I'll just drop you off to your car."

"Cool," Cole said, winked at Jason, and placed his nearly untouched food on the tray.

# Chapter 17

Back from lunch, Cole stepped out of Richard's truck into the heat of the afternoon. A rapacious afternoon sun fiercely reflected from the windshields of the trucks - and the few cars – that sat broiling in the sparse grass of the parking area outside of Richard's shop. In the shop the temperatures had dropped, but not enough. Gigantic fans that hung from the high ceilings and additional ones on stands whirred at high speed. Cole looked for Mr. Bean, wanting to welcome him back, but he was nowhere to be seen. He looked for Mr. Bean's big red truck outside where it would be parked in the shade of the one oak tree that everyone knew sheltered Mr. Bean's parking spot, but it was gone. That big red truck had stood apart from all the other vehicles in a show of steadfast reliability and conscientiousness, as unblemished and polished as the day it was new. Today, it had been a bearer of good news, a bright spot in a day filled with disappointment, but now it was gone.

Cole entered the cool office where Richard and Jason hovered next to Catherine's desk. Jason was pointing to his tool inventory notes, and

Catherine was wearing a wooden smile and nodding her head. They all turned to look at Cole as the door whispered closed behind him.

"I can wait," Cole said, and stuffed his hands into his front pockets. They continued to look at him expectantly. "Mr. Bean?" Cole asked. "I didn't see his truck. Just wanted to say 'hi' before I got going."

"Oh yeah," Catherine said, and turned to Richard. "He told me to tell you he'd be back soon. Didn't say why." The wooden smile spoke of disapproval. "Didn't say a thing about where he was going," she added.

"It's ok," Richard said. "I know he's got stuff to do." Then quietly, as if just to her, "Just like the rest of us." Cole silently wished that Richard would continue, along the lines of "only he's more prompt, reliable, competent, and diligent in his work than you." Catherine was another employee whom Cole would help Richard replace after the NAMM show. Jason, with his teenage flakiness, off-the-wall ideas, and tendency to mouthiness, would be better. At least he cared, in his own way, sometimes hidden beneath a veneer of apathy, but Cole saw that Jason surreptitiously paid attention, and if the tool inventory was any indication, he cared about his mission and how his efforts would be received.

"You headed home?" Richard asked.

"Yeah, got stuff to do," Cole said. He had a lot to do, too much to do, and his brain seemed stuck in first gear, unable to make a solid plan. In fact, today, Cole didn't want to be at home, looking at the four walls of his basement, stringing, tuning, assessing, and tweaking the Inflatables. And upstairs, there was plenty he didn't want to do as well. The ever-present dust that he kept meaning to get to be a daily reminder of so many things he had meant to do, but for which he hadn't yet found time.

He realized they were still staring at him expectantly. "Yeah, I'll catch you later," Cole said.

"Okay, later," Richard said. Cole walked back through the shop into the relentless sunlight, opened the driver's door of the Mustang and stood back as roasting heat poured out. After a minute, he got in and started the car, turned the air conditioning to high, and drove out of the parking lot toward home.

The thought of Frankie suddenly arose – but no Frankie would be waiting for him. Frankie and Jewell were a fresh loss every day, but Jewell had not been home all day every day of the last year hanging out in the basement with Cole like Frankie had. It was Frankie's peaked ears and liquid brown eyes and outpouring of happiness whenever Cole walked in the door that he most associated with coming home, and now Frankie's absence was a fresh punch in the gut every day he was gone. At Wendy's, Cole had nearly begun wrapping the box of fries in a napkin to take home for Frankie. Now Cole would go home to his quiet house, shower, and make a plan. Then he remembered that Constantine had asked him to come by…just for a few minutes. He was pretty sure that Constantine was just worried about him. So…okay, he would drop by.

Constantine's white van was in front of the house and fortunately, Jasmine's little truck was not. Constantine stood, shirtless and wearing cut-off blue jeans, on his small porch where it seemed he had been waiting in the oppressive humidity and heat, the mosquitoes, and the high-pitched drone of cicadas for Cole to drive up. But actually, Cole noticed, Constantine had his binoculars, so he was probably looking for the red-shouldered hawk that often perched in the high branches of a pine tree surveying the neighbor's open back yard for any small rodent that was not aware it was dinner.

Constantine held up his hand with the fingers curled forward like a claw, his characteristic greeting for Cole, a gesture he had borrowed from the sitcom 'Sanford and Sons', signifying that the aches and pains of life would one day land them both in rocking chairs where they would talk about their arthritis –

the rheumatism, he called it – and the failed adventures of their youth. Cole raised a claw back.

"What's new in the mysterious and wonderful world of the luthier-inventor?"

"Do you really want to hear it?" It was better to ask now than to sink satisfyingly deep in a morass of self-pity only to be interrupted by a visit from Jasmine.

"Just a minute." Constantine ushered him through the door and gestured toward Cole's usual chair and disappeared into the bedroom. A minute later, he returned wearing a baggy dark-blue t-shirt and brushing his long hair back with his fingers. "Wasn't expecting such esteemed company this early," he said. "Want a beer?" He opened the small beer fridge and pulled out a six-pack, rather a five-pack, and pulled two beers away from the plastic collar. He handed one to Cole, who sank deeper into the chair and peeled back the pop-top tab.

"Where's Jasmine?" Cole asked. He wanted to be genuinely interested in the success of Constantine's love life and the object of his romantic ardor, but at the moment he was more interested in learning if Jasmine's plans for the afternoon included dropping by to monopolize the conversation and all but push Cole out the door. And Cole equally dreaded the unwelcome news that Jasmine might have embarked on new adventures in South Florida where she could inflame the delicate detente that Cole felt had been forged with Jewell.

"She's at the lab," Constantine said. "Counting her sleeping fruit flies. Interesting, huh?" He grinned.

It was sort of interesting. "Do they sleep in the middle of the day?" Cole asked. "What time is it anyway?" Probably mid-afternoon, maybe late afternoon, Cole realized, since Constantine was home from school.

Constantine looked at the grandfather clock. "One-thirty," he said. "And I think that she puts them in a dark box during the day, so they go to sleep when she can study them without coming in at two in the morning."

"1:30…Really?" Cole asked. "What are you doing home, anyway? Don't you have school?"

Constantine hesitated, probably wondering why Cole had come by if he didn't think Constantine was home.

"I didn't think about school hours until just now," Cole confessed.

"Well, I'm free," Constantine said, looking as happy and relaxed and energized as if he had just been released from lockup. "Summer school session A ended today, and we put an end to their misery at noon." He raised his beer can toward Cole in a toast to his well-earned freedom.

Cole raised his beer can as well. "Congratulations," Cole said. "You survived another year of enlightening the youth of our fair city."

Cole relaxed into his tale of woes and Constantine listened. By the time Cole was winding up – Richard wasn't going to NAMM, Jason was going; Richard's big, air-conditioned truck wasn't going, the Mustang was; Jewell wasn't going, but a sense of foreboding that sat like a concrete sack in Cole's stomach was fully on board - Constantine and Cole were splitting the last beer. Constantine poured half into a glass for himself and handed the half-full can to Cole.

"I don't know," Cole said. "Hell of a time for Jewell to bail." He never spoke ill of his wife, whom he loved. Everyone knew that. But this was Constantine, practically his brother, sitting in his cross-legged Buddha pose on the sofa, his expression attentive and kind. Cole continued, "Ever since Gary and Peter, Jewell has been different. It's like she doesn't care anymore. After all we've sacrificed...one thing after another. For years." Cole fell silent, and they quietly sat and sipped beer.

Constantine broke the silence, "Let me ask you something." He placed his glass on the small coffee table. "Do you and Jewell ever talk about adopting a baby? Not even necessarily a baby…just a small human?"

"What has…?" Cole began to object, but he knew what Constantine was about to say. And of course, they had talked, or at least Cole had listened while Jewell had talked.

Constantine unfolded his legs and stretched one leg straight under the coffee table with the foot flexed, then the other. "Like you said…years of sacrifice." Constantine never belabored his point. He didn't need to. He had a way of brushing aside the B.S. and going straight to the heart of things.

Cole sat pinned into his chair under the weight of Constantine's softly spoken admonition. He should be working for Richard so that he could support Jewell in pursuing her dreams of going back to school. He should be seriously inviting Jewell's thoughts about adoption. He should be helping Maureen take care of his dad; helping Jewell's parents move their boat and batten the hatches; planting his mother's garden; really teaching Jason the joys of instrument making. He almost snorted a mirthless laugh. The joys of instrument making wouldn't be evident to anyone, not even to Cole, if he had only the ear-popping highs and gut-hollowing lows of the last couple of years to go by.

He was a luthier, but also an inventor. He was happy when he was building guitars…infinitely uplifted. But then an idea for something new would coalesce in his consciousness without regard to what he was doing at the time. It would not be ignored for long, and eventually he was down in the basement building some crude facsimile, just to see if it could work. These were endeavors of the heart, a galaxy apart from the murky, hazard-filled, dream-withering business world into which he had plunged, dragging Jewell and everyone he loved with him. Cole stared at the empty beer can that he tapped lightly on his thigh. "But it was fun for a while," Cole said. "Before Gary and Peter."

Cole couldn't pinpoint the exact month when he had entertained the first hints that the Heartbreak Guitar Company was an albatross, a magnificent bird that had once soared high in a cloudless blue sky until it faltered in its gliding flight, headed for inevitable collapse. Maybe the NAMM show was just another doomed effort. He didn't know.

Cole pushed himself out of the chair and placed the beer can on the coffee table. "Guess I better get back to it," he said.

Constantine stood up and arched his back with his hands clasped together and his arms stretched over his head. "Didn't Jewell go with you to check out the NAMM show last year, or was that the year before?" Constantine asked. He turned his head to look over one shoulder and then the other,

219

then stood on one leg and raised his opposite foot back and grasped it tight to his butt.

"Looks like you might hurt something doing that," Cole said, remembering that Jewell would go through the same contortions, only that with her long, graceful legs she resembled one of the waterbirds they could see from the riverboat at Wakulla Springs, whereas Constantine looked like a wounded warrior. Still strong but missing a limb.

"Yes, we went the year before last. That's how I know we should be in it." The show wore a little thin with Jewell after the first day, but she loved Nashville: lightning-fast guitar pickers on the street corners; balladeers in the Taco Bell or KFC; a bluegrass ensemble or solo soul singer in the cramped, dark bars where one might find the best burgers or – for Jewell – portobello mushroom cheese melt that she ordered sans cheese.

She loved the bookstores and the music stores that sold used vinyl and on their small stages hosted players with long gray ponytails or teenage guitar phenoms that weren't old enough to play in the bars. Nashville had an underbelly, a seediness that became apparent if one walked enough, as Jewell did, and traveled beyond the bustling music scene into blue-collar neighborhoods with clapboard houses clustered together in a community of those who had just enough to get by. Jewell could relate to that as well, and she reported that from some of the small, wood houses with sagging porches and scruffy yards she heard the loveliest music - a woman's Irish lilt accompanied by flute, or a full-throated country band, or haunting, rhythmic acoustic drumming. "She loved Nashville," Cole said. "I wish she were coming with me. You just don't know."

Constantine had clasped his hands together behind him and, with his back arched and his head thrown back, was stretching his long torso. "I haven't been to Nashville," he said to the ceiling.

The weight on Cole's heart lifted a degree or two. "Come with me, then. It would be awesome." Before he could say more, he remembered the limited space he would have for human beings, travel bags, guitars, amps, and all the rest. "It's just that," he almost couldn't say it. "It's just that I'm taking the Mustang. I don't think there's room."

"The van's in pretty good shape. Should get us there." Constantine smiled. "And back."

Cole closed his eyes and sighed a full exhalation, relaxing his shoulders, neck, and the tightness in his jaw, shedding for a moment his worries about money, his marriage, his parents, Jason, Richard's shop troubles, and the debut of the Inflatables at the biggest music trade show in the country. He let his imagination drift onto the oft traveled path of his dream, a succession of events culminating at the NAMM show, from which he would walk away with a new and vibrant plan that would bring about a restoration to whole cloth the tattered remnants of his life. His imagination was rekindled, lighting a fire inside him that he hadn't known had died down to the barest of embers. "That would be awesome," he whispered.

# Chapter 18

### Early evening

Cole pulled into his driveway and parked. It was dusk. The cicadas were singing, letting the chorus die away for a moment and then swell again, infused with happiness and hope. He headed up the walkway past the tall grass, brushing against dandelions that grew from cracks in the cement, releasing a puff of seeds borne aloft on fine tufted threads. There was a yellow document taped to his door, and he inwardly groaned. It would be another notification of electric service 'disconnect'. He pulled it off and entered the quiet house, where it was still cool. They must have just shut it off. But then, the air-conditioner cycled on with a subdued hum.

He placed the document on the dining room table and sat down to read it. It was an environmental code violation notice. He would be fined for every day that his grass towered above twelve inches, beginning on Monday. Seriously? They hadn't noticed the massive pine tree in the yard across the street that had been hit by lightning, turned brown and leaned toward the street...toward *his* driveway.

If it fell, it might even hit his house. The college boys who lived across the street didn't care, although after he urged them to call their landlord, they reported that she didn't want to spend the money to have the tree removed, and it turned out that the county had no ordinance against leaving it, regardless of its condition. Not only that, down the hill was a house with boarded up windows and holes rotted completely through the roof. It had been like that for years…empty, slowly deteriorating, beckoning to the local kids who needed somewhere to go to smoke pot. And an eyesore, let's not forget that. But apparently no more of an eyesore than Cole's patchy but not height-challenged Saint Augustine grass and his dandelions. Now that was an eyesore worthy of an environmental code, an ordinance, a fine!

Cole felt an affinity with every apparent ne'er-do-well with knee high grass – they all had too much to do and too little time to do it. Mowing hadn't even made the list. He'd already wasted half the day drinking beer with Constantine. Actually, not a waste at all since Constantine had either spontaneously decided to reward himself for a year amongst the city's apathetic youth with a road trip to Nashville, or he had just taken pity on a friend. Probably both, and Cole was okay with that.

No time like the present to satisfy the powers that be. Cole went outside, around back, batting away mosquitoes, and opened the door to the shed. There was the lawnmower covered in dust and some rodent droppings. He pulled it out and checked for gas. It was empty. Good. He wouldn't have to empty it of old gas. He grabbed a gas can and a siphon hose and walked around the side of the house through the grass and weeds, headed for the Mustang. But he stopped in the driveway and put down the gas can. It was clear that no regular mower would cut this grass without choking. Okay then, time for the weedwhacker, if he could find an extension cord long enough.

An hour later, it was fully dark, and Cole was through for the night. He stood in front of the house, and by the light of the moon surveyed the front yard. Not great, but better. He wondered if leaving all the grass clippings would be a code violation. It surely was not good for the grass beneath. He would deal with that in the morning. He walked into the house, peeled off his sweat soaked shirt and used it to wipe his face and neck. He would shower, grab something to eat, crawl into bed and with the curtains open, watch the moonlight pattern through the branches of the oak tree shift in a light wind that heralded a rainstorm. Time to just call it a day. A good one.

When the rain splattered the cement patio in front of the house, and the wind stirred the Corinthian chimes, he was reminded of the clanging of the depth marker in Biscayne Bay that they passed every time they went out in the boat with Jewell's parents. The thought of Jewell brought a fresh ache. He was ready for her to return. He had been ready since the day she left. Yet, it didn't make sense for her to come back now when in a few days the house would be empty…unless, perhaps, she preferred it to be empty. But there was no use contemplating her preferences or her thoughts. In twelve years of marriage, he had never felt so alone. Though they had been apart before, he had never felt so essentially separate, so completely in the dark about what she thought or how she felt.

The next morning, Cole was out early, finishing the weed whacking and raking the grass clippings into a pile around the oak tree and under the azalea bushes. He was acutely aware that today, Saturday, was only one of four full days left before leaving for Nashville. In addition to a visual and sound check of each Inflatable, he would have to undertake three urgent tasks before packing. He needed business cards, a brochure, or flyer to hand out to the retail store buying staff and anyone else who was interested. Secondly, he needed to finish the wood display case that he had built with mounts for six guitars to be held upright under a set of miniature theater-style spotlights he had picked up in a costume shop. And he needed to test the inflatable body he had made for the light and whimsical Diva. Diva would come first. He smoothed a wisp of hair that had floated onto his sweaty cheek and stuck there. And he needed a haircut.

It was a beautiful morning. Bright sunshine lit the tops of corpulent cumulus clouds that drifted only a few hundred feet above the ground. Humid and warm, but not yet roasting. Cole heard the plaintive peal of the telephone and headed inside. It was Richard.

"It's a huge thing to ask," Richard said, "but I need you at the shop today, just to keep things to subdued mayhem." Maureen had called and asked Richard to come to Pensacola for the weekend, and he was about to head out. Nothing was wrong, Richard said, she just needed an outing, away from Cole's parents, with another adult. "So, I'll be back in town tomorrow night, and back in the shop on Monday morning. Jason is coming with me."

Cole hung up the phone. "I don't have time for this!" he shouted. He picked up the sofa cushion and threw it against the wall. "Seriously, I don't have time!" He stood with his arms hanging from his sides, breathing deeply and slowly with his eyes closed like he had seen Jewell do so many times. He wondered if she also had her fists clenched tightly, ready to punch the wall. He unclenched them, breathed slowly several more times, then walked down the hallway toward the shower.

After showering, Cole changed into a fresh t-shirt and jeans, locked up, and headed for the shop, hoping to catch Richard before he left. When he parked in the sparse grass near Mr. Bean's oak tree, he noticed with a sinking heart that neither Mr. Bean's nor Richard's truck was in the parking area. But at least the shop crew was present. Three employees were working diligently at their workstations; another passed by the open roll-up doors driving the forklift with several sheets of solid surface material, driving fast and bouncing them up and down, a surefire way to crack them; and four more were standing near the coffee pot deep in conversation. He shouted at the forklift driver to slow down and approached the coffee drinkers.

"Hey guys, what's on the agenda today?" Two of them nodded at Cole and shuffled off toward their work areas. Two remained, slowly sipping their coffee. He reached for the jobs clipboard and flipped through the pages. "So what jobs are you working on?" When Cole spoke to Richard about these two, Cole referred to them as "bathroom guy" and "phone guy", given that personal business occupied so much of their working day. He wondered how Mr. Bean dealt with them. Until recently, Mr. Bean was not the official supervisor, and mostly he worked quietly and efficiently on his own countertops. But the guys respected him, and an occasional reminder from Mr. Bean, or even just a few seconds in the powerful beam of his disapproval, would often put them back on task. Before Cole could formulate a motivating speech, both men put down their coffee cups and headed toward the working part of the shop.

The office lights were turned off. Catherine and Laney did not work on Saturday. As the lights flickered on, Cole noticed a wasp-like buzz emanating from the fixture above Catherine's desk, evident only because of the quiet. Cole leaned over Catherine's desk to move papers, an aloe plant in bone-dry dirt, and a collection of small rabbit figurines out of the way so that he could stand on the desk and change the light bulbs, hopefully not the entire fixture. Typically, Catherine's desk would be neat, dusted, and free of work before she left for the day: no post-it notes or unopened mail or stray paperclips, as if she had nothing to do all day but answer phones and clip coupons. It was unusual to see any paperwork left out. Cole picked up Jason's tool inventory and the one that Catherine had typed and printed. Three installation trucks and a general-purpose truck, and not one of them was fully supplied, but it wasn't as bad as Cole had feared, and by assigning tools to each installer, instead of to the trucks, Cole hoped it would put a stop to disappearing tools. Cole clipped the inventories together and slid them into the top desk drawer to get them off the desk where he would be standing, but something caught his eye. He opened the drawer again and lifted out the tool inventory. Beneath it was a window envelope from one of the countertop material suppliers. It appeared to hold a check, and it was addressed to Laney.

Cole unlocked the door to Laney's office and entered. The small room had once been a large storage closet, but when Laney had worked from a desk in the main office with Richard and Catherine, he complained that he couldn't call customers with the office phones constantly ringing, answered by Catherine's coy little girl laugh, and with the stream of people who desperately needed to speak with Richard. Laney's separate office was just large enough for a dark mahogany desk, a low mahogany bookcase, and a small glass-topped table with a lamp, which had been left on. On the table were framed photos of Laney's happy family, studio shots of his smiling wife and two teenage sons, a wedding photo, and one wherein Laney is at the beach, squinting against the sunlight and grinning.

On his desk were several estimates that Laney was working on, with some countertop pricing sheets, some pieces of mail, a post-it note with a Wednesday doctor appointment, and a small, neat tray with compartments separating pens, pencils, paper clips, rubber bands, and a pad of pale yellow post-it-notes.

Cole opened the two large desk drawers one at a time. Most of the folder space was dedicated to past jobs with neatly labeled folders. There was also a section of folders for material pricing contracts with Dupont, Wilsonart, and Hi-Macs. And lastly, there was a folder labeled "Comms" which Cole picked out and flipped through. Laney earned both a base salary and sales commission from Richard, but that was not referenced in the folder. Instead, it held correspondence between Laney and the countertop material manufacturers. Laney was asking for a bonus if he secured volume purchases, money that would go directly from Dupont and the other manufacturers to Laney. The answers were polite, but firm. They don't do business that way. And why would they need to give out bonuses, Cole thought, when they already had a product that was wildly popular? Except for one, the new company simply named "Solid Surface Enterprises" that sold two colors, Arctic White and Cool Dawn, two products that Cole noted had been steadily going out the door and into people's kitchens of late. *They* had agreed to provide a ten percent incentive rebate, and they were willing to accept Laney's assertion that his employer allowed him to take that as his commission, so a separate check was made out to Laney and mailed quarterly rather than listing it as a line item on the invoices that accompanied each shipment.

It seemed unlikely that Richard had agreed to or even knew about this arrangement. Catherine received and dispersed all the mail and any that was directed toward Laney would go straight to him. There was plenty of mail that was addressed to him, probably most of the mail, including all the catalogues, safety data sheets, sales promotions, requests for placing ads locally to sponsor worthy programs like FSU baseball, Special Olympics, the Little League Awards Banquet, and the Community Theater.

Cole needed to speak with Richard, but it could wait until Monday morning. Give Richard one weekend away from the constant chaos. Anyway, maybe it was all kosher. Maybe Richard was completely in the loop. Cole did not really know what Richard knew. He would copy Laney's letters and discuss them with Richard on Monday.

He was standing by the copier, waiting for it to finish warming up, and staring out the windows beyond Catherine's desk at the towering cumulus clouds moving in from the Gulf of Mexico, when Alfie entered the office. "There you are," Alfie said. "I thought you'd gone home or something…then I saw your truck."

"What's up?" Cole asked.

"We're out of fine-grit sandpaper," Alfie said. It spoke for itself. No top would go out the door without the final polishing. It was one of Laney's jobs, researching prices and keeping general shop supplies in stock. Purchases of large and expensive items like the trucks and some of the shop equipment had to be approved by Richard, but cases of gloves, sandpaper, router bits, saw blades, countertop adhesives, and shop rags were ordered in bulk. At one time, Catherine had ordered the shop supplies, but for some reason, Laney insisted that he should do it. Cole wondered if other companies had been approached for "volume incentive rebates".

"Paper for the sanders, or by hand?" Cole asked.

"The sanders." Of course. It was the only way to finish a top to get an even finish. Hand sanding was theoretically possible, but only for very small pieces.

"You checked the supply room," Cole said, rather than asked. Alfie nodded.

"Okay, let's look on the installation trucks," Cole said. He accompanied Alfie into the stifling heat and humidity of the shop. Fortunately, in the installation truck bins, there was sandpaper both for the orbital sanders and for sanding by hand, not a lot, but enough to keep the fabrication work going. Cole distributed the sandpaper and helped one of the new employees clamp together his countertop pieces and prepare them for the adhesive.

It was only hours after he got home that Cole remembered Laney's correspondence, which he had left next to the copier. He could either go in now and copy the letters and return them to Laney's file folder, or he could go in early on Monday and talk it out with Richard before the others arrived, and let Richard decide. At the moment, he had other worries.

In the basement, he inserted the inside edges of the partially inflated cushion into the flanges surrounding Diva's small but solid guitar body. Black would have suited her androgynous presentation better than the rose – the only cushion material he had left - that now surrounded her straight-backed neck and body like a flaccid parasail. He gently pumped air to further inflate the cushion, sealed the valve, and placed her in a guitar stand to check on in the morning.

Cole was eating a tuna fish sandwich for dinner when he remembered that he had skipped breakfast and lunch altogether. He'd been losing weight. His jeans hung loosely on his hips. Even his shoes felt roomier…which reminded him…he should look for his dress shoes: shiny, black leather shoes, hard to find in a men's size seven, that he had bought over fifteen years before, along with a dark gray suit, to wear to Maureen's wedding, and since then had worn to various weddings and one funeral, that of a high school friend who had contracted HIV and died five years later. Then he remembered...the shoes were comfortable for about the first ten minutes of use, after which they deployed their arsenal of heel rubbing and toe compressing torture tactics. Tomorrow he would get some new tennis shoes and get a haircut. Everyone who could possibly care – Richard, Maureen, his parents, probably Jewell, most of whom were not present to *actually* care – would be so ecstatic that he no longer looked like he had just walked out of the Mojave Desert, they would not notice that he had upgraded his tattered and spattered but so comfortable tennis shoes to those that were elegant sportswear, perhaps blindingly white, most likely marketed as glacier white, arctic white, or heavenly white.

That evening he called Jewell, but no answer. Then he called Dan, who was at home with all three kids while his wife was studying in the library, away from the demands of three young children. She had decided to go to school at night and study accounting. According to Dan, she had scored a high-paying administrative job with just a bachelor's degree in political science, but she was incredibly bored there and needed something more. So instead of working on his dissertation right now, Dan was walking the colicky baby back and forth in the house, while the two boys were putting on pajamas and brushing their teeth.

"I can't talk long," Dan said. "What's up?"

"Mostly just called to say 'hello'," Cole said, which anyone, even someone who did not fall asleep with complex chemical formulas floating around in his hypnagogic brain – would know was not true. He had been hoping to ask Dan for the huge favor of making some business cards, and maybe even some brochures. He was willing to offer in trade some guitar parts, or even a guitar. But Dan literally had his hands full. "I just want to thank you again for your help with the website," Cole said, "and let you know that I'll be leaving on Wednesday for the show. I'll let you know how it goes."

"Yeah, man, I wish you luck, but you won't need it. It'll go great."

Cole heard a young boy shout "Stop that. I told you," and then there was crying, two children crying in syncopation. Dan said, "I got a situation here...have to go...good luck," And hung up the phone.

Cole slowly walked back downstairs, looked at the Inflatables, upright in their guitar stands as if waiting expectantly for their night on the town. He shut off the fan and the lights and walked back upstairs for a shower and bed. An emptiness had infused the house, or an unnatural quiet. He couldn't quite identify the perception of pause, the moment between breaths, a hush, the edge of a dream that hovered in the air throughout the house as he brushed his teeth while he locked the doors and turned off the lights. He climbed into bed and rested on his back, but then rose to open the window a few inches. Martina was in good form, shouting into the ionosphere, her lungs as healthy as ever. Cole inhaled deeply a wisteria scented draught that crept through the window opening. He slowly breathed it out. Within a few minutes, he drifted into sleep.

# Chapter 19

July 14th, Sunday
3 days before leaving

The early morning sunlight splashed a swath of amber on distant clouds and lit the top branches of the pine trees in the neighbor's yard. Cole stood in the kitchen, gazing out the window and grinding coffee when the phone rang. It was Jewell.

"I tried to reach you last night," he said.

"Yeah, we stopped by Dean's just in time for dessert," Jewell answered. "Have you been watching the storm?"

"It's pretty far west, right? Headed for the Yucatan?"

"That one's not even a hurricane now," she answered. "There's another one. Came up out of nowhere. We're moving the boat today if we can find a place to dock it."

"You can come home," Cole said. "I'll come get you. I can help move the boat and…,"

"Thanks, but we have to move it today."

"I can still come get you," Cole said.

"Aren't you packing?" she asked.

"Yes. Want to help?" he chuckled...keep it light.

She sighed.

Cole waited, but there wasn't more. "Richard's in Pensacola, coming back tonight," he said. "Maureen needed a break from Mom and Dad, the kids, everything I guess."

"So how is your dad?" Jewell asked, "and your mom?"

Cole hesitated. He didn't quite know. Basically okay, he thought...or someone would have told him. "Pretty good," he said. "Wish I could help, but I'd just be in the way."

"Say 'hi' for me next time you talk?"

"Of course."

"Mainly I called to tell you that we're staying with Dean 'til the storm's past, so don't try to reach me at my folks," Jewell said.

"How bad does it look?" Cole asked.

"We'll be okay," Jewell said. "It's too early to worry."

It was a good sign that she had called, knowing that he would worry. Or at least, he would have worried had he had known about the new storm. Surely, his ignorance was understandable, given all that was going on? He tried to hold onto the mantle of innocence, but it was thin. If something happened, the headlines would be painful to read:

"Man's wife runs from massive storm while he pursues improbable business opportunities."

"Man neglects to call as father struggles with broken hip and mother with crippling arthritis."

He definitely would call tonight.

For most of the afternoon, Cole changed the strings on the six Inflatables he would take to the show, inflated them, one at a time cranked them to full volume, strummed down hard, then picked each string and played some guitar riffs, a sample of Jimi Hendrix, Mark Knopfler, Carlos Santana, and Brian May, checking for buzzing or dead spots. He dusted them carefully, polished the bodies, and brought them upstairs where he placed them in the guitar display-stand he had built and painted earlier that week.

He kept the TV on in the bedroom, and each time he came upstairs, he walked to the back and stood a few feet in front of the screen to assess the progress of the storm. It was slow moving, not likely to hit the Keys and head toward Miami until Wednesday, if it made landfall there at all. Throughout the day it inched toward the north, a distant and still uncertain threat, so he turned off the TV at dinner time and tried not worry. Briefly, he called up the lines from a song he had written a few years ago - Put Your Worries Away – that seemed more achievable back then. That was before Heartbreak Guitars encountered The Investors. That was when Jewell was still enthusiastically helping him research cushion materials and glues, and at night, before dinner, when they were sitting out back with a glass of wine or a beer, watching the sun go down and birds flit from tree to tree looking for an overnight perch, she would tell him about the bird drawing she had started that day on her lunch hour. That was before Gary and Peter, before frustration boiled up like a tidal wave inside him, carrying his heart into his throat, pressing it against a jaw that was set like cement.

But during the early months of investor comradeship and bonhomie, a time when Jewell was still drawing and painting, she had created four or five different bird designs that she had sent to a custom guitar pick manufacturer. She had ordered picks with "Heartbreak Guitars" printed on one side and drawings and paintings, rendered in miniature, of an Anhinga or Blue Heron, Florida Scrub Jay, Purple Gallinule, or a flying Short Tailed Hawk on the other. They had ordered two dozen picks to give out to potential buyers, and then Gary and Peter had ordered a two hundred more. And Cole still had most of them, nearly a year later. He had no business cards or brochures to hand out at the show, but at least there were the picks. It was late, and he hadn't had dinner or taken a shower, but he trudged back down to the basement to look for them.

The next morning, Cole awakened to the muscular roar of a garbage truck, and the banging of the arm-and-claw mechanism that picked up oversized garbage bins and upended them into the mighty maw at the back of the truck. Seven o'clock. No sleeping in on Mondays, or even returning to sleep after awakening to the lumbering strain of a massive engine, the raucous squeal of air brakes, and the metallic clang and rumble of the pugilistic battle between the truck and the garbage bins. And no sleeping in when there were only two days left before leaving for NAMM!

Cole got up and slid on his jeans and t-shirt, stuck his bare feet into his tennis shoes, and shuffled down the hall toward the kitchen to make some coffee. The guitar display with the Inflatable beauties caught his eye as he passed into the living room. Sunlight sliced through an opening in the front window curtains and splayed across the display stand, lighting up the glossy finishes. Except for one, where in this bright light, there was a dull spot, like a large thumbprint smudged onto the headstock just above the Heartbreak logo. Shit! He walked over to examine it. As soon as the guitar, one of the Despair Sisters, was in relative shadow, the smudge disappeared, but in bright light…he groaned. He would need to sand and respray it. Sometimes spraying one spot was tricky, not quite blending with the rest of the finish. His one saving grace today - the headstock was not finished with a tint. Matching *that* would have been a nightmare.

Cole picked up Despair and together they descended into the basement where he flipped on the fluorescent lights and checked the headstock again. How had he missed it? And what else might he have missed? An hour and a half later, he had just finished the second sanding and spray coat when the phone rang. Before he even picked up, Cole knew it was Richard.

"Hey, I meant to intercept you," Cole said. "What time is it, anyway?"

"8:40," Richard said, "a.m."

"Did you find some papers in your desk drawer?" Cole asked. "Or by the copier?"

"That's what I'm calling about," Richard said.

"Yeah," Cole said. "Be there in a few." He hung up before Richard could say anything else, turned off the lights, took the stairs two at a time, grabbed his keys from the kitchen countertop, and headed out the door.

Catherine was still not in the office when Cole arrived at nine. She was always late on Mondays.

"Is Laney in yet?" Cole asked.

"He's stopping to look at a job on the way in," Richard said.

"Good," Cole said, not sure exactly how to approach the Laney issue. "So, I had meant to photocopy those," he indicated the papers on Richard's desk, "and put them back in his desk 'til we could talk. I was moving Jason's inventory from Catherine's desk so I could get up there and change the light bulb, and I saw an envelope in her drawer...looked like a check made out to Laney. So, I did a little more snooping. I thought you should know...or maybe you already do?"

Richard's elbow was on his desk, and his chin was cupped in his hand. He shook his head with his head still resting on his hand.

"I mean, it's ok if you knew...I just wasn't sure."

Richard sat back in his chair and sighed. He lifted up the letters. "How 'bout you make a copy of these and put them back in his desk. Think I'll make some phone calls."

Cole stood by the copier as it warmed up. "How'd it go in Destin?" he asked. "Dad doing better?" Cole realized that he hadn't called like he'd meant to, like he'd told Jewell he would do. It was better anyway, to find out the lay of the land from Richard first, then call when he got home.

"Everyone's doing okay," Richard said, "except Maureen. Don't get me wrong, she loves your folks. It's just wearing thin. Your dad is either going out for the paper without his walker, or looking for his glasses without his walker, or searching for the remote without his walker, or else he's sitting in the recliner expecting to be waited on. He pays Chrissie and CJ a quarter every time they bring him something he needs, so they're constantly plying him with drinks and snacks, his medicine, and the TV remote. Maureen just wants them to go outside and jump on the trampoline."

Cole looked out the window over Catherine's desk and thought about whether he could get to Destin and back before the show. He'd have to leave today and return tomorrow. It was the only way.

"Don't worry," Richard continued. "Maureen would be more worried if she were here than there. Maybe you could just call her. She'd like that."

The copy machine beeped, ready for action. Cole was copying the letters when the office door opened, letting in the shop sounds. The piercing whine of a saw and raised voices rose above a din of drilling, hammering, hissing, and squealing of machinery. Laney came inside and the door whooshed closed behind him. He ignored Cole but nodded to Richard. "Mornin'", he said, unlocked his office door and disappeared behind it.

Cole handed the copies to Richard. "Unless he needs to look in that folder today, he won't miss these. Or I can put them back when he leaves for lunch." Cole did not want to stick around the shop waiting for Laney to leave so he could return the letters to Laney's files…not with only two days left to get ready to leave town. But he couldn't just walk out the door either unless Richard had some kind of a plan.

Richard leaned back in his chair with his eyes closed and his head tipped back and resting on the chair back, ran both hands through his hair and sighed. After at least ten long seconds, he said, "Let me call this Solid Surface Enterprises company…then we'll see."

"Do you want me to stay?" Cole asked.

Another ten seconds. Still with his eyes closed and his head back, Richard answered, "I think it would just inflame the situation."

"Okay. If you're sure," Cole said. "You okay?"

"Yeah. Go on and pack."

"Let me know what happens," Cole said.

Richard didn't answer, so Cole slipped out, intending to head straight for the parking lot and go home, until he saw Mr. Bean across the shop, clamping several sections of solid surface material. Cole could see from a distance that the countertop was Arctic White.

He walked over to greet Mr. Bean. "Hey, Mr. Bean, welcome back!"

"'Mornin' Cole." Mr. Bean held out his hand and Cole took it and squeezed.

"You don't know how glad I am to see you." Cole spoke softly, "I heard about your daughter. I'm so sorry, man. There just are no words," he said.

Mr. Bean nodded.

"So, they let you out of the hospital," Cole said, wanting to move the conversation into a less painful space, not knowing what else to say about Mr. Bean's heart wrenching loss. "It's ok to be back now? You sure were missed." He gestured toward the shop.

"It's better to stay busy," Mr. Bean said. "You understand."

Cole nodded. "And your wife...she okay?" Cole wanted to ask if Mr. Bean had other children that he and his wife could lean on, but the realization that he didn't already know filled him with shame. He had known that Mr. Bean had a daughter because she'd dropped her dad at the shop a couple of times

247

when his truck was getting maintenance, and although Cole probably hadn't seen her in years, he still thought of her as a high school student. How had she grown up and gone out on her own? How had she joined a Church group on a mission in Africa?

When Cole had worked in the shop regularly, he was too busy putting out fires to stop and chat with his coworkers. That was how he remembered that time…day after day filled with an unrelenting series of problems to solve. Time was contracted, so that at the end of each day, when he or Richard locked the office and shop, he was surprised to find his coffee cup, nearly full of cold coffee, sitting on his dashboard where he'd put it that morning when he had parked the car and immediately became distracted by the sight of the forklift being driven with an overfull load or one of the shop workers tossing a large section of "scrap" countertop section into the dumpster.

"Hey, when I get back next week from Nashville, maybe we could grab a beer one day after work."

Mr. Bean nodded.

"Again, so good to see you," Cole said and reached out his hand and was met by Mr. Bean's firm handshake.

Cole glanced at the office as he headed across the shop toward the parking area. Laney was standing in front of Richard's desk with his hands on his hips. Richard was still sitting in his chair, doing the talking, gesturing with his hands. It didn't look too bad. Richard looked almost relaxed. Maybe a weekend in Destin was just what he needed. Maybe Maureen wasn't the only one who needed a few hours without chaos. Cole waved to some of the guys and said, "See ya," as he walked toward the parking lot and out into the sunbaked morning.

Once home, Cole called Maureen and just let her talk. There were a few stories about CJ and Chrissy, but they mostly featured their dad – often sweet, but grumpy and pig-headed too, Maureen said. "I heard that," Cole's dad yelled. Maureen laughed but lowered her voice. "I think it's a good sign that he wants to do so much. I might be heading your way in the next week."

"You want to come to Nashville?"

"Sounds exciting," Maureen answered. "But no. I just want to be home. I might not leave the house for a year."

"But you're okay?" Cole asked.

"Yes, but after you're back, come over here for a visit. They miss you."

"Of course, I want to. Let them know for me, okay?"

"Hold on, Mom wants to speak with you."

Cole waited a minute, two minutes. He could hear an indistinct conversation and the clattering of dishes or maybe pots and pans. He waited another minute as the conversation continued at a distance, heard the raised voices of kids and the drumming of running across the hardwood floor before the phone call cut off. He called back, but just got the answering machine. Now what? One more thing to worry about. He tried to channel Jewell and her "be in the moment mantra." But sometimes the moment just sucked.

Cole walked downstairs to check the finish on Despair's headstock. In the light of his basement shop, he couldn't tell. How had he managed to work at all in this lighting? Cole picked up Despair and carried her outside and squinted in the intense sunlight. He held Despair at different angles until he was satisfied that only a forensic examination of the headstock could detect the location of the repair to the finish.

Despair was soon nestled in place in the display stand. Cole stood back and admired the display. As he thought about setting up the display at the NAMM show, talking to a steady stream of musicians, musical instrument manufacturers and suppliers, and especially to buyers, a sense of calm came over him, a happy, excited calm. He walked to the bedroom and turned on the TV. Immediately, the radar image of a hurricane filled the screen. The calm ebbed away and was replaced by the familiar tension and worry. The storm was closer to the Keys now, but the path was still uncertain, and they couldn't predict yet which of the Keys or even the mainland might suffer the brunt of the storm, although all of South Florida was in for some heavy rain and wind. Jewell had said she would call if they needed to leave for a shelter. If he hadn't heard by tomorrow, he would call her.

After dinner, Cole called Constantine and they agreed that Constantine would come over the next day, Tuesday, sometime in the afternoon, and they would load up the van and be ready to get an early start on Wednesday. Then he called Richard.

"Don't have a salesman this week," Richard said. "It seems Laney already has another job. He's starting Monday, working at Thomason's Cabinets."

"That was fast," Cole said.

"Yep, he already had the job before he showed up today," Richard said. "I didn't even talk to him about his incentives payout," he continued. "We actually shook hands at the end. Looks like he's leaving on friendly terms…or so I hope. People who need cabinets also need countertops, so it's better if things are cool."

"You're going to change the locks anyway, right?"

"He gave me his keys, but I guess he could have others. One more thing for tomorrow."

"You got an ad out for a replacement?" Cole asked.

"Another thing for tomorrow," Richard replied.

Cole didn't want to say what he felt about Laney's departure - a big, fat, Hallelujah. "Could turn out to be a good thing," he said.

"We'll see," Richard said.

That evening Cole ran some laundry, folding the dry clothes while watching the storm on TV. It was lumbering slowly toward the north and wouldn't be a threat to land until Thursday or Friday.

He could pack most of what he needed in the one scuffed, brown suitcase that he pulled out of the attic, but he had forgotten it had a broken handle. He took it with him into the basement and replaced the frayed and broken handle with a dowel affixed to two small blocks of wood that he screwed into the top of the suitcase. It was humble, but it would work. He used the air compressor to blow off the attic dust and the debris from his repair, turned off the lights, and went back upstairs to pack.

# Chapter 20

Tuesday, July 16th
Last Day before leaving for the NAMM show

Cole awakened with a start. A bright morning light through the window blinds painted stripes on the pillow and sheets that moved gently with the breeze from a small rotating fan he had placed on the dresser. Crap. It was later than he had meant to get up. This was the final day to get ready and his list of unfinished business was long: pack the guitars, the display stand, the sound equipment; amps, cords, tuners, picks, straps, some tools, brochures, a map, paper and pen, as well as his suitcase and personal travel items, all of it and more stowed in Constantine's van; buy shoes and get a haircut; check with Jewell; check with Maureen; check with Richard and pray he didn't need anything; round up Jason and practically sit on him until they left in the morning; meet up with Constantine and pack everything into his van. First, he would have to find some blankets and beach towels to wrap around and cushion four of the six guitars. He had the one custom case made for Desire, and several more cases for standard electric guitars that could house the three Despair Sisters if he first carefully wrapped them in towels.

Cole turned on the TV and watched the local weather – hot and humid – and waited for the hurricane update. The storm had tracked a little to the west but the outer rain bands were still expected to sweep into the lower Keys by mid-day on Thursday. It was weakening, and was now a Category 2, but a strong storm surge was expected. Jewell and her family would undoubtedly be battening down the hatches at her parents' small house and then heading over to Dean's. Cole picked up the phone and dialed Jewell's folks. No answer. He called her brother. No answer.

Cole left the guitars, equipment, and accessories in the living room, locked up, headed out into the steamy stillness of a July morning, and drove the five miles to the Tallahassee Mall where they had at least five shoe stores. Fortunately, the Payless shoe store was accessible from the street, and soon he was back in the parking lot sporting a new pair of black tennis shoes. Next, he drove to the tiny white wooden building on Monroe Street, barely bigger than a garden shed, that was the one-man barbershop where he had been getting his hair cut for as long as he could remember.

Cole was greeted by a thin man with gray hair, wearing a short, white cotton jacket with a high collar and three-quarter sleeves. "Hey, Stranger. Long time, I'd say."

"Hey Mr. Whatley," Cole said. "Long time for sure."

"Looks like I got my work cut out for me."

"I'm afraid so," Cole said. "I just got busy. My wife's been cutting my hair, but then she got busy, too."

They talked about the heat and humidity, the FSU baseball team, Mr. Whatley's grandson's upcoming graduation, and a murder trial on which Mr. Whatley sat as an alternate juror. The trial had been suspended for some reason, but Mr. Whatley expected to be back the next day. "I'm not supposed to talk about the details," Mr. Whatley said, "but I just don't see how he can be innocent, you know what I mean?" Before Cole could reply, he continued, "Let me ask you something."

"Okay," Cole said.

"You ever been arrested?"

"No," Cole said. "Not yet anyway," he laughed.

"Well, me neither," Mr. Whatley said. "And they don't arrest people for nothing, so I just don't see how he can be entirely innocent."

Cole was nearly speechless. Is that what all the jurors thought? You get arrested and you're guilty? "Well, they do have to have solid evidence of the crime," Cole said. "Before a man gets sent to prison."

"Oh, I agree," Mr. Whatley said. "The trial just started so we haven't heard the murder evidence yet, but he looks pretty guilty to me."

Jesus, Cole thought.

He was still thinking over the flaws of the justice system as he pulled into Constantine's driveway. The side and back doors of Constantine's van were open, and Constantine was inside it with a black flexible hose that snaked out the van door to the vacuum canister sitting in the grass. Constantine climbed out of the van and turned off the vacuum.

"Ready to roll?" he asked and flashed his great smile.

"Gettin' there," Cole said. "How 'bout you?"

"Don't I look ready?" Constantine picked up the vacuum hose in one hand and the canister in the other and headed toward the front door, dragging the extension cord behind him. "Come in and I'll fix you something to eat. It's lunchtime, isn't it?" He looped the cord in a figure eight and placed it on the canister he had set off to the side, held the door open and waved Cole through.

"Nothing for me," Cole said.

"No, seriously," Constantine said. "I made stir fry for Jasmine last night and it won't keep 'til we get back."

"Okay," Cole said. He would eat a little, just to satisfy Constantine. "How's she doing? Jasmine." Curiously, he really did want to know. Both Jewell and Constantine saw something in her, apparently blinded to Jasmine's divorce from veracity and her need to be so intrusively in everyone's business. But...she made Constantine happy...or rather, Constantine generally existed in a world of upbeat rhythms, and she hadn't ruined that for him. Here he was, ready to embark on a road trip with an energetic curiosity for what the world had to offer – new places, new people, new adventures - a mindset that must serve him well when there were half a dozen barely civilized teenagers accompanying him on a trip to the Magnet Lab across town or to a math competition in Gainesville.

"She's doing okay," Constantine said. "A little stressed about her dissertation. One of her committee members is pushing for more experiments." He shrugged. "She'll get through it."

Cole briefly wondered if she would get through it by fabricating her research results. He squelched that uncharitable thought.

"Guess what?" Constantine continued. Cole had followed him into the kitchen where Constantine was heating up the stir fry. "She wants to go with us…just as far as Atlanta. That's where her folks live." Constantine opened the refrigerator door and pulled out a jar of hibiscus tea. He turned to place it on the counter and burst out laughing. "Oh, if I had a camera," he exclaimed. "The expression on your face."

"So…" Cole didn't know what to say.

"Don't worry." Constantine poured the tea into dark blue goblets that likely had once been his mother's. "I told her I would take her after we got back from Nashville."

After lunch, Constantine said "Sit just another minute. I have something for you." He headed for the guest bedroom he used as an office and came back with a box. Taking the lid from the box, he lifted a neat stack of papers and handed it to Cole. They were flyers featuring inflatable guitars – inflatable bird guitars – rendered in flight, with text beneath that described the guitars and Cole's contact information. "You can hand these out at the show," Constantine said.

"Oh, man. How'd you do this?"

"Jason let me in one day to take some guitar photos, and one of my students is a pretty decent computer whiz, so I paid him to incorporate the bird drawing to create the flying guitars, then I added the text and made the copies?"

"That looks like one of Jewell's birds," Cole said.

"It's from the print she gave me last summer. The one in the hallway. You like?"

"You just don't know! Thanks, man. Incredible. I don't even have business cards. This is huge!" Cole said.

"I kept it under the radar because I wasn't sure I could pull it off. Figured you didn't need more disappointments," Constantine said.

"But Jason knew?"

"Yeah, I'm telling you, apparently that kid can keep a secret."

Cole placed the box on the passenger seat, started the Mustang, waved to Constantine, and headed over to pick up Jason, thinking about how jazzed Jewell would be when she learned that her bird drawing was part of the flyer. It might even rekindle her interest in Heartbreak Guitars...that and the guitar orders he would bring back from the NAMM show.

Cole and Constantine agreed it made sense to pack the van first thing in the morning rather than have the instruments sit in the driveway all night. It was mid-afternoon, and once Cole could secure Jason in his orbit and stop by Richard's shop to let him say goodbye, they would go home for some dinner. Cole would call Jewell and Maureen, and he and Jason would make it an early night.

Cole pulled into Richard's driveway, got out and jingled his keys as he walked to the front door. He gave the doorbell a couple of rings, listened while inside it chimed a few bars uncannily similar to the 'Forrest Gump' theme song, and stood back. After a minute, he tried again. A few minutes later, he pushed it multiple times in rapid succession, but the sweet notes of the song did not convey the frustration and impatience on the outside of the door. After waiting a few more minutes, he called out for Jason, and walked around to the back yard. No one there, and no one to be seen through the sliding glass doors. But hey, they were not locked, so he went inside and called for Jason again and walked down the hallway toward his room. No one was home.

Cole called Richard's shop and spoke with Catherine, who said that Richard was out in the shop. He exited the house through the sliding glass doors, closed them, hesitated but left them unlocked in case Jason needed to get back into the house that way.

Cole started the Mustang and turned the A/C on high, wishing he'd remembered to roll down the windows, even for the few minutes he was inside the house. He cracked the windows to let out the heat and felt hot air blow on him as he slowly backed out of the driveway. It would take a few minutes to cool the car interior, and he was halfway to the shop before he rolled the windows back up and let the cool air dry the sweat on his face and blow its icy breath through his short hair. He glanced in the mirror. Rather than float like a golden lion's mane, his short hair rippled like a miniature field of wheat. Very civilized, Maureen might have said. He put his FSU ball cap on.

Richard's shop was roasting hot, and Cole was glad to see that Richard was sitting at his desk in the cool of the office. This might be one day when a glass wall would not seem to be the smartest office design, considering the sweltering heat on the outside of the office where the shop guys were toiling in the hot wind from the fans set up at nearly every workstation.

Cole walked quickly through the shop and entered the office. "Do you usually leave your sliding glass doors unlocked?"

Richard looked up, one eyebrow raised. "Say again?"

"I just went by the house. Jason wasn't there but I was able to get in through the back."

Richard sighed. "Okay, I'll talk to him."

"Where is the budding rock star today?' Cole asked.

"He went over to Jeff's house…lives just down the street. He said he'd be back right after lunch," Richard said.

"Jeff," Cole said.

"Jeff S.," Richard said. "There's Jeff S. and Jeff W. Maybe a whole lot of other Jeffs, I don't know."

"Well, it is definitely after lunch," Cole said. "Way after. And no one's home."

"How 'bout I bring him by later, maybe after dinner?" Richard asked.

"Thanks…that is, if you're sure. Have you spoken with Maureen?"

"Things are pretty much the same," Richard said. "Maybe a little better. She sounded sane anyway."

"I might try her tonight. If I don't get her, just tell her I'll be in touch in a few days. Six days. When I get back."

After dinner, Cole took a shower, packed some clothes, his toothbrush, toothpaste, and a razor, and aligned his small suitcase in the living room with the guitars and accessories. He turned on the television and watched the hurricane news. The storm was more disorganized, but bigger. The outer rain bands were brushing the southernmost Keys, and the storm was projected to continue to the north and west, sparing the upper keys and the east coast of the highest winds. They still would get plenty of rain and the storm surge threat was significant. He called Jewell, trying first to reach her at her parents, where she should not be if she was tucked in safe and sound at Dean's. Then he called Dean's. Dean's wife, Randie, picked up the phone. She was a beauty in every sense of the word. Dean and Randie had been high school sweethearts and had been named King and Queen of their high school prom, which had caused a ripple in Warner Robbins, Georgia because he was white and she was black, and Warner Robbins wasn't quite ready for that much integration.

"Hey, this is Cole. I'm just checking on the status down there. Is everyone safe and sound, ready for a hurricane party?"

"Hey, Cole. We're mostly ready," she said. Cole noticed that she was keeping the volume low, almost a whisper. "Looks like the storm has stalled," she continued. "Now it's just sitting there battering the Keys. If it turns and tracks up the west coast, we'll just get a little wind here and a lot of rain."

"You sound a little hoarse...are you coming down with something?" Cole asked.

"No," Randie whispered. "The baby just fell asleep on my shoulder. As soon as I'm off the phone, I'll move her to the crib. Let sleeping babies lie, I say."

"Amen," Cole said. "Just one question. Did they move the boat?"

"Dean and Jewell and Dad moved it today – we have a friend on the Intercoastal waterway. It's more sheltered there."

"Are they back yet?"

"They're on their way. How's your dad doing?"

"Maureen tells me he's ready to rock and roll. Whether he should or not is a different question. She's talking about coming home in a week or so, so he must be better."

"Jewell will be glad to know. You doing okay, ready for the big show?"

"As ready as I can get," Cole said. "I guess I should let you go. Thanks, Randie."

"Sure. Good luck at the show."

Randie hung up and Cole realized that he hadn't asked her to tell Jewell to call. It didn't matter in the big scheme of things. He just longed to hear her voice. The quiet of the house seemed to magnify his loneliness, as if his emptiness had grown beyond him, making each room an echo chamber of solitude. Jewell and he had been separated one time before this, when Randie was sick with the flu she had caught in the hospital delivering Maya, the first of their three girls. Dean was trying to work during the day and at night help Randie and the baby, and feeling completely overwhelmed, so Jewell had gone down for a week to take care of the baby and let Randie sleep. Randie said that Jewell had saved her life and possibly her marriage. Cole knew how she felt. With a quiet energy, Jewell could just calmly take care of things, tuck every part neatly into place and get it all humming again. Until the Heartbreak Guitar Company - or rather until Gary and Peter - had sapped her energy and wrung the joy from the vision she and Cole had nurtured.

Cole sat on the sofa and stared at the guitar stand. He was usually uplifted and filled with a desire to strum one of the Inflatables and let her music fill the room and lift his spirits on her light and lilting wings. Tonight, he was tired, too tired to think, to plan, to talk, to do much of anything beyond take a shower and head for bed. It was as if he had been deflated, ready to be packed into a guitar case and shipped off to Music City. Despite his emptiness, he hoped that Jewell would not call back. He was drained of the desire to open his mouth and force out the words, any words. Nevertheless, he had to gather up enough energy to greet the soon-to-be-delivered Jason, or he could call Richard and let him know that they would come get Jason in the morning on the way out of town. He walked over to the phone to make his call.

# Chapter 21

Wednesday, July 17th
Day of Departure for NAMM

Another hot and humid day, with no hint of a tropical storm, yet. If the storm hit mainland Florida, even if it was a glancing blow, Tallahassee could eventually get some rain, perhaps a lot of rain. It didn't matter to Cole. They were headed north through southern Georgia on U.S. 319 under blue skies and spectacular towering white clouds. Traffic was light; Constantine was driving and tapping the steering wheel to music that played only in his head; Jason was listening to music through his headphones and drumming his knees; and Cole had nothing to do but look out the window at the soft green mounds of peanut plants lined up in rows, the immature cotton plants in more rows, and fields of corn that bravely stood in the blistering heat.

Hour after hour, they drove through rural Georgia, stopping for lunch at Bailey's Best Bar-B-Q, and then continuing toward the foothills of the Appalachian Mountains in north Georgia. Constantine was determined to avoid the interstate and was resolute that they would not drive through Atlanta, but he gave up when they got lost north of Atlanta and wasted an hour and a half backtracking until they were caught up in the rush hour traffic on the west side of the city.

"We are not going to Atlanta," he declared as he passed a sign that indicated a turn for the Atlanta Zoo and Downtown Atlanta. Too late. They were sucked into the city as if into a black hole. Constantine's van waded into the traffic and inched forward for another hour, until the traffic suddenly cleared, and the van and other cars poured onto I-75 north of Atlanta. It would take them to Chattanooga, and they would take I-24 from there to Nashville. They wouldn't arrive until after nine or ten.

Jason was pleasantly quiet, uncharacteristically so. After they had waded through the Atlanta traffic and were heading north, he looked up from his Gameboy and said "I'm hungry. And don't you guys ever stop for the bathroom?"

"Good idea," Cole said. "Next exit."

They stopped at a Texaco station for gas and a bathroom break. Across the street there was a laundromat, a thrift store, and a Vietnamese restaurant with a hot food bar that looked promisingly inexpensive. "Better than McDonald's,"

Cole said, and held the door open for Jason and Constantine.

"Not to me," Jason said, but he loaded up his plate with noodles and grilled beef with broccoli, Pho pork, rice and shrimp spring rolls, along with chocolate milk, sweet corn pudding and mango cake.

"You think you've got enough to eat there?" Cole asked.

"Probably not," Jason said.

Cole had hoped that after dinner, Jason would continue to quietly play on his Gameboy, perhaps even fall asleep, compelled by his overwhelmed digestive system to hibernate while he slowly assimilated his dinner.

"I wonder what my dad is doing now?" Jason mumbled.

Sweet, Cole thought, that he was already missing Richard. Cole was kind of missing him, too. And as much as he had at first wanted to head up to Nashville unencumbered by Richard's enthusiasm for tracking overhead, variable costs, net profit margin, and market penetration, Cole now realized that now he, Cole, was the most experienced businessman in the van. Scary. "Did I ever tell you about the guitars I gave away?"

"No," Jason said. "But if you're just giving them away, I'll take one."

"So, Jewell and I cooked up this raffle," Cole said. "We planned to give one Inflatable to the winner, which basically just required an entry form that could be emailed to us. It was meant to be a way of advertising, get us some radio time, and put a spotlight on our unique product, and we scheduled the raffle to be announced on FSU's V89, but it turned out that they announced the raffle the day after the scheduled drawing. We ended up sending a perfectly good guitar to this college student in Jacksonville who hadn't even heard the radio ad. He had accidentally found our website and sent an email for the raffle. No one else heard the radio spot until after the deadline, so he was the only ticket holder to email his entry on time."

"Bummer," Jason said.

"Oh, that's not all. We got a letter from a prison chaplain in South Florida, asking for a donation of a guitar for their gospel prison band. He had seen our website, too. Jewell really wanted to send him one, and she reminded me that Merle Haggard had been in prison and later played guitar and cut records and became well-known, with a crazy number of fans, so – yep - the prison got one, too."

"If I get sent to prison, I can have one?" Jason said.

Heartbreak Guitar

"Yeah, if you get sent to prison, you can have a guitar. And anyway, they're a lot lighter now than those early Inflatables. But I'm pretty sure you'll have to join a gospel band, and you better practice now so they'll let you join when you get there, because they have some seriously good players. And start learning some gospel songs."

Constantine burst into song, slow and low, employing his best Elvis impression: "Farther along we'll know all about it...Farther along we'll understand why...- *everybody now* - Cheer up my brother...live in the sunshine."

Cole joined in for the last line, "We'll understand it...all by and by."

It didn't stop there. Constantine gave voice to another prison favorite, this time with the more upbeat tempo as performed by the "Man in Black". "I hear that train a comin'"... he belted it out in his rich baritone. Cole was impressed that Constantine remembered all the words, and that he could so well emulate Johnny Cash. He could barely gasp out the last low note, however, so he stepped up the pitch – and his enthusiasm - for the next verse and began slapping the steering wheel to keep the beat.

"You're still driving, you know," Cole exclaimed. "You do know that, right?"

Constantine grinned at him and continued with gusto.

Jason was again wearing his headphones and playing on his Gameboy.

After Constantine finished the last verse, he rendered the melody one more time mimicking the train whistle with zest.

"I can drive if you want," Cole interjected.

"Hey, man," Constantine said. "If we don't practice, we won't be ready for the big show."

"What big show?" Jason had his headphones off again.

"Any big show," Constantine said. "The big show of life!"

"Oh." Back on went the headphones.

They pulled into a motel, the Savannah Inn, about thirty miles from Nashville. Only two rooms were available, one with one King size bed, and the other with two doubles. They checked in to the room with double beds, brought in the guitars, the amp and electronics and stacked them on and around the small desk in the corner. It was nearly eleven.

"Who wants first shower," Cole asked.

"The driver always gets first shower," Constantine said. "But I need to stretch my legs, so I'm going for some ice."

"Jason, it's you or me," Cole said.

Jason had already put his bag on the bed nearest to the bathroom. He had picked up the remote and was flipping through the TV channels. "You can go first," he said.

By the time Cole got out of the bathroom, Constantine was back with snacks and a six pack. "There's a Food-Mart next door," he said, and pulled out a bag of corn chips and popped open a Miller's. "Got you some Sprite," he said to Jason. "No caffeine."

"I'll just take a beer," Jason said.

"No can do," Constantine said, and handed Jason a Sprite. "How about a cold one?" he asked Cole.

"Just one," Cole answered. "Then we need to hit the sack. But first, let me check the weather."

"It's hot," Constantine said. "And humid. Just like home."

"Not for here. South Florida, Miami, the hurricane," Cole said.

"I'm taking a shower in the morning," Jason said. He kicked off his shoes, pulled back the spread and top sheet, and climbed into bed in his jeans and t-shirt.

Cole watched the weather and the news while Constantine showered. A few minutes later, Constantine came out of the shower wearing some baggy cotton shorts with the ends of the drawstrings hanging down. "What's the storm doing?" he asked.

273

"They only showed the local weather, then the news. I called Richard. He said he would get back to me if there was anything to worry about, and he hasn't called back.

"So that's good news," Constantine said. He climbed into the bed near the window. Cole nudged Jason to move over.

"I'm not sleeping with anyone," Jason declared. "I'll sleep on the floor first."

Cole sighed and looked over at Constantine. "No problem, brother," Constantine said, "I'll be the big spoon and you can be the little spoon." He moved to the far edge of the bed. Cole was relieved to see that Constantine had rolled onto his side with his back to him, so no spooning. Cole slid into bed.

Cole awakened to a sickly blue light that flickered on the window curtains, the wall, and the door. It emanated from the television, without sound. He looked over at Jason, who had pushed two pillows against the headboard and was half-sitting against them staring at the silent screen.

Cole whispered, "I thought teenagers slept in. I'm guessing it's not even eight."

Jason shrugged. "Who could sleep with both of you snoring like…I don't know…like a horse with a cold. Two horses…with really bad sinusitis."

Cole laughed, trying not to shake the bed.

"Worse than my dad," Jason said. "Seriously."

"I'll let him know you said that." Cole sat up and picked up Constantine's watch from the nightstand. Seven-thirty. "Your dad will be glad to know that *he* doesn't snore like a horse." Cole pulled on a clean t-shirt and jeans and put on his socks and tennis shoes. "Get dressed and come with me for coffee."

Jason dressed, slow as ever, and they headed out the door. They entered the motel office and walked over to a countertop where there was coffee, hot chocolate, and a plate of wet-looking powdered donuts and dry-looking cinnamon swirls. Cole poured two cups of coffee and held up a third, but Jason shook his head. When they returned, Constantine was dressed, and the instruments and amps were already loaded in the van.

"Don't know if this is drinkable," Cole handed a cup of coffee to Constantine. It wasn't.

They had only driven two blocks when Constantine saw a Dunkin Donuts. "Now you're talking," he said and swung into a shaded parking space in the far corner of the lot.

Soon they were back in the van with a box filled with donuts and pastry, headed for NAMM...expected arrival – less than an hour.

Janice Dodge

"Any idea exactly where we're going," Constantine asked. They were in heavy traffic ambling toward the city center.

Cole had a map spread across his lap. "The Renaissance Hotel and Convention Center. Commerce Street and Seventh Avenue. Just stay on I-24 heading downtown. Looks like we take State Road 70 and turn left onto Broadway. If you get to Church Street, you went too far."

Within a few minutes they had pulled up to the front of the Renaissance, which appeared to occupy most of a city block. "Wait here 'til I find out where we go," Cole said, hopped out of the van and walked quickly toward a wall of glass doors into a stately two-story lobby that smelled faintly of new plastic. There were people everywhere, multiple sets of bags on the floor, and several people at the reception desk waiting to check in. Cole spotted a sign indicating the NAMM show with an arrow pointing to the NAMM Show office.

"Okay then, check with Registration," he overheard one of the hotel staff say, directing some other bewildered soul toward the show office.

At the registration desk, a young woman in tan slacks and a dark blue t-shirt with the NAMM logo stitched neatly near the collar asked for his identification and his booth number. "Three of you, correct?" she asked.

"Yes, three," Cole answered. He wondered if he should mention that the names would be different from the registration material he had sent at the beginning of the summer. It would not be Cole, Gary and Peter as provided on the original registration. And it would not be Cole, Jewell and Richard that he had subsequently submitted as a correction, and that were now printed on the name tags hanging from lanyards that the staffer was handing him. He remembered that NAMM had sent several emails about tighter security since nine-eleven, and they had emphasized the importance of avoiding last minute name changes. When he got back to the van, he handed Richard's name tag to Constantine, and handed Jewell's to Jason. "I know," he said, reading both of their faces. "Before you say anything, I'll fix it later. For now, just put it on so we can unload our stuff."

Jason and Constantine looked at each other wearing matching expressions of mild indignation. Constantine held out his hand for Jason's name tag. "Give me that thing," he said. Jason handed him Jewell's name tag and Constantine passed back to him Richard's name tag. He pulled the lanyard over his head so that Jewell's name tag rested against his own shirt. "Jewel in the Lotus," he said. "It's a Buddhist thing." He patted it. "Let's go," he said cheerfully.

At registration, Cole had been instructed to find some parking first and then bring his product through the hotel entrance. "The large companies ship their stuff," someone waiting in the office had said. "Then they can just use a forklift and take a whole box full of stuff from the delivery truck straight to their display booth. You didn't ship, did you?"

They found a parking space about a block away. "I think we can do this in two trips if we all carry stuff," Cole said. "If we need to, we can leave the brochures, picks and effects pedals to bring with us in the morning."

Jason, aka Richard, took hold of the handles to two of the guitar cases, one in each hand. Cole picked up two more guitar cases in one hand and pulled the amp and a canvas bag filled with electronics and extension cords toward him with his other hand. Constantine grabbed the last two guitars in his left hand, holding them by the twine that was snugged around the towels that wrapped the small guitar bodies. He reached his other hand for the amp that Cole was struggling to lift. "Put it down. I got this," he said and pulled it gently from Cole, leaving Cole to carry two guitars and the canvas bag. They locked the van and headed back to the Convention Center. They would have to come back for the display stand.

"Where to Kimosabe?" Constantine asked.

"Booth #2006," Cole said. "It's on the second floor toward the front." It was late morning. They lumbered under their load in the heat and humidity of the parking lot and were relieved to get inside where the air conditioning dried the sweat that had dripped down their necks and tickled the back of their legs. They located Booth #2006 in a large second floor room with high ceilings and recessed lighting, which provided a pleasantly muted light. The booths were three-sided alcoves that opened onto wide walkways. These were reserved by new-to-the-trade-show companies as well as some that were already established and highly respected. The big-name companies were in a gigantic hall on the first floor.

Everywhere was controlled chaos. Boxes were stacked next to many of the display booths and a cadre of men and women were unpacking them. Electricians were checking the floor outlets. NAMM employees wearing their signature dark blue shirts delivered paperwork, electric cords, and more chairs, answered questions and provided directions for the stream of exhibitors who, like Cole, were wandering the aisles with bewildered expressions.

He had not realized before he was actually looking at Booth #2006 that he had the good fortune to be assigned a space on the corner of two wide intersecting walkways. His booth had only two curtained "walls" with a narrow but long display table set against each of them. On one he could easily fit the Inflatables display stand with the amp behind it and the effects pedals on the floor. On the other, he would put the flyers and picks, and also the mini air pump that he would use to demonstrate the ease of filling the inflatable guitar bodies. That still left plenty of empty floor space to demo the guitars and talk to potential customers.

Cole nodded at the crew of two men at the table next to his who were setting up a display of guitar accessories: tuners, capos, strings, preamps, picks, straps, cables, metal and ceramic slides. Across from him was a table with two beautiful mahogany bass ukuleles on display, and presumably more in the cases behind the table, but no one in sight.

He looked around at the bustling scene, wondering if everyone, except him, knew what they were doing. And now that he was finally here, would the Inflatables soar in the attendees' hearts and imaginations as he had dreamed? And if they did, would he be able to take them to the next step – out of the basement and into a real shop, one with capacity and manufacturing know-how?

He looked again at the disorder around him that matched the internal disquiet he felt so keenly. This whole endeavor was a long shot. Maybe he wasn't ready, but he was here. And something told him that his big moment would come, and then all the heartache, all the fear would dissolve into the background of life experiences. The show would change everything.

Back at the van, Cole suggested that he and Constantine each take one end of the display case to carry it from the van to the booth, but Constantine placed it on top of his head and held it there with his hands to keep it steady as they walked across the parking lot and entered the Renaissance. Jason and Cole carried the boxes of flyers, picks, and electronics.

The elevator was held up on the third floor, so they took the stairs to the second floor and slowly made their way around the carts and boxes to Booth #2006. As they had planned, they placed the display stand on the table, angled so that it faced the intersection of the two walkways. They placed the amp behind the display case and the effects pedals on the floor near the corner. The tools and cases went under the table, where they were hidden behind a dark blue skirt that draped the table to the floor. They stood for a few minutes in front of the booth and admired their display while Cole changed the angle of the display case slightly one way, then the other. "Which way catches your eye?" he asked.

Jason answered, "both."

"Yeah," Constantine said. "Both. It's good, man."

They headed out on foot to look for a place to eat. Cole remarked that they could eat PB&J since they had everything they needed in the van. "Tomorrow," Constantine said. "And every day after that."

By late afternoon they had walked all over the downtown, stopping in a musical instrument store where Cole was interested in seeing what kind of exotic guitars they would have on display. Disappointing. There were some great guitars - Martins and Taylors and Paul Reed Smiths - but those could be purchased in Tallahassee far from the music mecca of Nashville. Then he spotted a locked glass case showcasing one guitar they were told belonged to the store owner, built by master luthier Don Manuel Rubio. Cole would have loved to get his hands on that one.

A few blocks away, they picked up some ice cream and sat on a bench by the Cumberland River, hoping for a breeze. Heading back in the general direction of the Convention Center, they walked slowly past restaurants and bars where there were small stages. Even with the doors closed against the heat, they heard all kinds of great music: A drummer wielding his drumsticks at a blistering pace; a pair of silver-tongued singers crooning country ballads; and some old timey pickers putting their skills on display. There were musicians playing solo, others playing duets, banjo and guitar or guitar and mandolin. There was even a Mariachi band playing on a shaded outdoor stage behind a Mexican restaurant. They were drawn to a poster showcasing the music talent at Robert's Western World, a restaurant and music venue, and oddly, also a clothing store. Constantine offered, then insisted that they go inside and let him treat them to an early dinner. They ordered burgers and basked in the cool temperatures as they listened to traditional country ballads with tight harmony sung by Cat and Flora, two musicians they had never heard before. He was playing the guitar and she the violin. By dusk they were back at the motel.

In the morning, Cole called Richard and learned that the storm had moved into the Gulf of Mexico, and it was now threatening the Florida west coast. Miami was getting drenched but had escaped the damaging winds. Jason talked briefly with Richard but hung up after a minute, saying that Richard had another call coming in. Constantine had gone out for coffee, and he came back to the motel room with a box of Dunkin Donuts and three cups of coffee. "One cream and sugar," he announced as he handed a coffee cup to Jason. He opened the box of donuts and passed it around. "Not the healthiest," he said. "But pretty cheap."

"Thanks," Cole grunted. He was sitting on the end of Jason's bed, jiggling one foot up and down, tapping a pen against his knee. Even without coffee, he was wired…ready to get to the show and plunge headlong into a world of musical instrument wheeling and dealing, where he had a small corner carved out for the willowy and evocative Inflatable ladies. He accepted the coffee but waved off the donuts. "We'll get something better later," he told Jason.

Jason was carefully licking glaze off his upper lip with his eyes closed. He opened his eyes, glanced at Cole, nodded, and then reached into the box for another donut.

# Chapter 22

They found a parking space two blocks away from The Renaissance. They donned their badges and were waved through by the security staff and ascended a set of wide stairs to the second floor. "Why can't we stay here?" Jason said, turning his head to view the expansive lobby they were leaving as they ascended the stairs.

They stepped onto a display floor that had been transformed since the previous afternoon. The boxes and carts had been removed, electric cords had disappeared, and a green and turquoise geometric patterned carpet had been rolled down each walkway. The booths were draped with dark blue cloth backings and displayed banners indicating the company names. Polished instruments and an array of accessories were displayed on tables or stands.

Cole looked around at the sea of exhibits, stunned and somewhat demoralized by the professional showcasing of musical instruments, sheet music, accessories, amplifying systems, and more - an awe-inspiring universe of musical instruments and music products. Here were the music merchants, the companies large and small that were displaying their products and hoping to catch the interest of the attendees, comprised primarily of music store buyers, school band instrument buyers, and the lucky employees they brought with them.

Cole looked at Constantine and Jason, who were standing in front of his booth side by side, hands in their pockets, silently taking in the view. Did they also sense that the Inflatables might be less than ready, that when the show officially started at 10 a.m. they would be peddling a product that was essentially a prototype, hastily assembled and still smelling faintly of lacquer? Maybe it was better that they didn't know how unsettled Cole felt by this unveiling of his product among the luthier greats whose guitars would be in the show, and the guitar buyers who would be prowling the aisles in just a couple of hours.

Additionally, Cole later came to realize, some among the general public had managed to snag tickets. Some were musicians, some were journalists, and a few others in attendance Cole never managed to connect to the music industry. Perhaps investors like Gary and Peter could find a way to get in and prey on other hopeful designer-inventor-builders. But Cole knew that Peter and Gary were too cheap and too full of themselves to consider spending a few days at NAMM.

The morning passed quickly. Jason sat on a stool at the back of the booth with his Gameboy. Constantine flashed his great smile and handed out flyers as people streamed by, winding their way among the booths, many holding the exhibitor booth map, stopping to study it, clearly on a mission to find particular products on display. Others were just browsing, and more than a few stopped to stare at the Inflatables. Cole felt the unease in his stomach solidify. He periodically wet his lips by taking a small sip from a water bottle he kept behind the amp. He drew up the corners of his mouth into a subdued smile as he tried to make eye contact with the approaching attendees and attract them to his booth.

"Try to look relaxed," Constantine said. "Just now? Looks like you could use an aspirin."

Cole rubbed his forehead with his fingertips, shrugged his shoulders and let them drop. He stood with his arms at his sides and looked up at Constantine with a weak smile. "Better?"

Constantine laughed. "A little. Enjoy the moment, man. It's what you've been waiting for."

Cole found that he could snag the attention of many of the attendees by inflating the cushion-body of Desire just as they were approaching the booth. Some of them stopped to watch, and then strapped on Desire or Diva or one of the Despair sisters and strummed some chords, and with a look of surprise,

287

Janice Dodge

ran some notes up and down the frets and launched into full out picking. Cole would edge up the volume a few decibels at a time until – across the aisle - Ukulele Luke gave him the "cut it" sign, his hand slashed horizontally across his neck, which indicated that the NAMM sound police were headed his way.

Despite them, there were more than a few eddies of sound in the room. With so many instruments being test-driven by interested attendees - all of whom were musicians, perfectly happy to strut their stuff - the noise was surreal at times, with remarkable dissonance, as if composed for the Tower of Babel. Cole wondered how the sound squelching NAMM staff managed to determine which booth held the offending amplifier that sent out sound waves exceeding eighty-five robust decibels. When one's neighboring booth was loud, one had no other choice but to crank up the volume on his or her own amplified product. It was survival of the loudest, and woe be unto those who were simply trying to talk to a potential customer about tuning forks or sheet music.

Cole was flushed with nervous energy as the day wore on despite having had an unsettled stomach all morning and skipping breakfast. He could eat any day. A number of music store buyers had been enthusiastic, picked up flyers and a couple of picks and said they would give Cole a call after the show.

Cole hoped that they meant it. Just now, something positive and definite would be heartening.

Among the attendees were some truly fine musicians who had stopped in front of the booth and eyeballed the display in amusement as Cole tried to discern which instrument held their attention, and then wondered if that particular guitar would sound as rich to their ears as to his. And would these musicians, who had probably already checked out a number of truly spectacular guitars at the show, appreciate the incredibly small space in the "heart" of the Inflatables into which he embedded the electronics? Cole hoped that they would recognize the resourcefulness required to finesse the Inflatable design. Heartbreak Guitars were different from anything else at the show…extremely light but still beautiful and with great sound. Players would surely recognize those attributes…solidly delivering sound but offering something different and exquisitely useful. Something they *must* add to their guitar rosters.

Some of them let Constantine wave them into the booth and watched as Cole removed the diminutive Diva from her place on the guitar display stand where she was tucked near the middle as if she were simply a shelf for the storing of electronics. Cole inflated her with the mini air pump, activated her tiny amp, and handed her to the bemused attendee for a close inspection and some music magic. On one such occasion, when he placed her into the hands of the teenage offspring of a guitar buyer from a music store chain in Ohio, Cole realized that the volume of the mini amp would be no match for the thundering din in the room. Where were the sound police when you needed them? Fortunately, Cole had installed an earphone plug in what he delicately thought of as Diva's derriere, and he handed some earphones to the young woman standing before him wearing a tank top and miniskirt.

By mid-afternoon, Cole became aware that Jason had disappeared. Jesus! Didn't he have enough on his plate? Cole waited half a minute for Constantine to finish flirting with a NAMM show staffer, then interrupted to ask, "Have you seen Jason lately?"

"He said he was getting some lunch," Constantine said. "I think he was bored."

Cole remembered the food court they had passed on their way in this morning, where he had noted they had nine-dollar hamburgers, five-dollar soft drinks, and eight-dollar 24-ounce beers. Cole's stomach rumbled despite his aversion to the idea of lunch. "Did he by any chance say where he was getting lunch?" This came out more tersely than he'd meant.

"Don't worry. He promised not to leave the premises." Constantine looked past Cole, nodded, and produced an impersonal smile for a group of men in suits who were ambling by the booth wearing somber expressions. Cole recognized them as members of the Steinway team, whose grand pianos were tucked into a corner practically under the stairs. No wonder they didn't look happy.

Cole returned Diva to the display stand. "When we see him again, let's tell him to check in every hour or so." Seeing Constantine's expression, he said, "Ok, every couple of hours, and he should let us know in advance where to find him."

Across the aisle, a Ukulele player ripped a jazz-boogie-woogie fusion on a bass uke. Ukulele Luke had the sound cranked up, and the stream of attendees slowed, then stopped to watch, creating a small traffic jam in the aisle, not an uncommon sight when so many fabulous musicians were test driving the products, but disruptive to the flow of attendees passing by Cole's booth.

Just as the demonstration ended and the crowd was separating and drifting away, Cole noted that a commotion had erupted in another part of the room. Where there had been a heavy metal phenom cranking out some massively distorted psychedelic noise, now the music had stopped, and Cole could hear yelling. He stepped out of the booth to see the source of the disturbance. At a booth a dozen yards away, he spotted Hans, the German tremolo inventor and business owner with whom Cole had spoken a few times last winter when he was trying to snag some tremolos in trade for a guitar. Hans was stomping around in front of the booth and yelling, first in English and then in German, at the NAMM staff, undoubtedly the sound police, who had shown up just as the heavy metal performer, flown all the way from Germany to demo one of Hans' custom tremolo-fitted guitars, was taking it through its paces. A minute later, the tremolo booth was down to a staff of two as the NAMM personnel escorted Hans toward the stairs.

Cole remembered that somewhere in the NAMM registration contract was a list of consequences for breaking the rules: warnings, expulsion, and blacklisting from future shows. So, was an invitation to accompany the NAMM staff to the show office a warning? Cole hoped that would be the case, and occasionally looked for Hans throughout the afternoon, wishing for him to be returned to the booth where he would see that there was a brisk interest in his tremolos even without the ear-splitting demonstrations that disrupted Cole's – and everyone else's - sales pitches and distracted the potential buyers.

"You want to get some lunch?" Constantine asked. "I'll hold down the fort until you're back."

"I'm just not hungry," Cole said. In fact, his stomach had still not settled, and he regretted having drunk three cups of coffee before the show. "You go," he said. Constantine saluted and disappeared among the attendees that were headed for the stairs. He returned an hour and a half later with Jason trailing behind holding some bags and a box. Jason dumped them onto the floor in the corner of the booth.

"You can't leave those there," Cole said. "Put them under the table, behind the drape. What is that stuff, anyway?"

"All kinds of stuff," Jason said. "Look at this." He held up a notepad with a sheet music score on which one would write his inspired music and lyrics, guided by the lines of the treble staff. He had a bookmark covered in eighth notes, a saxophone key chain, sunglasses adorned with Treble Clefs, a cloth carry bag with a pink sequined mic on the side, and a Wish-you-were-here greeting card with a delicate pop-up piano. He held up a mylar drumhead on a stick, decorated like a lollipop, and tapped it using a drumstick with a purple rubber tip. "They're going to have a drum circle later," Jason said. "What time is it anyway?"

"Almost four," Constantine said.

"Gotta go," Jason said, and took off with his drum and drumstick, loping toward the stairs at a speed Cole had not previously witnessed in Jason.

"I'll go with him," Constantine said. "Meet you back here."

By five o'clock, Cole's energy was depleted. He had inflated and deflated various of his guitars, handed out flyers and picks, periodically tuned his guitars and polished off the fingerprints, and had shaken enough hands to make Maureen cringe at the thought of the microbial life that now resided on his hands and on his instruments. Until this moment, he hadn't given a thought all day to Maureen, CJ, Chrissy, Richard, Cole's parents, Jewell, Jewell's parents, or Frankie, and he wondered what they were doing in their ordinary lives while he was finally here, making music history, if only in a small way. Especially Jewell…if she could only be here.

He looked through the small stack of business cards he'd collected. He was certain that the Inflatables had succeeded in winning the hearts of at least a few buyers and musicians, but he didn't have one actual sales order. He winced as he remembered that the NAMM show had advertised sales seminars held yesterday. He hadn't checked them out and instead relied on his countertop sales experience instead. He looked through the business cards again. Fender and the other big companies would have ushered these potential buyers into their private meeting rooms and had them sign a contract on the spot. Tomorrow he would push harder for a commitment, as hard as one can push with no name recognition, a completely new and untested product, and a small prototype shop with no financial backing.

Today was just a warm-up. Some positive interest...that was a good sign. But tomorrow would be better. Tomorrow he would look for the moment when a buyer is on the verge of decision...and with the right mixture of incentives and charm, the sale would be made. In some ways, it *was* like selling a countertop, except that the customer didn't walk out of the store with a sample of the merchandise. The "installation" would come later, after the product discussion, after negotiating the specifications and delivery time and price, after the sales order was signed. After he had taken a stack of sales orders to the bank to secure a loan and gear up for production.

But now he was spent. He thought of his dim and quiet basement with a yearning, and realized that it would be okay with him, just for the last hour, if the NAMM sound checkers would just shut everyone's power outlets down, let a hush pass through the hall like a gentle calming breeze so that everyone could recoup his or her non-sales persona and talk quietly among themselves, or just sit with closed eyes and – as Constantine might say - 'let mind be like sky'…spacious, empty and serene. But although the sound checkers were out and about, overheated music continued to erupt sporadically throughout the room, and the NAMM staff would stifle one overly exuberant demonstration only to have to hustle to the other end of the room to address another one.

It was nearly six when Constantine and Jason returned. "That was so cool," Jason asserted. He tapped his drum with the drumstick a few times. "There were at least two hundred people out there."

"Apparently they do this every year, rain or shine," Constantine said. "The Remo Drumhead Company."

"Where'd they have it?" Cole asked.

"There's a huge courtyard," Constantine said. "Don't know if they'll do it again this weekend, but we can find out. I could watch the booth while you and Jason drum. It's good for the soul."

"Yeah," Jason said. "You can feel it in your bones." He glanced at Constantine, and it was obvious to Cole that Constantine had regaled Jason with stories of his own experiences in drum circles in Tallahassee. At one point, Constantine had joined a band of percussion players, with two didgeridoo players and a handful of drummers with various sizes and types of drums, and Constantine and half a dozen other players would take their drums to Lake Ella on a brisk November night, and drum in unison under a full moon.

A few minutes after six, they and their exhibitor colleagues flowed out of the Renaissance Hotel and Convention Center onto the sun-drenched sidewalks. They followed their fellow music lovers around the block and stood at the entrance to the parking lot. "Back to the hotel for sandwiches?" Cole asked.

"Let's walk around first," Constantine placed his hands on his hips and arched his back, and then stood straight and stretched one arm overhead, then the other. "I'm not used to sitting that long."

They fell in behind an all-girl accordion band marching down Broadway. There were five accordions, a snare drum player, a bass drum, and a cymbalist marching single file and banging out an Irish march. Jason had begun walking behind to the beat, and Constantine placed his hand on Jason's shoulders and said something to him that Cole couldn't hear. Jason stopped walking, and after the band had moved further ahead, they resumed walking at a respectful distance.

On the next block they joined a group of admirers of an eight-piece band all wrapped up within one wiry little guy. He sat in front of multiple drums with pedals which he engaged with perfect rhythm while playing a musical instrument that appeared to have been made from a cardboard box held together by decals, bumper stickers and sticky-backed coupons. It had two necks, each with four strings. He had bells strapped to his biceps, a harmonica in a harness strapped around his neck with the harmonica positioned only inches from his lips, and a small-brimmed hat bearing a Brazilian rattle which kept the beat as he moved his head. He occasionally let up from playing the main instrument – the cardboard box - to reach to tap out a few melodious notes on a set of small gongs to his right.

They were mesmerized, even Jason, who minutes earlier had slumped his shoulders when confronted with the idea of just walking around. He'd made a show of wiping his brow with his sleeve and pulling his shirt collar away from his neck, although they had not yet thawed out completely from the chill of the convention center. "They don't play like this is Tallahassee," he said.

"They play like this everywhere," Constantine said. "Everywhere people are, there's music."

"Not like this," Jason said.

"Seems to me I remember someone telling me about his very own dad drumming on a circular saw housing and bending a handsaw until it sang," Constantine said.

Jason glanced at Cole and looked at the sidewalk. "It's not the same," he said quietly.

Constantine motioned for Cole to start walking. "C'mon Jason," he said, and they moved down the block.

They decided to head back to the motel, eat their sandwiches, and call Jewell, Jasmine, and Richard, and then head back into town to take in some of the big-name performances listed in the NAMM show Directory. They pulled into a crowded parking lot at the Savannah Inn. The room was stuffy and hot. "Did anyone turn off the air conditioning?" Cole complained. He simply wanted to sit – or preferably lie - in a somewhat dark room and do nothing. Just for an hour.

"Not me," Jason said.

"Nor me," Constantine said. He was pushing the buttons on the A/C unit. He checked to make sure it was plugged in, and just in case, he unplugged it and plugged it in again and pushed the buttons without success. "Okay, I'll find someone in the office to take care of this."

A few minutes later, he returned and with a grumpiness rarely seen in Constantine, declared, "Pack your stuff. We're heading out." Cole rose stiffly from the bed, and together they packed everything into the van and headed back toward

Nashville. "What are we doing?" Jason asked. Cole was wondering the same thing.

"They couldn't fix the A/C and said they were too busy to come to look at it. And there weren't any other rooms, so we're finding another place."

Cole essentially agreed, despite his desire to just be horizontal. Lying in the grass outside of the motel room would have been more pleasant than baking inside all night. "Good idea to get something closer anyway." He relaxed a little in the cool air emanating from the van's air-conditioner. "It's a waste of gas to drive back and forth." Right then, he could have just driven around for the next hour luxuriating in the A/C.

"Someone at the show told me about this motel that was really close to the convention center and really cheap," Constantine said. "Scotties, or Scotsman, or something like that. It's on 70."

They drove on in silence.

"Scotsman's Inn?" Jason said. "We just passed it."

"No problem," Constantine said. Twenty minutes later, after driving around a confusing matrix of streets near the river, they were headed back on 70 toward the Scotsman's Inn.

"Looks pretty full," Cole said. "But it wouldn't hurt to check."

"I think we should stay at the Renaissance," Jason said. "But this is alright, I guess," he quickly added.

The Scotsman was not a step up from the Savannah Inn. Instead of a gigantic pink and green neon palm tree in front of the motel, there was a neon red and gold figure of a stout little man, wearing his plaid kilt and a flat plaid hat. They pulled in at the office and Constantine went inside. He came out shaking his head.

"No luck?" Cole asked.

"I got us a room," Constantine said. "See here, this little key? Just one, and not even attached to a keychain. They wrote down the room number. Room 103." He handed Cole a piece of paper. They parked in front of room 103, but the room lights were on, and they could see through a part in the curtains that there were people inside. "OK, what's the number?" Constantine asked Cole. "On the paper I gave you."

"103," Cole said.

"I thought that's what she said, but maybe the three is a five. Give it to Jason. His eyes are better."

"103," Jason confirmed.

"Dammit," Constantine declared. "I'll be back." He walked purposefully toward the motel office.

Fifteen minutes later, Constantine was back. "They have another room for us, but it won't be ready for another half hour or so. We can eat our sandwiches and either wait until it's ready or go find some music."

Jason groaned. "Really?"

"There's some really great stuff tonight," Cole said. "Muriel Anderson and a whole bunch of other great guitar players will be at The Ryman, Carnegie Hall of the South, first home of the Grand Ole Opry. Some of the best players anywhere. One of them playing tonight won a national picking contest last year."

Jason didn't respond. They could leave him in the room to watch TV, but it just didn't seem right to Cole. "We won't stay for the whole thing." Cole said. "I think it goes to 1 a.m., but…well, let's just see."

The Ryman auditorium was only a few blocks from the Convention Center. They waited in a crowd that was a slowly moving protoplasmic mass jostling toward the entrance. Near the door, they saw that everyone in line was handing tickets to a distinguished elderly man before being waved through. Cole leaned forward and asked the young man standing in front of him where to get the tickets. "At the NAMM show. Breedlove and Brian Moore

Guitars had tickets at their booths. I think Tacoma had them too."

"Okay, thanks," Cole said. He looked at Constantine. "We should have gotten the tickets today at the show."

They turned to leave but spotted Ukulele Luke making his way from the parking lot. Cole waved and waited for Luke. "Turns out we should've gotten tickets at the show," Cole said.

"I got extras," Luke answered. "My guys are sick. Might be food poisoning."

"That sucks. You feeling okay?" Cole asked.

"Not great. Probably won't stay long, but my girlfriend's holding my spot." He pulled the extra tickets from his back pocket and handed them to Cole. "See you tomorrow," he said and walked toward the front of the line.

The auditorium, although not small, was informal and intimate, with a large stage in front, soft lighting, and wooden pews arranged in a wide semi-circle facing the stage with each row of pews sitting slightly higher than the row in front so that there was a gradual rise in seating from the stage to the back. A large balcony also held rows of wooden pews, and at the very back were tall stained-glass windows. Inside the auditorium most of the seats were taken. There were several available seats scattered among the pews near the back, but none that were next to each other.

Cole really would have liked to sit but wasn't keen on being hemmed in by total strangers, having to shake their hands and make small talk...or any talk. "I'm okay standing," he said, and motioned for Constantine and Jason to take the open seats.

"I'm good here too," Jason said.

They stood behind the seated audience with a perfect view of the stage and remarkably clear sound and listened to the welcoming remarks and introductions of the musicians. Finger-stylist Muriel Anderson was a wisp of a woman with an enormous guitar, from which she elicited an intricate symphony of bell-like harmonics simultaneously with resonant bass notes to blend with mid-range notes as she played melody, harmony, and everything in between, covering familiar melodies like "Imagine" and "Moon River" and original compositions.

Following her incredible performance came Richard Smith, who was the national finger stylist selection the previous year. Phenomenal. Cole looked over at Jason's rapt expression and wondered if watching and listening to such fine musicians dampened Jason's enthusiasm for his own uphill path to guitar playing proficiency or if it awakened his sensibilities and inspired him. Indeed, in an auditorium stuffed to the rafters with musicians, all of them admiring the brilliance of musical prowess that tweaked previously untouched audio circuits in their brains, could anyone sit through such a sound cornucopia without a twinge of envy threaded through his sense of awe? Richard Smith, at age eleven, had played onstage with Chet Atkins. Age eleven. Now he had achieved warp speed in his finger picking. And there was more to come.

They managed to peel themselves away just before midnight, and head back to the Scotsman to take showers and fall into bed, this time with Jason sleeping on a cot that Constantine had added to the room tab, and Cole and Constantine each getting an entire, luxuriously wide double bed to himself.

# Chapter 23

The second day of the NAMM show began smoothly. In the morning, Cole snagged two more business cards from interested music store buyers, one from a music store in Italy and another from Elderly Guitars. Both stores specialized in sales of unique instruments. After the guitar buyer for Elderly shook hands with Cole and walked away, Cole recognized a feeling he'd not encountered in a while, not since he had sold his last countertop – the sense of having closed the deal. Today would be a good day.

By late-morning, almost a third of the flyers were gone. Throughout the morning, a number of well-known musicians – James Taylor, John Sebastian, and James Burton - had passed within a few feet of Cole's booth as they weaved between attendees and walked past with barely a glance at the booths. They did not stop to check out the products on display, and briefly waved to enthusiastic fans as they rocketed toward their destinations, undoubtedly to the performances that had been scheduled by Fender, Paul Reed Smith, Gibson, Tacoma, Seymour Duncan, EMG, Lace Sensor or other hugely successful manufacturers. Cole knew that most musicians in attendance would be under contract to one of these big-name companies, but he hoped that just one player – just one – might be independent, seeking out a new product that would be emblematic of the player's unique music. If he could capture the interest of Jerry Donahue or another of the Hellecasters or elicit a "thumbs up" from Emily Strayer or Tony Rice…then CJ, Cole's mother, the bag boy at Winn Dixie, and everyone else who had told him to just get someone famous to endorse the product would have been right all along. He would be happy to declare to the universe the folly of his prior unwarranted pessimism, his crazy skepticism, his over-reliance on what was tangible, and his total lack of magical thinking.

Just one well-known player at his booth, strumming on Desire with a smile on his or her face, that would be awesome. That one moment alone, with or without an endorsement, would affirm his dream, all that he had been striving for, and all the sacrifices that he and Jewell had made.

Just before lunch, a tanned, middle-aged couple paused in front of the display stand. They were dressed as tourists from some tropical paradise - he with his Hawaiian shirt, khaki shorts and Jimmy Buffet sandals – she wearing a white sun hat, a sleeveless, flower-splashed sundress draped with a purple Hawaiian-style lei and holding a small camera in one hand with a strap looped around her wrist.

"These are cute," she said to Cole. "What are they?"

How did these people get past the front desk? Even if they had flown straight to Nashville from an atoll in the South Pacific, one might think that anyone in attendance at a music trade show would recognize a guitar. And perhaps some ukuleles. But they had not stopped at the booth across the way, where the most melodious uke at the NAMM show was showing off its musical chops, played by Luke himself. Luke must have wondered about this couple in the same train of thought. Hawaii? No, probably not. Nevertheless, a couple with money and a fondness for Hawaii. He locked his gaze with Cole's as he continued to strum-pick. Cole gave him a nod. "Have you checked out the ukuleles?" he asked and motioned toward Luke's booth.

The man briefly turned his head and nodded at Luke, then turned back to watch Constantine inflate the cushion around one of the Despair sisters. "You know," he said, while still watching Constantine. "I had a '57 Fender at one time. Played it for years before I lost it in the move to Vermont."

Vermont! Cole would have put Vermont 50th on a list of likely home states. The man droned on about his beloved Fender acoustic guitar with its warm tone and gorgeous volume, and Cole nodded every now and then, but his attention had wandered as he realized that this couple was just sightseeing. The man fell silent and glanced at Cole and then to the beautifully inflated and alluring Despair, and back to Cole. He must have asked a question.

"Sorry," Cole said, but didn't know what else to say. He pulled his lips into a worn smile. He was tired of hearing about '57 Fenders and '71 Martins and wonderful old Gibsons, Epiphones and Gretches. They were great, absolutely! But even Fender, Martin and every other manufacturer had new models at this trade show. They didn't just keep selling the oldy goldies. Well…they did, actually. But they also continued to build, to experiment, to create, just like Cole had done. If they couldn't talk about the actual products on display right under their noses, perhaps these Hawaiian wannabe's and every other nostalgic music show interloper should trek on over to the vintage guitar shops on 8th Avenue and reminisce to their heart's content.

Cole sighed, reached behind him, and pulled one of the Despair sisters from the display stand and held it up next to a newly inflated Despair model. "Here's your next travel guitar," he said without enthusiasm. He felt a gentle tap on his shoulder and turned to see Constantine's worried frown. He turned back to the man and nodded to his wife. "Would either of you care to strum a little?"

When they demurred, Cole selected a pick and played a verse of "House of the Rising Sun" and handed the pick and a flyer to the woman to drop into her enormous straw bag. She could fit all three Despair Sisters in that thing. "They're small, fun to play, easy and light. What more could you ask for?" Cole said.

"Sure," the man said.

"Thank you so much," the woman gushed. They shuffled away, caught in the undertow of the demonic music that had erupted from Hans' tremolo booth. Forget the fancy pickers rendering intricate, ethereal, and haunting melodies. And save your money on the big-name songwriters with whispery golden voices whose performances had been advertised in NAMM show literature and on Nashville radio spots. Hans' player, whomever he was, needed nothing more than his untamed enthusiasm, a deep affinity for his wah-wah pedal, and a Pavlovian addiction to the tremolo. If the other exhibitors were paying any attention – and Cole was certain that they were - then next year, the NAMM show would need an army of sound police.

Cole looked across the aisle toward Luke, who still held the now silent ukulele. *"The man who hath no music within himself, nor is moved with the concord of sweet sounds, is fit for treasons, strategems, and spoils.*"

Cole felt his stomach grumbling and remembered that he'd only eaten half a donut with his coffee that morning. Maybe he and Jason could get a quick bite for lunch. Cole could take him somewhere nearby – or rather, let Jason take *Cole* to lunch, Jason being the most knowledgeable of the three of them regarding the local food landscape. He turned to ask Constantine if he knew where Jason had gone, but Constantine was nowhere to be seen. He very likely had stepped out to find the men's room or find another equally interesting place to be while the tourists were puzzling over the Inflatables and blocking the Heartbreak booth from the view of more serious buyers. Or maybe Jason had returned, and he and Constantine had together gone out to find something to eat. If so, they would bring something back for Cole, he was sure. Just in case they had not gone far, he leaned out of the booth and looked first down the aisle toward Hans' busy exhibition space, always a magnet for...well, for just about anyone. Then he glanced down the other aisle.

That's when he spotted Ricky Skaggs walking slowly down the wide aisle, waving at passerby's, signing someone's NAMM show map, and stopping at one booth and chatting with the two

311

smiling young women clad in high collared, sleeveless blouses and long, flowing skirts, who handed him first a mandolin and then a banjo, and who nearly quivered with excitement when he plucked a few notes to please them. *If music be the food of love, play on.*

Even if Ricky stopped at every stringed instrument or accessories booth on the way to the Heartbreak, he would pass within a few feet of Cole's booth within minutes. Cole would be ready.

The foot traffic among the booths had increased considerably, and Cole fervently wished for Constantine's return so that Cole did not, himself, have to demo the inflation of the guitar bodies while simultaneously chatting with the attendees about the portability of The Inflatables and the Heartbreak commitment to sound and quality, and while also trying to keep an eye on Ricky Skaggs, whose progress from one booth to the next seemed glacially slow. Even so, it would only be a few minutes at most before Ricky arrived at Cole's booth. Cole thought about which Inflatable he would thrust into Ricky's hands. Desire! No question.

Just when a small group of attendees had peeled themselves away from his booth, flyers and picks in hand, and Cole had perused the thinning crowd for Ricky, the music accessories booth owner to whom Cole had previously waved and said, "Good morning," but never actually conversed in the day and a half that they had been booth neighbors, appeared in front of him and whispered excitedly, "Ricky Skaggs just came by the booth! Can you believe it? I gave him one of our custom capos." He was practically hopping up and down as he held up a capo for Cole to inspect. "Our company name is engraved on it. Unbelievable!" Cole looked past him at the receding back of Ricky Skaggs, who, moments later was hidden from view by a stream of attendees, all of them undoubtedly wonderful human beings, but not Ricky Skaggs. How could Ricky have failed to stop at Cole's booth? There was only one explanation...his booth neighbor had blocked Ricky's view just as he passed. Probably not on purpose, even so it was the most colossally thoughtless and ungracious act Cole had yet experienced in...he didn't know how long. He was more than disappointed. He was speechless, held in the grip of a wave of anger, more than anger, a bitterness that burned through his heart like hot coals. There were no words or actions that could the convey the thoughts that were brewing inside his brain, building energy like a chemical reaction in one of Constantine's classroom demonstrations that started with a lump of yellow crystals and if not carefully controlled, would proceed to an explosion rather than the beautiful green flame that was the desired outcome.

But when there was heat, and bubbling, and a wisp of smoke, the first signs of the reaction going sideways…what would Constantine do? There with all his young students eyeing him from their desks, collectively holding their breath, hoping for a small explosion and a quick exit from class to wait on the soccer field until the fire department declared the school to be safe again. What would Constantine do? Constantine would just turn off the heat, cool the reaction vessel with lukewarm water, tell everyone to open their lab notebooks and write up the experimental design and to speculate on the potential reasons for why the experiment had not produced the lovely verdant flame. *Heat not a furnace for your foe so hot that it do singe yourself.* Cole stepped back from the accessories-booth owner whom a moment ago he would have liked to punch in the face. He took a deep breath and let it out slowly. "Great!" Cole mumbled. "Just great."

Constantine and Jason appeared with a bag of food, take out from a barbecue place a few blocks away. They were both wearing smiles as wide as the Grand Canyon. "Guess what we got," Jason said.

"Smells like barbecue," Cole said grumpily. "Looks like a carry-out bag decorated with a pig in a chef's hat, so I'll guess barbecue."

Jason pulled his hand from behind his back and waved some rectangular pieces of paper in front of Cole and pressed them against Cole's chest until Cole slid them from Jason's hand.

"What are these?"

"Concert tickets. Seymour Duncan concert tickets!" Cole had learned that same morning that to get free tickets to the Seymour Duncan music extravaganza, one had to head straight to the Seymour Duncan booth on first arriving at the NAMM show. Tickets went fast, and if you didn't make a beeline for them early on the first day, you were out of luck. Of course, he was hearing this on the second day.

His mood had drifted like a dense fog into a subterranean chamber in his brain, where he had been ruminating on the opportunities – so many, it seemed - that had materialized briefly and then slipped away while he watched in despair. But here Jason had handed him tickets to the Seymour Duncan music bacchanal and opened a small window into the above ground world of light. "Thanks, Bud," Cole said. He handed the tickets back to Jason. "Why don't you take care of these. And thanks for the food." He took the bag of barbecue from Jason and tucked it under the table to be eaten later, outside, when traffic slowed down. It never did.

The afternoon hours rolled by, slow and steady, inexorably headed for the end of Day 2 of the NAMM show, when attendees and exhibitors would be propelled into the July heat and bright sunlight where they would hustle to their cars and turn on the air conditioners or linger in the shadows of buildings and restaurants while they consulted their maps and itineraries. Day 2 had brought more traffic by his booth, and Cole had exchanged business cards and answered questions and given demonstrations and landed two almost solid commitments. And, early in the afternoon, he believed he had snagged another sale, although this one had not felt quite as strong as the promise of a deal with the Italians or Elderly Guitars.

He wished from time to time that Dan could have come to enthrall passersby with his evocative playing. As Day 2 began to wane, a sense of time slipping away from him filled him with angst, a steady simmer of disquiet that fell short of desperation. He had shaken a lot of hands, given out picks and literature, created smiles... but he hadn't had that Ricky Skaggs moment, a NAMM show collision of possibility and serendipity that would propel him and the Inflatables into the "Big Red

Book of Lutherie" or "Bluebook of Guitars", place Heartbreak on the list of serious instrument manufacturers, and wipe the smug smiles off the faces of Gary and Peter, should he ever see them again.

He could call Dan up now and beg him to get on the first morning flight to Nashville. But would a really good, unknown player make any difference in the traffic to the Heartbreak booth? Cole wondered what advice Richard would have for him. He could call Richard, who would pontificate for thirty minutes on what a good salesperson could do (or have done), how he should think, what he should care about. However right Richard might be, Cole would not call him.

Constantine had done a credible job of chatting with potential buyers, showing them the Inflatables, and flattering their egos when they told stories about some unique landmark in their hometowns, or how their families had supported their aspirations, or the difficult paths they had traveled to succeed. Their businesses, they said with satisfied smiles, had been built on big dreams and sacrifice, and on blood, sweat and tears. Constantine nodded and smiled. Had he not occupied a front row seat, borne witness to Heartbreak's real-life performance as a fledgling business trying desperately to spread her wings and fly? He was empathetic as only Constantine can be – interested, kind, irresistibly friendly, exuding knowledge of another place to park one's psyche where it could rest in the shade and drink from a clear mountain stream and – refreshed - pick itself up for further travels into unknown steep canyons, blistering deserts, and rough mountain terrain. Cole wondered where Constantine had parked his psyche while the travails of the music store journeyman fell upon his ears. Constantine did not have the nimble string-picking fingers and ear for music that Dan had been born with or the business acumen that Richard had cultivated, but he was a good friend, and in no small way, a teacher in the school of human nature.

"Where are we eating?" Jason asked. They were headed for the van. "I'm just asking because we can walk to just about any kind of restaurant from here. And even the Taco Bell has live music, I'm pretty sure," he continued, "if that makes you happy. Me? I can eat in total silence."

"That's good," Cole answered. "Because we're going back to the room for sandwiches. We can be very quiet there."

"I can't eat another peanut butter sandwich," Jason said.

"No problem," Constantine said. "We've got apples, dried apricots, some cashews. And donuts. Don't forget about them."

Jason didn't reply, and Constantine drove into the MacDonald's drive thru a block from the motel. "What's your order?" he asked Jason. "We're eating peanut butter," he said to Cole.

At the Scotsman, Constantine and Cole fixed peanut butter sandwiches. Jason ate his cheeseburgers and fries in silence, then lay back on the cot and stared at the ceiling.

"You okay?" Constantine asked.

Jason didn't say anything.

Constantine tapped his leg. "I'm talking to you," he said.

"Yes," Jason replied. Then added a gruff "A-O-K."

"Good, cause we need to get showers and get ready to go."

"I don't need a shower," Jason said. "And I'm not going."

"Seriously?" Cole said. "After you did such a great job of getting us tickets?"

"You go," Jason said. "I'll stay here and watch TV."

Cole looked at Constantine. Constantine shrugged. "We'd really enjoy it more if you came with us," Cole said.

"But I don't want to," Jason said. "I'll be fine here."

Up until then, Jason had surprised Cole with his general good nature and his enthusiasm for everything the NAMM show had to offer: the performances, both those advertised and spontaneous; the free goodies and souvenirs; the freedom to disappear into the crowd and report back about some new musical gadget he had discovered or the scantily clad, big-bosomed women in the Galactica Drums booth who were posing for photos with attendees. Jason had a photo to prove it. He had also become something of an expert on where to get the cheapest food, who was performing at various booths, and even the NAMM show gossip. He said that Hans had reached some agreement with the NAMM show staff to lower the sound generally if they could ignore the rare song ending acrobatics that generally resolved in a final scorching sustained chord. "And there's this guy on the first floor who can't use his own name for his business," Jason said. "It's kind of crazy because he's down there selling stuff using his name but someone else owns his company and he's not supposed to use his own name."

"Bill Lawrence," Cole said.

"Yeah, you heard of him?"

"Oh yeah," Cole said. "He invented various guitars and electronics, but his company went bankrupt, and his partner bought it or somehow got it, and supposedly the partner owns it now."

"Well, they're still fighting over it," Jason said. "He has all these guitars in a big booth on the first floor, where he sits around playing guitar and acting all grumpy, kinda like you were earlier today."

"What are you talking about?"

"When we came back with the food. Good thing we showed up. You must've had low blood sugar or something. Mumbling something about Ricky Skaggs."

"I wouldn't mind having a booth on the first floor," Cole said. "I wouldn't be grumpy down there."

By the time they had finished eating, Cole realized he was exhausted. Any other time and any other place, he would not be planning to go out and listen to music, and would have opted to kick off his shoes, stretch out on the bed, close his eyes, and think of nothing. But this was Nashville, and they had Seymour Duncan tickets. Cole put the lid back on the peanut butter jar and returned it to the food bag. He sipped from a cup of water and ate a dried apricot. "We can't leave you here," he said.

"It's easy," Jason said. "You get in the van, start it with a key, and drive on down the highway while I stay here and enjoy the peace and quiet." Jason languidly stretched his long body and draped his arms and legs from the cot to the floor. "I don't know what you think would happen if I sit here all by myself and watch TV."

"OK, so we *can* leave you. We would just rather not," Cole said.

"It's just TV," Jason exclaimed. "My parents leave me home alone all the time. Nothing ever happens. Ever."

An hour and a half later, Jason was watching "Ghostbusters" when Cole and Constantine headed out the door.

The Wildhorse Saloon, once a warehouse, was an airy arena with a gigantic stage at one end, and two tiers of balconies around the three sides high above the main floor where the rows of seats were pretty much packed.

"Let's go upstairs," Constantine said. The second-floor balconies were filled, so they headed up to the third floor, where they had one balcony section almost to themselves – they and three young men standing at the back smoking cigarettes.

"I didn't think they were letting people up here," one of the smokers said.

"They're not. These guys must be part of the crew," another one answered.

# Heartbreak Guitar

Cole and Constantine waved and moved down the balcony steps and leaned on the balcony railing, high above the crowd, with a fantastic view of the stage.

One phenomenal musician after another took the stage: Victor Wooten, in whose hands the bass guitar was a completely new instrument. He played the melody to "Amazing Grace" using harmonics while pulling in deep bass notes and continually tuning and detuning strings. Thom Bresh played an incredible "Dueling Banjos", both the banjo and guitar parts alternating first and then combining to play both parts at once. Even his guitar was a stellar instrument, the "Super Dualette", two guitars joined back-to-back like Siamese Twins. He was joined by Tommy Emmanuel for a ragtime duet. There were more players: Nokie Edwards, Muriel Andersen, Randy Strom and the phenomenal Ben Lacy. Cole looked over at Constantine. He was transported, as were they all, as if the ever-expanding universe had been sped up, energized by music. The audience was a small mass of humanity reduced to its essence, there to absorb the waves of sound that washed through it – each person, one by one, receding from the egos of their conscious brains to become a sound receiver as the reverberating energy rippled and roiled through them.

Janice Dodge

Seymour Duncan, dressed in sweatpants, appeared onstage, where he and a panoply of musicians absorbed the attention of the audience. Cole leaned over to Constantine. "Think we should go check on young Jason?" They waited for a raucous country song to finish and while the audience was whistling and clapping, they rose from their seats and headed toward the exit.

In the motel room, the television was tuned to Comedy Central, but it was playing to an empty room. Jason was not in the room, nor in the bathroom. They stood for a moment, surveying the emptiness, while tedious "fat" jokes were recounted on TV by an overweight young woman with poorly timed punchlines who was squandering her fifteen minutes of fame. Cole sat heavily on the bed and rubbed two fingers across his brow as if to straighten the creases that had appeared there. "Can just one thing work out as planned?" he said glumly.

Constantine sighed audibly, picked up the remote from Jason's cot and turned off the television. He sat on the bed next to Cole, then stood up abruptly. "Wait here," he said. "I'll go to the office and ask if they've seen him."

Ten minutes later, Constantine opened the door and made a sweeping gesture with his arm, and

Jason entered the room. "I just went to get a Coke," he said. "You guys are worse than my parents."

"Good, be sure and tell them that when you see them. I think they're counting on it," Cole said. "We have one more day here before we head home. I really need you to be where we can find you. Are you good with that?"

"Okay, okay," Jason said. "It *was* just a Coke!"

Cole continued to sit on the bed, staring at his shoes. It was just a Coke. That pretty much represented every minor blow, inconvenience, disappointment, missed opportunity, hardship, and betrayal. They were all small and petty, but they were many. One raindrop was nothing to get excited about, but thousands, tens of thousands, millions drumming down from the once spectacularly cloudless sky was significant, damaging, defeating…slowly eroding his ambition, his dream, his hope. Cloaked in a heavy sense of gloom, Cole peeled off his shoes, shirt, and jeans, slipped into bed, and rolled over to face the wall, while Constantine and Jason talked quietly for a few minutes before turning off the lights and settling into sleep.

# Chapter 24

It was eight o'clock on Sunday morning, the last day of the NAMM show, and sunlight shown like quicksilver on the chrome hood ornaments and grills of cars in the parking lot outside their hotel room. It lit up the dust and pollen on the large windowpane that a few minutes before had seemed invisible in the shade of an overpass behind which the sun had risen. It was going to be another hot one. Cole and Constantine were having the complimentary coffee made in a small coffee pot on the countertop beneath a bank of fogged mirrors just outside the steamy bathroom that Jason had exited wearing baggy shorts and with wet hair dripping on a towel draped around his neck.

"So…..," Jason said. "You guys having peanut butter sandwiches for breakfast?"

"I think we'll save that for later," Cole answered. "Interested in some coffee?"

"Do we have anything else, like Mountain Dew?" Jason asked.

"I don't think so. Look in the cooler," Constantine said.

Jason flipped the lid to the cooler with his toe. "Just a couple of beers," he said. "I can have one of those."

"You can check out the complimentary breakfast," Cole said. "They probably have milk or juice. Can you bring back some milk for the coffee?"

"The breakfast stuff they have is worse than cow manure, worse than Dad's peach wine, worse than the school cafeteria!" Jason exclaimed.

"Does your dad know you were into the wine?" Cole asked.

Jason briefly looked at Cole with a small smile and declined to answer. He checked the pockets of the jeans he had worn the day before, pulled out a small wad of bills and some coins, slipped his bare feet into his untied tennis shoes, and headed for the door.

Cole started to comment on Jason's clothing, or mostly lack of it, but sat back and sipped his coffee black, and watched the cars move slowly, bumper to bumper, across the overpass.

It was Day 3 of the NAMM show, the last day of first impressions…the last day to secure one's place in the known luthier's universe. Cole wanted just a small corner in that hallowed space, just a toe dipped in the ocean of success, a tiny ripple in the big pond. He wanted simple recognition for having created something new – definitely a novelty item, but not simply that. In fact, what he had created was a well-designed, fun, and fully functional instrument, as anyone should be able to see and hear. He wanted Heartbreak to rise above its obscure and humble beginnings and be spoken of by the musicians and journalists and instrument makers and even the public once he left Nashville. He wanted Heartbreak to "break hearts" only in the sense that Heartbreak instruments would open one's heart to their unique design and extraordinary sound.

The show had gone okay so far, with two pretty solid commitments and some maybes. He had hoped for more, but it was a start. But Cole longed for that Ricky Skaggs moment…one incredible memory that would stand out from all the rest, and that would represent having reached the summit after all the months and years of strife and striving and climbing over one obstacle after the next. One incredible moment that would justify all that he and Jewell had gone through. That was all. And today would be his last chance.

At the Renaissance Center, there was the usual bustle and noise as vendors checked their products and their equipment…Bach fugue-like chords followed by a few runs and trills on the piano keys; some familiar guitar riffs with deep distortion;

all kinds of drumming, and cymbals crashing and simmering; and in nearly every corner, stringed instruments were being tuned. A new odor crowded out the static-clean aroma of the previous days: bacon and sausage, sweet baked goods, and freshly brewed coffee. Cole felt the lump in his stomach that was the stale Fig Newtons he had gotten from the Scotsman vending machine, and the handful of cashews he had snacked on in the room while they waited for Jason to return. Jason had appeared with a bag of leftover hash browns and a large drink from Chick-fil-a. Cole had declined the hash browns, but instantly regretted it, and watched while Constantine polished them off.

Cole and Constantine took up their usual positions in the booth: Constantine inflating guitar bodies and Cole nodding and smiling at attendees, shaking hands, narrating the Heartbreak story, strumming Desire, and watching others take her through her paces, offering picks, pressing brochures into all the hands that would take them. It was uplifting and exhausting. Not infrequently, he would listen to tedious stories of a beloved Fender Tele or Gibson Les Paul that was tucked away in a safe place or hung on the wall for show, or those that had been played and loved and passed to a daughter or son. Often in the middle of such a guitar love-fest recounting, Constantine would gently nudge the increasingly exasperated Cole to move him aside and let Constantine stroll down memory lane alongside the enthusiastic but banal storytellers. Constantine managed to listen with a genuine-looking smile of appreciation, and Cole managed to swallow back "I'm trying to sell something here, you moron," and mutter it later, after the offending raconteur had departed the booth.

At 11:30, Jason showed up with a plastic harmonica and a penny whistle. "For CJ and Chrissy," he said, and tucked them behind the amplifier. "Hey, you guys missed the pancake breakfast!"

"Did we know about the pancake breakfast?" Constantine asked Cole.

"Probably," Cole sighed. "In the literature somewhere."

"And I saw some old guy hanging around talking to everyone," Jason continued. "At least, everyone wanted to talk to *him*. Maybe he works here. I think his name is Lou Reed."

"From the Velvet Underground," Constantine said. "It was a 60's band."

"Let me know if you see him coming this way," Cole said glancing up and down both aisles.

Jason stayed for about twenty minutes, said he wanted to check out the booths with the real guitars, "you know, the ones that don't fold up into a long stick with strings." He laughed at Cole's expression of disgust, stood, and stretched. "Yep, I like heavy guitars. What fun would it be to smash an Inflatable on stage? You probably couldn't even get it to break apart with all the cushions around it." He was edging out of the booth, quickly turned, and was subsumed in the stream of attendees.

"Tell me honestly," Cole turned to Constantine. "What do you think the average music store buyer thinks when I show him or her Desire? Or the average guitar player?

"They think… 'this is wonderful, a Heartbreak in a love story filled with ordinary Fenders and Fender posers.' Jason is having his fun, but he doesn't know what he's talking about."

Just then two lanky young men wearing nearly identical black t-shirts, baggy jeans and boots stopped in front of the booth. Constantine smiled at them and inflated the small and elegant inflatable body around Diva. Cole started his spiel about the portability of the Heartbreak Inflatables but stopped when both men burst into a fit of laughter.

"Of course. You could take it practically anywhere," one exclaimed.

"Like on a cruise ship," the other man said.

"Seriously," the first man said. "And you could use it as a float if the ship sank."

"Or to paddle your lifeboat," the other one said, laughing.

The first man burst into a long, machine-gun roll of laughter, and held his stomach as he sputtered "just throw away the neck and wear the inflated part as a life vest."

"God yes!" the second man roared. He turned to Cole. "If you made them glow in the dark, the search planes could find them at night." They were now so weak from the hilarity of their repartee that they leaned on each other, arms around the shoulders.

"And make the neck edible," the first man gasped. "In case the rescue…" he couldn't finish. "In case…," he could hardly breathe for laughing so hard, "…sustenance." Several people had stopped walking and looked at Cole with amusement, hoping that this was part of a performance they hadn't seen on their itineraries. Cole glowered at them, and they moved away.

One of the young men gave Cole a dismissive wave and they stumbled off, still guffawing, enjoying their idiocy.

Constantine put a hand on Cole's shoulder. "Take a break," he said. "I've got things covered here." He offered Cole a twenty-dollar bill. "Check out the sights. Grab a beer. You've been working hard, man." Cole had not moved, so Constantine stuffed the bill into Cole's back pocket. "You need to go," he said. "You won't do any good here at the moment."

He was right, and Cole knew it. Cole was nearly at the point of testing out just how smashable his guitars might be. There's smashing and then there's the equally satisfying slashing. For a moment he closed his eyes and imagined channeling all his frustration and heartache into one high-intensity guitar-smashing work out. But even in his imagination, he couldn't do it, not with Desire, or Diva, or Despair. Give him a Stratocaster or Les Paul or Gibson SG or PRS. He was sick of hearing about them. The whole guitar-making world was sick of hearing about them. The big companies had blanketed the planet with their guitars, so that the small companies were mere seedlings in a towering forest of brand-name guitars that starved them of sunlight.

Cole sighed and said "yeah, okay." He looked around the booth, sighed again, and headed for the exit. He descended the stairs and walked into the huge arena of first floor vendors, noted that here were the brand name guitar manufacturers that were worshipped as if deities, all with expansive displays of dozens of gleaming instruments. Down here, there were no music police because each manufacturer was equipped with a sound booth, or more than one, for test-driving their instruments at whatever earsplitting volume would be desired. And there were areas set aside as small stages for the musicians who would be performing later in the day. Maybe he could take this in later, but right now, he just could not. He started back up the stairs, but noticed the food and drink pavilion, a softly lit, relatively quiet oasis in a sea of merchandising and deal-making. He walked up to a counter, slid onto a high stool and ordered a pricey lager. He looked at the sandwich menu, but he wasn't really hungry, or not hungry enough for a burger that cost nine dollars.

Cole finished his beer, thought about ordering another, but decided he would rather save the money for dinner out tonight. They could take one final stroll down Broadway and blow the rest of their food money on a meal while they listened to and watched some fabulous display of musical artistry…medicine for the body, heart, and mind. He left a dollar on the counter and walked along the aisles of the second floor, avoiding for now the intersection that – like an undertow - would draw him back to his own booth.

There was a breathtaking array of musical instruments, electronics, music accessories, even music-themed clothing. At one such apparel booth, there was a display featuring a life-sized cardboard

Johnny Cash next to a rack of black long sleeved cotton shirts and black vests. There were the spangly right-hand white gloves made famous by Michael Jackson. There were buxom dolls dressed in slinky dresses and fulminating a mass of blonde curls.

Cole stopped by Hans' booth to say hello, but he could see that Hans was deeply held in the grip of a serious conversation with two men in dark gray suits, whom Cole hoped were corporate buyers or investors with real money and the sense to see that the entrepreneur standing before them knew what he was doing, and they could keep their grubby hands off the product.

Cole glanced down the aisle toward his own booth and noted that Constantine was chatting it up with a lanky young woman who, like all women, appeared to be practically melting in Constantine's penetrating gaze, one that conferred the undivided attention that Constantine gave to any companion - man, or woman. She had no way of knowing that.

Cole followed one of the outside aisles to a set of stairs that led to the third floor. He imagined that the booths on this floor were booked late in the reservation period and would be populated primarily by late-comer small companies like Heartbreak, who either had to beg or borrow the money for registration or had given up on perfecting their products by the summer deadline, and had decided to bring their prototypes, each of them costing ten times more than they could possibly recoup in a real-world sale. Cole had been lucky in landing a booth on the second floor, he believed, and he attributed it only to an unrelenting perseverance – some might say pigheadedness – along with a strong belief early on that the NAMM show was where he would make his mark. That, and the use of his worn out - at that moment back in spring still active - credit card for the initial deposit. He didn't quite know what to expect on this floor, and he wished he had saved one of the NAMM show booth maps that everyone seemed to carry around and consult as if they were on a scavenger hunt. In fact, he had barely glanced at the map to check his own booth location before he had crammed it into the van console with the state highway maps. He stood at the top of the stairs and perused the landscape of booths…more drums, more guitar straps and picks, all kinds of hats and scarves, auto harps and dulcimers, flutes and rattles, cigar-box electric guitars…electric and acoustic instruments and accessories as far as the eye could see. An eruption of an amplified drum roll brought the sound police scurrying down one aisle, only to be followed by a bellowing electric guitar, something outfitted with humbuckers, bringing more NAMM show staff to a nearby offending booth.

Cole considered whether he wanted to wade into this sea of sound and lights. He was not in the market for anything, so was it reasonable to saunter down the aisles and watch the hopeful smiles light up in booth after booth as if activated by a motion detector? Was that really fair, given that he knew the minor cut that each indifferent passerby would inflict on the psyche of the aspiring peddler of entrepreneurial dreams? He could justify his third-floor tour as taking a look at the competition, but actually there was no direct competition given that his product was unique. That was precisely the aspect of Heartbreak Inflatables that had intrigued Peter and Gary. They didn't have to take his word for it, and they hadn't. They had researched it themselves and realized that although there were hundreds of guitar makers with all manner of guitar designs, there were no other guitars just like Heartbreak's.

Cole took one more sweeping glance. He couldn't see down all of the side aisles, but he had a pretty good idea that this floor was just like the second floor, filled with a lot of bright and glittering musical ideas strung together by wishes, prayers and reveries. He headed back downstairs to join Constantine and, if Jason was back, to send him out foraging for some inexpensive food: sandwiches, burgers or even salads. Cole's appetite was back and almost any food would be fine.

He reached the booth and waited while Constantine wrapped up his sales pitch to a couple of teenagers who were infinitely more polite than the two imbeciles that had thought of themselves as veritable comedians.

"Have you seen Jason?" Cole asked.

"He should be back any minute with lunch," Constantine answered. "Did you see anything interesting…I mean particularly interesting? Spectacularly beyond anything in the known universe?"

"No," Cole said. "But I didn't actually see everything, just walked around. Hey, I'm starving. What time is it?"

Constantine looked at his watch. "Almost 1:30," he said. "I could eat myself. Well, not myself. I could eat."

Shortly after 2:00, Jason returned with two pizzas, one with pepperoni, and the other with mushrooms, onions, and olives. "This one's healthier," he said as he peaked in the box with the vegetable laden pizza, reached in and blotted congealed grease with a stack of napkins.

"Just don't tell your parents that this was the healthiest meal you ate," Cole said.

"I would have bought wine," Jason said, "but…you know." He shrugged his shoulders. "It's not like I never had it before." He glanced at Constantine and smiled. "These places take themselves so seriously."

"Yeah, so does the liquor license board," Cole said. "Anyway, you know we can't eat in the booth. So maybe you guys could…"

Constantine interrupted, "how about you go with Jason and eat. I'll hold down the fort 'til you get back. Not much traffic anyway."

The latter statement wasn't quite true, but it was Constantine's gentle way to claim his sales spot. A broad-shouldered, broad-everything man wearing a cowboy hat stopped at the booth and gazed at the display. Constantine stepped up to show him Desire.

"Let's go," Cole said to Jason, and they carried the pizza boxes down to the first floor and outside where there were benches under the shade of some Japanese maple trees.

"It's hot out here," Jason complained. "And I couldn't get drinks. I only have two hands, you know."

"Let's just eat and then get something to drink and get back so Constantine can eat."

They ate pizza and watched a family, a couple with two small children that had seated themselves across the hot expanse of white concrete, pull out sandwiches and cartons of juice from a small cooler. Cole waited for Jason to complain again of thirst, but Jason quietly took another slice of pizza – pepperoni, Cole noticed – and steadily consumed it.

"I took a break earlier," Cole said. "From schmoozing with the rabble, otherwise known as attendees. Checked out the other floors."

"Oh yeah, did you see the inflatable guitars?" Jason asked. He was wiping his mouth and cleaning his fingers with the one napkin he had saved from the grease blotting. "I'm dying of thirst here," he said.

"What do you mean, inflatable guitars?" Cole barked. He had stopped eating and turned toward Jason.

"On the third floor. Not exactly like yours," Jason said warily.

"Show me," Cole said as he stood up.

"What about the pizza?" Jason said, closing the box lid and stacking the two boxes.

"You can leave them or bring them. I don't care which." Cole wiped his fingers on the greasy napkin, then on the back of his pants and headed for the entrance.

"Wait up," Jason called as he hustled to catch up, carrying the pizza boxes. "Damn."

Cole took the stairs two at a time until he reached the third floor, where he waited for Jason, who ascended slowly, like a man headed for sentencing. "This seems weird," Jason said. He set the pizza boxes on top of a large trash can before they headed down one aisle and then another. At one intersection, Jason paused to get his bearings, then motioned for Cole to follow him as he walked toward a booth in the very back.

There was Gary – the actual Gary of 'Gary-and-Peter', former investors - smiling and glad-handing a rotund woman and stick-thin man in corporate black suits, and at the back of the booth, Peter was sitting on a stool talking on his cell phone. On the display table were half a dozen inflatable guitars. As Jason had said, they were not exactly like Heartbreak's. They were grotesque, made of brightly colored plastic with contrasting colored inflatable cushions. Each had a guitar strap patterned with flowers or hearts or lightning bolts. One guitar on display was connected to a small two-way pump that filled it with air and deflated it within seconds, as if the instrument was breathing. In their essence, however, they were Cole's guitars made cheaply and drained of the artistry of guitar building so that they were totally without a hint of musical soul. So no, they were not *exactly* like Heartbreak's. They were a mockery of it.

"You sons of bitches," Cole hissed. Gary looked up in surprise. "You bastards," Cole said. "Liars, cheats, fucking crooks!" he shouted.

"I can't believe this! I fucking can't believe it!" Gary had backed up in the booth and stood just in front of

Peter, who was still holding the phone to his ear, but staring at Cole as if frozen in place. The couple had scurried away and stood at a distance to watch.

"Did you think I wouldn't find out?" Cole shouted. "Well, I found out, you scumbags!" Cole turned to look at the crowd of attendees who had stopped walking and were standing at a safe distance. He noted that the sound police were headed his way. "You'll need a special decibel meter," he yelled toward them. "One that detects lying, thieving scumbags! Hey everyone, come and do business with these guys, they'll lie to your face and steal your ideas. THAT…" he indicated a small white inflatable guitar with a furry pink cushion body, "*THAT* is a patented design. MY PATENT! My patent which these creeps said they would invest in, signed the contract, and then went behind my back and stole my idea. Fucking morons!"

By then, the NAMM staff had planted themselves in front of Cole, whilst still at a distance. "Sir, you have to leave the area," the young woman with a ponytail said.

"Me? How about these liars? How about them? Do you rent a booth to every rip-off artist who sends you a check?" Cole shouted. He was striding back and forth in front of the booth. "Better make sure the check cleared," he said forcefully. "Lying, stealing snakes," he hissed.

"Sir, this is your second warning to leave the area now and come with us."

"I think he's drunk," Peter said.

Cole had plucked the frilly pink and white inflatable off the table and pointed the headstock at Peter like he would spear him with it. "Really? Really? That's what you have to offer? That's your wise observation?" Cole turned toward the gathering crowd. "Sign a contract with them at your own risk. Be forewarned," he intoned with the fervent roar of a fire-and-brimstone preacher. "Sign a contract," he roared, "and the next day they'll steal your company, leave you penniless and in debt, and ignore your phone calls. I wouldn't trust these SOB's to live up to their contract if it was witnessed by the Pope!"

In a nearby booth stood a lanky young man poised to play a beautiful hollow body electric with a quilt top, Cole noticed. The melody line of John Hiatt's "Perfectly Good Guitar" arose, at first like a small whisper in the dark, and then it swelled on the refrain "it breaks my heart to see those stars smashing a perfectly good guitar." He nodded at Cole as if encouraging him to smash the ludicrous inflatable to smithereens. A distant drum picked up the beat, a bass guitar and a few more percussion instruments added support until the whole nearby section, and perhaps the one adjacent to it, was playing John Hiatt's song. Cole realized that Peter and Gary were not popular among their NAMM neighbors, who actually seemed to want Cole to smash that fluffy little inflatable, practically a toy! "They'll sign on the dotted line and stab you in the back," Cole continued his preaching, wondering briefly if he had exceeded 85 decibels.

"Sir, this is your final warning!" the woman declared. She motioned to her companion who was speaking into a walkie-talkie.

"By the way," Cole shouted toward Peter, "I only had one friggin' beer, and I had to borrow the money for that! So fuck you!"

"Sir!"

Cole turned to answer her but caught a glimpse of Jason's shocked expression. He placed the guitar back on the table, plucked a couple of the strings, grimaced at the deadness they evoked, and allowed the pony-tailed staff person to take his arm and lead him toward the stairs. "Perfectly Good Guitar" was in full swing. From behind him, Cole heard Jason say, "they *did* steal his idea," as they headed down the stairs to the office on the first floor.

# Chapter 25

The NAMM show office was small, and inside the glass walls that separated the office space from the hotel lobby, Cole felt like an exotic bird on display. The blonde pony-tailed woman, Sarah Grant he noted on her name tag, pointed to the seats across from her desk. She looked older in the bright light of the office than he had at first thought, with gray hair mixed through the blonde, and with small pouches beneath her eyes.

"It's okay," she said to the two security guards who Cole realized had joined their entourage somewhere between the third floor and arrival in this office. They hesitated, but after an unintelligible squawking came over their walkie-talkie, they turned and left the office. One took up a position just outside it and spoke into the walkie-talkie before relaxing his shoulders and standing at ease.

"So," Sarah began as she leaned forward to look at Cole's badge.

"Cole," he said.

She nodded and said "Okay, Cole...and Richard," she said, now reading Jason's badge. Jason stayed quiet. "Can you explain what just happened up there?"

"The short version is that those scumbags stole my idea," Cole said. "They were investors in my company and just walked away from our contract last winter, and now they show up here parading around with my guitars. A version of my design, I should say, because their products are shit!"

She sat back in her chair and studied Cole for a second. "If what you say is true…"

"Oh, it's true," Cole interrupted. "I can't prove it to you this second, but I have all the documentation needed to show that I have a patent on the design that they not only stole, but transformed into the bastardized, corrupt piece of crap you saw displayed up there."

"Nevertheless, we can't allow the behavior you exhibited! If you have a business dispute with another exhibitor, there are procedures for resolving those by submitting a formal complaint to NAMM and…"

"What good would that have done? They are still up there hawking their imbecilic, phony inflatable plastic guitar toys. Would you have kicked them out?"

"You can file a complaint, but you cannot verbally or otherwise assault another exhibitor," she answered. "And I'm sorry to say that you can't remain on the premises. NAMM staff will review the incident and let you know if you may exhibit at a future show. You were warned."

"So you're kicking me out? Is that what's happening here? I have to go, but they can sit up there and lie and cheat to their hearts content?"

She held up her hand for Cole to stop, scanned one of the papers on her desk, flipped a page and scanned again, and sat back in her chair. "You registered with Jewell. Is that your wife?"

"That's my partner," Cole said, glancing at Jason, who remained quiet and stared at the floor.

"OK, it's like this," Sarah said. "You cannot return to your booth or remain in the building, but your partner can continue to exhibit your products. The security staff will help you find the exit from the building." She motioned for the security team. "If you return, you will be trespassing. I will escort this young man back upstairs or he can leave with you."

"I'll go upstairs," Jason said unhappily. He turned to Cole. "We can meet you at the van after the show."

"Okay then," Sarah said and stood up. She signaled the security staff person who stood stiffly at the office door and waited for Cole to join him. "Just a minute," she said. Cole turned toward her. "If you wish to file a complaint, I'll send the documents you will need. And of course, you may respond to the correspondence I send once we have reviewed your case. And you can appeal a permanent ban, but of course, that has not been decided."

Cole turned away and walked toward the exit.

Day three of the NAMM show ended at 5:00 p.m. Sunday. Cole had spent one hell of a long, hot afternoon walking around Nashville. He stopped and entered a dark tavern and sat at the bar and sipped on a Heineken, then two more, while he listened to the sweet sound of nothing. No performer, television, jukebox or preselected bar favorites. Just an occasional word or comment from two men playing chess at a table near the back, and the low murmur of a couple of patrons who – like Cole – were taking respite from the unrelenting brightness and heat of a brutal July mid-afternoon in a big city. At 4:45, Cole left a tip on the counter, walked into the bright sunshine, and headed toward the Renaissance. He found the van and waited.

Eventually, Jason appeared with a cart loaded with the amplifier and guitars. Jason rolled the cart to the back of the van, slid Constantine's keys out of his pocket and unlocked the back doors. "I was going to tell you Ricky Skaggs came by the booth." He looked quickly at Cole. "But he didn't, so Constantine talked me out of it," he said.

"Thanks for that," Cole said. He put the amplifier inside the back of the van, then climbed in and pushed it forward against the backseat. Jason passed the guitar display stand to Cole, and then the guitars in their cases. Jason seemed uncharacteristically quiet. "How'd it go?" Cole asked tentatively.

"It was weird," Jason said, "but mostly in a good way. I think some people came by just to see your guitars because of all the talk about it, you being kicked out and everything."

"What did Constantine say?"

"He just sighed and looked worried. Then he said, 'let's sell some guitars,' so we did." Jason handed Cole a bag filled with electronics, and several bags of souvenirs. "I have to go back for the rest of the stuff," Jason said.

Half an hour later, Jason and Constantine were walking across the parking lot, carrying guitar cases and a briefcase with the leftover flyers and the newly acquired business cards. Cole stood by the van until they reached him, and held out his arms for the guitars, which he stashed in the back of the van, then the briefcase and the last satchel of electronics. He turned to look at Constantine, who threw his arm around Cole's shoulders in one of his famous one-armed bear hugs, then stood back, jingled his keys, and said, "ready to go?" They rode silently back to the Scotsman, entered the room, turned up the air conditioning and sat on the bed.

"I made a spectacle of myself," Cole said softly.

"You had every right," Constantine answered. He pulled two Miller's and a coke out of the cooler and wiped them with a hand towel. "At least to be angry. It was an outrageous betrayal. Unbelievable…even for Peter and Gary."

"I didn't see it coming," Cole said. "Maybe I should have, but I just didn't see it."

"You still have a patent," Jason said. "You could sue."

"It takes money to sue," Cole said. "And they know that. I was an idiot to believe a word they said or wrote, or that a mere contract, a piece of paper, would mean anything."

They fell silent and sipped their drinks.

"You made a definite impression," Constantine said. "More than one person came by the booth saying they wanted to check out the real inflatables. And I got the sense that no one was very impressed with Peter and Gary's stuff anyway."

"Yeah," Jason added. "I think they'll remember you."

"How could they not?" Cole said. "All those months getting ready for the show…" he lay back on the bed with the beer resting upright on his stomach. "*Years* getting ready…everything we sacrificed, and it ended up like this."

Cole was not hungry, so Constantine and Jason, discerning that no celebratory dinner would be in the offing, went out to pick up food to bring back to the Scotsman. It was decided that they would all get to bed early, get up early, and be home by late Monday afternoon or early evening.

Cole drank his beer and thought about the ignominious ending to his luthier's dream. In all those months of preparation for the NAMM show, he had carried uncertainty and worry like a troublesome tooth that flared frequently and deeply ached, most notably in the middle of the night when he was alone with his thoughts. Until he and Constantine and Jason had actually driven north on U.S. 319 and crossed the Florida-Georgia state line, he had not been absolutely certain that he would have the wherewithal to display his products at NAMM. He had never actually questioned the wisdom of going to the show. Even in the dullest of his fantasies, he had always believed that Desire and her sisters would need little from him to seduce guitar enthusiasts, and that their debut at the NAMM show would secure his spot in the annals of guitar makers.

As much as he had hoped for financial success, or at least the promise of it, what he longed for most was an acknowledgement of the art of guitar building and the problem-solving perspicacity that was required to create a fully functional, beautifully toned instrument out of a two-by-four and some air-filled bags. He had created something beautiful; he had cobbled together a way to come to the show and display his product; he had acquired some solid guitar-buyer leads; and then he had blown it.

Peter and Gary had brought into the world the ugly spawn of Cole's creation, like a mutated and pathogenic virus that had escaped into nature and threatened to spread, music store by music store, or – given the cheap, plastic, not-musical nature of the product – marketed in every Walmart and Dollar General throughout the land. The latter would be preferable in the sense that it would be clear to all that the Gary and Peter's merchandise was never meant to be a real instrument. Leave the actual music stores for the real instruments manufactured by Heartbreak. But Gary and Peter would never agree to limiting distribution. They would place their product wherever they could, go cheap on manufacturing and big on advertising, and drown out any efforts Cole might make to establish Heartbreak as the original and rightful owner of the inflatable guitar.

The jangling phone startled him, and he spilled beer onto his shirt and jeans. He reached for the receiver and cautiously spoke, "hello?"

"Cole, I'm so glad I got hold of you," a slightly raspy male voice struck a familiar note.

"Oh, hey," Cole said, hoping that the next sentence or two would clear up the mystery of the person behind the voice. He should know who this was, but…

"I have someone here who wants to speak with you, but I wanted to jump in first…oh, Em just called her from the back patio…"

Em. Okay, that helped. Emmaline was Cole's mother-in-law whom everyone referred to as Em or Emmie, so the mystery voice was Cole's father-in-law, Jack. Jack was typically reserved, letting Emmaline convey important family news like that of a grandchild who lost a tooth, or that a family pet – usually the accursed cat – had given them a scare when she went missing for almost a day and was found locked in the utility room. Emmaline also planned the family dinners and vacations and researched the best school districts for the grandchildren and announced to her grown son, after the last baby, that it was past time for him to get a vasectomy. But this was Jack, a man of few words, and Cole knew that when he did speak, it was deliberate and important.

"Before Jewell gets back, let me just say something," Jack said.

"Sure," was Cole's half-hearted response. It wouldn't be surprising if Jack were to lecture Cole about his selfish dream that might have cost him his marriage, or perhaps urge him to start a new countertop business, or one building cabinets or even custom furniture…a business that would support Jewell so that she could go back to school and study art.

"I just want you to know how proud I am of what you have done there." Jack said. "It takes some guts and perseverance to go the distance like you did. You faced an uphill battle all the way, but you kept at it, and we just couldn't be more proud."

Cole cleared his throat, ready to protest the undeserved praise.

"Also," Jack continued, "I know that you and Jewell fell on hard times, and she needed a break. But you should know that the whole time she's been here, she's talked about how hard you have worked and how extraordinary and beautiful your guitars are."

Cole let out a long sigh that – before he could stop it – turned into a moan. His shoulders shook as he silently sobbed, wanting desperately to stop, but unable to stem the emotions that filled him until there was no space for air in his lungs. "Just a minute," he gasped, and he pressed the phone receiver against the bedspread and wept openly. After a minute, possibly two, or what seemed like forever, Cole wiped the tears away, blotted his runny nose on his sleeve, cleared his throat and picked up the receiver. "Jack?" he said.

"You okay there?" Jack asked.

"Yes," Cole said abjectly. "Thanks, Jack."

"Jewell's not back yet," Jack said. "Em must have her setting the table or some such thing. Very urgent, you know?" He chuckled.

"It's okay," Cole said. "I'll be here all night. And thanks again Jack. What you said…that really means something to me."

Cole peeled off his shirt, stripped and headed for the shower. He knew there would be more tears, maybe not tonight, but later, back at home, when Jewell and Frankie came walking up the front steps.

Half an hour later, Constantine and Jason returned. Jason called Richard, and learned that the storm, downgraded from a hurricane to a tropical storm, had traveled north through the Gulf, and was expected to move inland somewhere in the panhandle, but it had lost most of its punch. Cole sat in the room with them, picked at enchiladas, chips and salsa, sipped on a Pepsi, and tried to think of nothing. In truth, he was totally exhausted, almost too exhausted to care that they still had to carry into the room his amp and guitars for safekeeping. After they finished eating, he would solicit Constantine and Jason's help, and then turn in for the night, comforting himself with the thought that his family was safe from the storm despite his neglect and a single-minded obsession with his own mission. They were safe, and Jewell and Frankie would be home soon.

# Chapter 26

## Leaving Nashville

The next morning broke over them sunny and hot as they packed the instruments and all their stuff into the van and drove south. Cole noted that shreds of gray-white clouds scudded across the sky, and as they descended from the mountains around Chattanooga, more clouds amassed on the horizon and blocked the sun. The sky ahead darkened as towering thunderheads mushroomed into the atmosphere, threw down lightning, and emitted a low, growling thunder.

"Doesn't 'tropical storm' evoke a happy, Margaritaville, sunshine, sand, and waves kind of vibe?" Constantine asked.

"Not really. I've lived in Florida my whole life," Cole said. "So...no."

Jason pulled his Walkman out of his travel bag and untangled the cord to the headphones. "It usually means a day off from school, though," he said. "So I'm cool with it."

Just then gigantic raindrops splatted on the windshield, and within a few minutes water splayed

357

from the tires of semi-trailers that had slowed to forty miles an hour. Trees and billboards were buffeted by wind, and lightning ripped open the sky and struck the ground.

A massive anvil cloud ahead towered over the road. Cole watched as it rolled toward them and loomed over the cars and trucks, over the puny lives of the humans hurtling to put themselves in its path as if their endeavors were consequential or even measurable against the epochal sweep of the storm. He was struck by the provisional nature of his own existence in this body, in this van, hurtling toward the storm with Constantine and Jason. How much did it really matter what had happened at NAMM, and would his life have been demonstrably changed if he had met Ricky Skaggs and watched him politely demo a Heartbreak Inflatable, or if Peter and Gary had been selling garish t-shirts and guitar straps instead of inflatables, or if, upon seeing Cole, they had wilted into a puddle of shame as they should have done?

His life story would unfold moment by moment, day by day, just like the life of every other human in every car or truck on this highway, just like the life of every living entity on the planet.

Cole noticed Constantine's hands tense on the wheel as wind buffeted the van. Pelting rain gusted into the van through Constantine's cracked window, bringing cooler temperatures and the aroma of wet earth. Constantine was exhilarated by the immediacy of atmospheric disturbances, and Cole imagined that he was enthralled by the oncoming storm that darkened the sky, and curtains of rain that swept across the highway like billowing sails. Rain seeped into the van and soaked Constantine's shoulder and seat back, and Cole was struck by the notion that Constantine sought this connection to the turbulence around them as they drove on a drenched roadway that rushed toward them like a river. Constantine immersed himself in an experience, now in the storm, and later - Cole imagined - sitting cross-legged on his patio sipping Merlot and studying the hawk in his neighbor's pine tree as dusk enveloped them in a peaceful twilight.

Cole turned to glance at Jason, who had moved from the seat behind Constantine - where he was getting an occasional spray of rain - to the center seat. Jason had donned his dark green hoodie, unperturbed by the cool wind or fine mist coming through Constantine's window. Instead, he appeared to be enjoying the ride, exactly as he had been on the first half of the trip driving north, apparently untroubled by Cole's final act at the NAMM show and what it might portend for Heartbreak or to Cole's aspirational yearnings. To Jason, Day 3 of the NAMM show had been just another day. Events had

359

transpired, some of them interesting, but nothing so seismic as to shift his view of life off-kilter or require soul-searching ruminations or a collapse of his belief in his stewardship over the trajectory of his life journey.

Cole turned back to the front and gazed through the water-sloshed windshield. For Cole, the blustering wind and torrential rain were among the many forces beyond his control, but no more so than the events of the last year that had culminated in the NAMM show debacle and an implosion of his luthier's dream.

It had once been Jewell's dream as well. What Jewell had given up and all that Cole had risked burst into his consciousness with full force like an exploding rocket, spewing disappointment and despair. Heartbreak had overtaken Jewell's plans to study art and her wish to illustrate nature books…even her desire to be with her friends, stroll Maclay Gardens, picnic at Mashes Sands, or wander the aisles of the Goodfinds thrift store. Her aspirations and desires had withered as their Heartbreak adventure claimed most of their energies and all of their resources.

Could they get back what had been lost? Next week, or the week after, would they come home from work – she from FSU, or even better, from art school, and Cole from Richard's shop – to Frankie's unrestrained and joyous greetings, and lie together in the hammock he had promised to string between the backyard magnolia and the water oak, but that was still in its box in a corner of the shed? If he installed the hammock, would they lie in the shade of the Loblolly Pine, skin to skin, watching the clouds drift high overhead and the blue jays and cardinals dart between the Magnolia and the Ligustrum?

Cole looked at the worsening traffic that signaled their approach to Atlanta. He thought it would be wisest to stop now, if they could get over to an exit, before they were caught up in the Atlanta lunch-time rush hour melee. "You going through Atlanta or taking the back roads?"

"Straight up the middle," Constantine said. "Back roads didn't work out so well last time." Constantine put on his turn signal, then glanced in the rearview mirror and side mirror to check the traffic in the next lane, and eased into a space between a motorcycle and an RV. "You guys need to take a break?"

Cole tapped Jason on the knee. "Need a bathroom break?"

Jason looked up from his Gameboy. "I could go." He put the Gameboy aside and looked out the window. "Where are we, anyway?"

"Somewhere in the Peach State," Cole said. "Long way to go yet."

Constantine worked his way to the far-right lane, exited the highway, and drove into a Jolley's gas station, where there were two vehicles parked not far from the store entrance. Constantine pulled the van adjacent to a gas pump that displayed a soggy handwritten sign that read "Out of Order", so he moved forward and parked close to the double glass door entrance. They exited the van on stiff legs, and Cole limped through the rain and followed Jason and Constantine into the store.

Constantine hadn't locked the van, so Cole hovered near the door studying the rain as it drummed on the van roof and windshield. After a minute of watching, it was clear that even here, his guitars would rest safely without tempting a second look.

They took turns in the bathroom and wandered the aisles of chips and candy, white bread, beef jerky, and pork-n-beans. Cole selected a small bag of peanuts and a Sprite and got in line behind Jason, who was directing the cashier to wrap up a gigantic slice of warm pizza to go with the Coke Jason had set on the counter.

Constantine was still browsing the snack aisles while stretching his arms overhead, and then bending to touch his toes, and back up with his hands on his hips and leaning first to one side, then the other. Cole and Jason paid for their food, exited through the glass doors, and stood for a moment under the overhang just outside the store and watched the steady rain.

Cole tucked his peanuts in his pocket. "Ready?"

Jason looked at Cole and nodded, and they both sprinted to the van and climbed in.

The rain and wind had diminished when Constantine strode toward the van, holding a bottle of water and two yellow apples, and climbed into the driver's seat. "Easier to eat and drive," he said, brandishing the apples like a rare find.

"I can drive," Cole said.

Constantine bit into his apple. "It's okay, man. I got it."

It was still raining, but the storm was notably less intense. As they merged back into traffic and resumed speed, Cole observed that the skies were lighter directly overhead, but more storm clouds were amassed in the distance, and just up the road gray scraps of clouds, like detritus from the storm band through which they had just driven, hung low in the sky.

They drove toward Atlanta, and Cole watched as the silhouette of two large birds flew across the highway above them. Jewell would have delighted in seeing these birds. She would have happily relayed the salient facts about why they were

363

flying so low, and why they might have ventured out in the storm, and where they would find shelter. Her excitement would be contagious, and their ride the rest of the way would not seem as long and dreary...and somehow, even in the storm, the landscape would be less drab.

Soon she and Frankie would be home...a day or two at most. Tomorrow, Cole would retrieve the bird feeders from the shed and hang them in the back yard and fill them with birdseed he would borrow from Maureen. He would hang up the hammock, mow the lawn, and pick whatever flowers were still blooming to place in the Aztec vase. After that...he just didn't know.

He slumped in his seat and gazed out the windshield with his eyes half closed. There were the dark clouds on the horizon. The birds had disappeared, and a light rain seemed to fly toward them. It softly spattered on the windshield and fanned out across the glass. Drop by drop, the pattern on the windshield was mesmerizing. It reminded Cole of the feather-like pattern in one of the exotic woods given to him by Constantine's grandfather that rested on a shelving unit in the back corner of the basement.

Among the boards were ones from a tree that Constantine's grandfather had told Cole had withstood windstorms and fire, was strengthened by a will to flourish, and held its crown high. Cole remembered taking the wood to a spot directly under one of the basement lights where he had studied the wood grain. It was beautiful, with a scarlet blush, and an unusual feather-like pattern, as if it had captured the essence of a nearby bird or had arisen from a small seed imprinted and dropped in flight by a Summer Tanager or a Scarlet Macaw. It was impossible to think about this highly figured wood and not attribute to it these ethereal and dreamlike origins. This wood could become a beautiful instrument top if it stood the test of strength and flexibility. Cole would not know until he had made from it the thin layer of wood that he could test for hardness and suppleness. But he had a gut feeling. The wood spoke to him, in the same way it had spoken to Constantine's grandfather...barely more than a whisper, but it was musical, as if imbued with the haunting notes of a melody carried in a storm by the wind.

*"If you can look into the seeds of time and say which grain will grow and which will not, speak then unto me." William Shakespeare*

CPSIA information can be obtained
at www.ICGtesting.com
Printed in the USA
JSHW022302200523
41779JS00010B/138